saint morrissey

mark simpson

Mark Simpson is the author of several
critically-acclaimed books, including:

MALE IMPERSONATORS   "Brilliant." - *Observer*

IT'S A QUEER WORLD   "You'd have to be a chronic
                                       depressive not to laugh."
                                       - New Statesman & Society

THE QUEEN IS DEAD   "Something of a masterpiece."
                                       - Independent

ANTI-GAY   "The year's most controversial book."
                                       - BBC Radio 5

SEX TERROR   "Every page has gem-like sentences Zadie Smith
                                       would give her white teeth for."
                                       - Independent on Sunday

www.marksimpson.com

saint morrissey

mark simpson

First published in 2004
by SAF Publishing
Reprinted 2004

SAF Publishing Ltd.
149 Wakeman Road,
London.
NW10 5BH
ENGLAND

email: info@safpublishing.com

www.safpublishing.com

ISBN 0 946719 65 9

A CIP catalogue record for this book is available from the British
Library.

Cover photographs:
Front: Eamonn J McCabe
Back: Alex Crick

Printed in England by the Cromwell Press, Trowbridge, Wiltshire.

For the other Steven in my life.

Also a ruffian butterfly collector.

acknowledgements

I'd like to thank Mum and Dad, Mark LeFanu and the Society of Authors, the late Shulman Livesey, Alan Jackson, Meirion Todd, Suzi Feay, Paul Simpson, Jake Arnott, Mary Lawton, Lorraine Gannon, Simon Blow, Brian Pera, Dave Clemens, David Baker, Simon Casson, The Readers Wifes, David Tseng of Morrissey-solo.com, David Toube, Tim Lusher, Daniela Bernardelle, Mr Hughes, Mr Lowe, Mr Bulcock, Mr Mitchell and very particularly Mr Zeeland.

contents

'Saints should always be judged guilty until they are proved innocent.'

George Orwell, *Shooting an Elephant*

'Every great man nowadays has his disciples, and it is always Judas who writes the biography.'

Oscar Wilde, *Intentions*

i am a living sign

1

Morrissey.

The name, like the artist, like the unmistakable if somewhat dated hairdo, stands apart. Aloof in an age of ghastly accessibility. Aristocratic in an age of dumb democracy. Inimitable. Indigestible. *Irredeemable.*

Instead of being famous for being famous, Morrissey has the breathtaking petulance to be famous for being Morrissey.

And this from a pop performer! The former frontman of Manchester indie legends The Smiths and long-distance solo artist since their demise in 1987, is the anti-Pop Idol: a reminder that pop music might not just be something you have to do, like expensive dentistry, or cheap sycophancy, to become what everyone *really* wants to become these days — a TV presenter.

A reminder that pop could in fact be literally an end in itself: a (dangerously careening) vehicle for someone's prodigious, provocative, poisonous perfectly beautiful scorn. Like his hair, Morrissey has succeeded in fashioning his shyness into an elegant weapon.

Truth be told, Morrissey should never have been a pop star at all — he should, by his own admission, have been a librarian, like his mum (though perhaps, given the gallows humour of much of his lyrics, he did end up following in the footsteps of his hospital porter dad). Of course, librarians are very dangerous people, and bear more grudges than High Court judges — so you can imagine what happens when one ends up on *Top of the Pops* with the words 'MARRY ME' scrawled on their scrawny chest in magic marker.

Morrissey was the last, greatest and most gravely worrying product of an era when pop music was all there was and all anyone could want. As anyone young enough to remember that time knows, sex, drugs and materialism are pisspoor substitutes for pop music. Gloriously, terrifyingly, pop music was invested with far too much meaning and significance by a whole generation of young people back then. And no one had over-invested pop music with more meaning than Steven Patrick Morrissey, who spent the Seventies in his box bedroom in his mother's Manchester council-house listening to the New York Dolls and Sandie Shaw and wondering how he was going to become that strange, transfigured, transmitted thing, a pop star.

In that brief window of opportunity called the early Eighties the ultimate fan somehow spectacularly managed to become the ultimate star — one with a global following that to this day displays the kind of devotion to him unmatched by the fans of any other contemporary artist. The kind of devotion that only dead stars command. Or deserve.

Worse, this criminally shy working class Anglo-Irish boy from the mean Manchester suburbs of Stretford managed to become a pop star on his own terms, in his own right and in his own words: bizarre enough back then, but an unheard-of outrage in today's music business.

Bookish, reclusive-but-pugnacious — avowedly *celibate* — with an almost Puritan disdain for cheap glamour and armed with a deeply unhealthy interest in language, wit and ideas Morrissey succeeded in perverting pop music for a while and making it that most absurd of things, *literary*. Some were moved to talk of how much Morrissey owed that blousy Anglo-Irish nineteenth century torch-singer and stand-up comedian Oscar Wilde, the 'first pop star'. Arguably, poor Oscar was merely an early failed and somewhat overweight prototype for Morrissey.

✳ ✳ ✳

Now that the Twentieth Century itself has already been counted down like a particularly tedious Sunday evening singles chart and the world has woken up to a Hit-me-over-the-head Parade of Boy Blands and Girl Gropes, even to his enemies Morrissey is looking more and more like the man he told us, again and again, he was: the celibate climax to the once-splendid and now well-and-truly spannered tradition of English pop.

The man from whom, in other words, pop music and England never really recovered.

You think I exaggerate? You think me partisan? Well, of course.... But even the *NME*, Britain's most famous music newspaper and his sworn enemy since the early Nineties when it tried to assassinate him in one of the greatest *crimes passionel* in music history, in 2002 finally faced facts (and all those torrid Morrissey centrefolds they ran in the Eighties), naming him the 'most influential artist ever'.

Morrissey may stand apart and aloof, but he still casts a long disdainful shadow over the current British music scene *almost* without trying, even from the distant, sybaritic comfort of Hollywood where he has lived since the late Nineties, partly to be closer to his largest fanbase, partly to be within idolatrous distance of the grave of his secret heroine Bette Davies the 'difficult' diva who defied the studio system and almost won, but mostly because of a fabulously sulky desire to continue punishing the English for their ingratitude by the most painful means possible — depriving them of himself.

But then, one of the central paradoxes of the Morrissey phenomenon has been that whilst no one gives more of themselves in their art and their performance, no one is more selfish in the purest sense of the word. Morrissey is possibly the last privately owned company in a world where artists are floated on the stock exchange of public opinion.

As a result he has somehow managed to hang on, not only to his integrity, but also his privacy — in an age where transparency and confession is increasingly compulsory even for mere nobodies, let alone artists who have been globally famous for nearly two decades. Even in an hour-long TV documentary on Britiain's Channel 4 in 2003 (his first major TV appearance in sixteen years) he managed to give nothing away except his relationship with hairdriers. Like his private life, his personality remains for most a puzzle to be unlocked. To the world, Morrissey remains a baffling enigma, an almost *occult* mystery.

Yet there is something rather pertinent here which everyone except his fans seem to have overlooked: *Morrissey is not a mystery at all.* There is no need to train a telephoto lens on his bathroom window or rummage through his dustbin looking for evidence of lesbianism. To get to the melancholic heart of Morrissey's condition, to get inside the wasteland of his head — or his bed — there is only one thing you need to do.

Listen to him.

Granted, this requires a certain amount of recklessness. Not only is Morrissey one of the greatest pop lyricists — and probably *the* greatest ever lyricist of desire — that has ever moaned, he is fully present in his songs as few other artists are, in a way which fans of most other performers, quite rightly, wouldn't tolerate for a moment. In an age when 'truth' is whatever keeps the customer (vaguely) satisfied, Morrissey resolutely delivers only his own. Frequently unpalatable, it is often as hilarious as it is mortifying; after all, since desire is his subject — or rather his tormenter — frustration is frequently his material.

Morrissey's work is his life: there is no 'clocking off', as he puts it. That is the key to his greatness and to his tragedy. Morrissey is a record to be played, never a life to be lived. One day perhaps, in spite of all the evidence to the contrary, a fascinating secret life of scandal and debauchery may be revealed (and I suspect that no one would be happier than Morrissey at such an exposé). But who would bet money on it?

In his singular *oeuvre*, which must include his interviews, in themselves frequently riotously entertaining performances, Morrissey offers himself up, dandy Christ-like, as a fascinating, foppish 'fuck up', atoning for all our neuroses. As the novelist and Morrissey's 'sister in-law' Michael Bracewell has suggested, for his audience Moz represents not only the ultimate pop star but the ultimate patient, one they want to kiss better: *I am sick and I am dull/and I am plain/how dearly I'd love to get carried away....*

Hence like its subject, *Saint Morrissey* is not a conventional biography. Instead it is a 'psycho-bio' — one that does not presume to put

13

the performer on the couch as he's already chained himself there, but does try to listen carefully, and informed more by literary than clinical psychoanalysis offers an interpretation and a kind of diagnosis of this famous patient's extraordinarily creative if rather disturbing symptoms. And how he has succeeded in turning them into a global epidemic.

Saint Morrissey is an inquiry conducted through words, images, and music into the beautiful but damaged soul of a man who has willed *himself* out of words, images, and music. It is a history of a man as a history of ideas, not all of them terribly wholesome.

It does not, however, promise any cure.

* * *

But before any of *that*, before we start rummaging around inside Mr Morrissey's enormous head, please indulge me for a moment as I presume to lie on the couch myself and tell you something about Mr Morrissey and me...

on a hillside desolate

I think writing about unhappiness is probably the source of my popularity, if I have any. After all, most people are unhappy, don't you think?

PHILIP LARKIN

All people are lonely in some ways. Some people are lonely in all ways.

NOW VOYAGER

2

I remember it clearly. All too clearly. Seems like only yesterday and several lifetimes ago all at once. It was tea-time November 1983, I'd just turned eighteen and hardly ever been kissed. It happened in my parents' sitting room in Upper Poppleton, a nice sleepy normal village in North Yorkshire where such things aren't even supposed to be imagined.

I was minding my own business slouching on the sofa, picking wax out of my ear and watching a pop music programme on Channel Four called *The Tube* while I waited for my tea. Then, without warning, this pale, emaciated James Dean double, clearly much more in need of my fish-fingers and chips than I was, wearing some woman's blouse, a plastic necklace, a pair of jeans two sizes too large and a head three sizes too big, leapt out at me with his mouth open: *when in this charming car this charming man...*

I stopped picking my ear. Of course, I should have jammed my fingers in both ears.

He was singing at me, right at me, in the most indecently direct and alarmingly fey way. He'd singled me out for his warped attentions, I could tell. And it wasn't just any old pop lyric you could hear at that time — the sort of thing that's a bit pretentious like The Associates, or daft, like The Cure, or kinky and daft and pretentious like Soft Cell — but basically harmless. Oh no, it was, well... *bloody poetry*. How are you supposed to get over that?

Bloody poetry like I'd never heard before, but which spoke directly and assuredly to a happy-sad part of me that I barely knew existed myself — so how the hell did he know it was there? *Why pamper life's complexity when the leather runs smooth on the passenger seat.* Such a strange thing to sing in a pop song. Such a disturbing thing. Such a thing that shouldn't really mean anything but which, you couldn't help but notice, even without those intense, over-expressive beetle-black eyebrows aimed at you, meant far too much. Such a thing that made it sound as if I'd never heard a pop song before.

And that voice, coasting, feet off the pedals, over the chiming, tearful, bright guitar chords that also sounded entirely new and familiar, young and ancient all at once; so naïve and wise, wistful and lustful, carefree and very, very controlled — and this is the really ill part — so clearly taking pleasure from the feeling of the words in his mouth: *this charm-ming mmann...* A pleasure in possession, for these were incontrovertibly his words and nobody else's, with more lyricism in a single syllable than most popsters had in their entire back catalogue: *It's gruesome that someone so handsome should care.* This was an alliteration of the soul.

Oh yes, I knew he was a wrong-un. But I couldn't help myself. There he was, blouse billowing, junk jewellery jigging, economy-sized Adam's apple bobbing and his skinny arm windmilling a poor abused bunch of gladioli round and round and round, like a floral mace, hitting me over the head again and again until I felt so dizzy that I didn't know what was the right or wrong thing to do any more. Petals were raining everywhere, like fairy dust, like free drugs, like jism, like poison. And all this well before the nine o'clock watershed.

I was alone with this man for less time than it takes to boil an egg. But he knew what he was doing alright, and he made sure it was two and a half minutes I would never get over.

Accomplices? Well, I have a vague memory of three fresh-faced, slightly shifty lads looking on, smirking behind their instruments. I think he must have hit them over the head with his gladioli too as whenever they stole glances at him they had big, round dazed eyes, as if they'd do anything he asked. I tried to get away, really I did. But I was rooted to the spot, like an especially pathetic victim in a Freddie Kruger film. This strange man's sense of abandon, his openness, his archness, his tenderness, his viciousness, couldn't be resisted. I just couldn't look away. He was, simply, the funniest, saddest, smartest, loveliest, deadliest thing I'd ever seen.

Of course, I also knew the moment I saw him that he was the man my parents had warned me about: the man who steals children from their destiny, that makes good sons bad. But when I tried to open my mouth to call out for help, I just found myself singing along: *Will nature make a man of me yet?*

I can still hear that unearthly noise he made – YOW! – a falsetto animal yelp of release and abandon, not heard since Little Richard found God, Elvis joined the Army or Ziggy climbed back inside his spaceship. It was the cry of something unwholesome, unearthly and unfed, unleashed upon a world too flabby and too soft to get away, to want to get away.

A yell of triumph, I think, at having caught me: I'd accepted the ride this charming-alarming man had offered me.

As if there were any other response possible.

* * *

Like many such victims, at the time I was in deep denial about what had happened. I pretended it was just a bit of fun, a laugh. That it was just 'pop music'. I tried to forget about it. Put it down to experience. After all, I didn't have time for such foolishness. I was Going To University. I was Going to Experience Life – or at least leave home, make some new friends, get drunk and maybe even get laid. I certainly wasn't going to let this blousy madman spoil it all.

Of course, the reality was that I'd taken a lift to somewhere I'd never quite be able to come back from; I'd just met someone that I would never quite manage to get rid of.

Within just a few months I was to give up higher education as a bad mistake and find myself in January 1984 on the dole and shivering in a rented room in Levenshulme, a depressed and dilapidated district of South Manchester without the romance of Whalley Range. I kidded myself that I was still in control, that I was hot on the trail of Real Life now — and somehow managed to overlook the fact that I'd ended up in Morrissey's hometown.

And then The Smiths' eponymous debut album was released.

I can't remember how I came to buy it. I didn't plan to, it just happened. In a haze. But listening to/mainlining that album, as I did constantly for weeks, I was happy to be shipwrecked in Manchester, and Morrissey was both Siren and Man Friday to me — the seductive architect of my doom, and my sole, loyal companion in the wilderness. I lay on my mattress gasping and panting as I listened — above the sound of my teeth chattering: *under the iron bridge we kissed/and although I ended up with sore lips/it just wasn't like the old days any more/no it wasn't like those days/am I still ill?'*

Who needs heroin or analysis when you have lines like these? With their curiously hypnotic self-sufficient, self-mocking nostalgia they speak of a longing for something lost that was almost certainly never possessed in the first place, and which could never be recaptured anyway even if it were. The mixture, the intimacy of longing and lack is so acute, so intense that it even produces 'sore lips'. It's a song of innocence and experience that is entirely adolescent but at the same time seems to do away with adolescence altogether.

The pathology at the root of 'Still Ill' and *The Smiths* and Morrissey's art is the familiar modern malaise of self-reflexivity — an illness that the singer makes entirely his own but somehow universal at the same time. It's melancholia mixed with nostalgia and incubated in Morrissey's heart, head and mouth to produce... melanalgia. *Does the body rule the mind/or does the mind rule the body?/I dunno....*

Sickness never sounded or felt so good. For my part, sharing that box room and mattress with him, I was like thousands of others at that time rapidly developing a full-blown case of melanalgia myself. I may have felt unloved and unlovable but I also derived an exquisite, narcotic satisfaction from the knowing of these things and the ability to laugh under my breath at the perversity of that knowledge. Instead of feeling eighteen and inept, I felt a thousand years old and wiser

19

than the hills, and somehow this allowed me to float above the pathetic reality of my life. To this day, Smiths songs reek to me of cheap hair gel, unwashed sheets, damp walls, badly ventilated gas fires and impossible, intoxicating expectations. That's to say, a time when I had everything.

I had precisely one love affair to my credit at that point. Yet, according to Morrissey, in that one long, drawn out, pathetic, spotty disappointment, I had experienced everything there is to experience in Love. He cooed in my ear that yes, adolescence, like The Smiths and pop music, might be a moment that passes, that one day you might be laughing and dancing and finally living, but that feeling of aloneness and the bitter-sweet prospect of a life of disappointments stretching out before you, like a football supporter who chooses the wrong team to follow, is the purest, truest, noblest feeling you will ever have.

In other words, he told me terrible, venomous, mad things that innocent teenagers should never ever be told. Precisely because, of course, they're true.

In fact, *The Smiths* and The Smiths were experiences from which not only I but, I'd like to think, the whole of Western civilisation never recovered. *The Smiths* was not so much an album as a serious illness — the kind that you secretly relish because in the grip of its fevers and sweats, its aches and agues, it transforms your view of the world and leaves you so charmingly debilitated, so thoroughly exhausted, that afterwards you almost find the idea of yourself quite likeable. To this day there are precious few Smiths songs that can't mist my vision; but pretty much every track on *The Smiths* can have me abashedly wiping my eyes — if I make the mistake of really listening to it.

Not because they are 'sad' or 'miserable', but because they are so unutterably, unfeasibly, unlawfully *handsome*. Which is the deadliest drug of all. If ever there was proof that Keats's assertion that 'beauty is truth, truth beauty' is anything more than just a trite line, or simply wishful thinking, then it is in *The Smiths*.

* * *

The Smiths is the greatest of The Smiths' albums, making it of course the Greatest Album of All Time. The first Smiths album had to be the best. It's the most immediate, the freshest, the purest and the most depraved. Its power and poignancy is in the final emergence into the light, blinking and gasping, of all the passions and preoccupations that consumed Morrissey for years, alone in his darkened bedroom.

Like the first single, 'Hand in Glove', the first album has an evangelical brilliance, an urgency and malice that fills you with a lust to go out shoplifting expensive perfume with which to spray bus-shelters, or seditiously stay in bed all day picking your nose. With bafflingly beautiful tracks such as 'Still Ill', 'Reel Around the Fountain', 'Suffer Little Children' and 'I Don't Owe You Anything', *The Smiths* did nothing short of reinvent desire and turn it into something palpable, something communicable, something transmissible, something catchable — the inevitable effect of capturing the fickle, fleeting essence of it so definitively.

The much mentioned poor production on the album, apparently a source of great disappointment to Morrissey and Marr themselves, sounded and still sounds perfect to my ear. Its very lack of hi-tech professionalism, the slightly muffled, distant quality, especially of some of the vocals, even the rough balancing that allows Mike Joyce's drums to dominate too often, lends it an innocence and energy which underscores the remarkable depth of its knowledge, as well as reminding you where this album is coming from — someone's bedroom, someone's past, someone's bottomless frustration. *The Smiths* represents a once-in-a-lifetime explosion of suffocated ambition, disappointed desire and blocked aggression that could never be repeated, not even by Morrissey.

The official 'rock critic' best album, *The Queen is Dead* (decreed 'Best Rock Album Ever' by *Melody Maker* in its Top Albums of the Millennium list), is a very fine album, and in fact the second best album in the world. But the problem, or rather the slight and minor flaw with *Queen* compared to *The Smiths*, is that it sounds just a little too accomplished, a little too professional, a little too grown up.

Not content with just reinventing-perverting desire, Morrissey also reinvented-perverted the Eighties — or at least the version of it that I and other losers like me inhabited. Thousands of young people fled to Morrissey's version of that decade, abandoning in self-righteous disgust the shiny High Street one that everyone else seemed to live in: the wake-me-up-before-you-go-go-kajagoogoo-morning-in-America-do-they-know-it's-Christmas-the-price-is-right-for-I-am-your-laydee-and-yoo-are-my-maan-this-lady's-not-for-turning-gotcha-this-time-you've-gone-too-far-Alexis-red-gold-and-green-cruise-missiles-are-the-guaran-tors-of-peace-we-begin-bombing-in-five-minutes-just-rejoice-at-that-news-you're-about-as-easy-as-a-nuclear-war-isn't-Princess-Di-pretty-Eighties.

It was a difficult decade for idealists, and not only because crass-ness and shoulder pads were all the rage. Margaret Thatcher's constant tuneless refrain 'No Alternative' was the biggest-selling single of the decade. The crushing weight of mainstream stupidity was becoming increasingly impossible to resist with marginal eccentricity, quaint lyri-cism and a sketchy knowledge of the works of Pierre Joseph Proudhon. In bitter hindsight, it's possible to see that the Eighties was nothing less than a glacier composed of icy common sense and hard commer-cial realities which smoothed and ground the culture flat and feature-less ready for the Nothing Nineties...

But before that glacier did its terrible work, there were still quite a few young people who dared to be different, to dream, to be . . . well, *prats*. Even punk's nihilism had been based on an essentially idealistic belief in the sacred role of youth — young people's divine right to rebel, reject, purify and generally behave like a bunch of total wankers.

The post-punk early Eighties may have been an increasingly disil-lusioned and cynical period, but it still boasted the last generation of young people who were naïve enough to believe that there was an alternative — and that a pop star prophet would come and save them from dowdy darkness and take them to the lacy light with his fey ways and magic spangly cod-piece. This was the last generation to actually listen to pop records, all those who came after would merely shuffle tracks. And I mean really, really, listen, in a way which young people today would, quite rightly, consider merely 'sad'.

This intensity was partly down to the fact that young people in the early Eighties had nothing better to do (Ecstasy had not yet been added to potato crisps and watching your parents' home-made pornography on the Internet was not a common teenage hobby back then), and partly because they really did believe that if they listened hard enough and often enough they would hear The Answer.

It was the measure of both his genius and his dangerousness that Morrissey, the latest, last − and most pre-eminent − in a long line of pop wrecks turned pied pipers, wrote lyrics that finally justified this kind of hopeless attention, right at the very moment when pop as a whole was descending into pointless gibberish. The situationist, anarchic stunts and poses of punk had long run out of steam; the glamorous, post-modern sashays and simpering strategies of the New Romantics had been shown to be ultimately empty if rather gorgeous attention-seeking, while the initially exciting urgency and icy aestheticism of electro pop was about to descend into a disco inferno.

Morrissey saved pop not just by making it lyrical and melodic again (with help from Marr's sacred guitars), but by making it intellectual, by making it literary − something from which it would never recover (even Bowie's 'cut-up' lyrics had been merely artful where Morrissey's were inspired; coldly contrived where Morrissey's were wittily, deadly accurate; ironically, or perhaps inevitably, in making pop music, for want of a better word, intellectual, Morrissey succeeded in provoking some of the most passionately emotional responses to pop music ever). As a final proof of his destructive creative genius, Mozzer, the greatest enemy of the Eighties and everything it represented, would ultimately come to be remembered as its greatest artist.

Morrissey was the pop Anti-Christ in a way which a contemporary controversy merchant like Marilyn Manson cannot hope to be, no matter how many gallons of eye shadow he sprays on of a morning. Manson offers only a grotesque pantomime and travesty of everything that a pop/rock star is supposed to be; a reductio ad absurdum, in which all the drama of rock music is externalised − which may be ironic and, frankly, fucking hilarious but is no more inspiring or subversive for that. Morrissey on the other hand was the actual, fleshly (though maybe not that fleshly) antithesis of everything that pop and rock had come to stand for. He was bookish; he wore NHS spectacles and a hearing aid on stage; he was celibate. Worst of all, he was sincere. He said what he meant and passionately meant what he said. Especially when he was joking. Some thought him an arch ironist and stylist, a sultan of insincerity, like his Wildean role model, but they weren't quite right. Even though hyperbole was his idea of a healthy balance, Morrissey wasn't making it up as he went along.

In assaulting pop's nostrums and clichés and remaking it in his own image, Morrissey made it about the one thing both parents and pop music had been united against: intelligence. Forget drugs, forget promiscuity, forget green hair and safety pins, and certainly forget androgynous silver body-suits. As Morrissey himself demonstrated incontrovertibly, Thinking Too Much was undoubtedly the most degenerate, most anti-social habit any teenager ever picked up.

This was the vengeful virus of Moz Pop: he made pop music which was so intoxicatingly melancholic, so dangerously thoughtful, so seductively funny that it lured its listeners, most of whom were not really damned just slightly cursed, into a relationship with him and his music instead of the world. The Pop Pied Piper knows that life doesn't imitate great art, it is destroyed by it.

* * *

It certainly did for mine. I was the barely living proof that whether or not an unexamined life is not worth living, an over-examined one simply isn't lived. During my Manchester embalmment I foreswore the corruption of the world in the form of meat and lived on a diet of curried lentils (which didn't help the condensation problem), and heady books (which didn't help the alienation problem). There were a limited number of reasons for actually leaving my room. Shopping for food wasn't really necessary, as a large bag of lentils lasts approximately fifteen years.

I would however visit second-hand clothes shops or Manchester's Central Library, both mortuaries of dead people's fancies. There were hours of bleak fun to be had in sifting through the detritus of loves, hates and passions just like mine. Wearing clothes worn by people now perished, and reading books written by hands now melted, wasn't simply an economic necessity, oh no, it was a symbolic protest against the Way of the World and a championing of the dejected and down-trodden in a decade in which shopping and superficiality were rapidly becoming the national religion.

Like much of early Eighties youth, in other words, I was unemployed.

Difficult to believe, but back then unemployment and a certain kind of poverty was actually fashionable, so much so that even southern career-girls Wham! noticed and one of their early singles, 'Young Guns', extolled the benefits of a life on benefits and the hipness of the DHSS (the government department which then paid them). Which was quite fortunate really, given that three million people were on the dole – most of them in the North, and most of them, unlike me, not through choice.

But the great thing about being unemployed in the early Eighties was that you could devote yourself to the noble and sacred and artistic pursuit of Being Yourself. And Being Yourself was undoubtedly a full-time occupation: England owed us all a living and the fortnightly Giro was really an Arts Council grant. Certainly, being surplus to capitalism gave you plenty of time to practise your chords and stage moves. Or at least think about practising them. Finding a real job rather than planning your pop career was considered a compromise at best, collaboration at worst. After all, being a pop star was the only way you would get paid more than Supplementary Benefit for Being Yourself (though as the history of pop shows, making it as a pop star is actually about Becoming Someone Else – or in Morrissey's case, Becoming the Person You Were Meant to Be).

I discovered an amazing fact while on the dole: if you just ate lentils and porridge, walked everywhere, wore second-hand plastic shoes and nursed a half pint of beer all evening on the only night you went out all week, you could in fact save money. It was, I suppose, another way of cheating The System. It was also very Northern.

Essentially, the trick to saving money on the dole was to minimise your life functions until they could barely be measured. This meant staying in bed for most of the day, while wearing two layers of clothes, with your overcoat over the bed to save fuel. In other words, you had to actually die, in an economical if not a clinical sense. (Hence it seems very likely that Morrissey was rather good at saving money during all those years he was on the dole).

My mate Herman, so dubbed because he looked a bit like Herman Munster, was another expert at saving money on the dole. Perhaps this was because he'd been on the dole for longer than anyone else I knew. Herman was a few years older than me and had been on the dole since the Seventies, which seemed to me like another century. There wasn't anything Herman didn't know about minimising your life functions. People used to come to him from as far a field as Stockport for tips on how to avoid eating for three months without going into a coma, something which would actually have been a very desirable, very economical condition if it hadn't meant that you would miss signing on and therefore have your dole stopped. After all, Herman had managed to buy equipment for his band, Three Fish, out of the money he'd saved on the dole. It had taken him about five years in bed.

The only activity that Herman actually recommended when you were trying to save money on the dole, other than staying in bed all day holding your breath, was visiting the dentist. This was because dental care was free for the unemployed. 'We may be starving,' Herman would grin, proudly showing off a set of gleaming pearlies that made his vitamin B12-deficient skin look even greyer than it was, 'but we got perfect teeth!' A Wildean sentiment that no doubt Morrissey would have endorsed.

* * *

Manchester itself was somewhat malnourished in the early Eighties: a vicious economic recession engineered by Morrissey's love-hated Margaret Thatcher, designed to get rid of the troublesome working class and turn Britain into a post-industrial service economy based on finance, property and hairdressing, had hit the North harder than anywhere else.

Its front teeth weren't in good shape either. Apart from the occasional tatty pub and Job Centre, and a confusing number of bus and railway stations whose purpose seemed to be to evacuate people from the centre rather than bring them in, its heart seemed to be mostly a collection of boarded up warehouses and abandoned Victorian office-buildings — glazed red-brick Neo-Gothic edifices that were once full of people working for life assurance companies, but whose sightless windows now bore testament to a society that had given up on the future. Most commercial life seemed to have retreated to the climate-controlled windowless refuge of the day-glo orange shopping centre hell known as The Arndale, a structure clearly based on a prototype model for *Space 1999*'s Moonbase Alpha, one discarded because it didn't look convincing enough (mercifully it was bombed by the IRA the following decade).

Manchester, the Los Angeles of the nineteenth century, the city to which the world once looked as The Future, the hub of industry and enterprise where Engels lived so as to study capitalism at its most dynamic, was at its lowest ebb, deprived of a future by its own past. The perfect Diamond Dogsian backdrop, in other words, to the arrival of Morrissey, a prophet of doom drunk on nostalgia.

Of course, from the perverse pop view of things, which weaves joy out of misery, beauty out of boredom, this was Manchester's Golden Age, one that had begun in the late Seventies with The Buzzcocks, Joy Division, The Fall, and the presiding mad genius of Tony Wilson's Factory Records, and would last at least another ten years. If English pop was essentially Northern, and it was of course (just like Englishness itself), Manchester in its doldrums had become its pop capital. It wasn't only The Smiths that formed in the unemployed early Eighties: James and 'baggy' stalwarts of the early Nineties 'Madchester' scene the Stone Roses and the Happy Mondays also decided to take on the world at this time. If you have nothing it's easier to demand everything.

Twenty years later, those warehouses are million pound loft apartments, those abandoned red-brick neo-Gothic buildings are designer bars, cafes and hotels. Brand spanking new buildings sheeted with green glass that look like giant top-of-the-line Swedish stereo systems shoot up overnight. Manchester, thanks to the IRA and an explosion of design terrorism has been improved out of all recognition, and quite possibly, existence, and is now a place where a London hairdresser could happily live. And many do. Manchester City Centre these days looks like a place that has everything.

But perhaps it also has nothing. Pop music is of course over. It isn't needed any more. What is the point of an aesthetic rebellion against the world if the world has been aestheticised? How can you deploy your youth to refuse the world — or demand it — when the world is much better looking than you could ever hope to be? Manchester, so much to answer for, has upstaged its inhabitants.

* * *

As for me, well, I'm not sure I ever made it out of the early Eighties, thanks to you-know-who. I did however make it out of Manchester. Sort of. After a few months in Levenshulme I decided that there was more to life than lying in bed all day farting, and sold my stereo and *The Smiths*, repaired that punctured bicycle, started eating meat again, and then ran away to sea, working as a deckhand on sailing yachts in the Mediterranean, hoping nature would make a man of me.

It very nearly did. But when I got back to Blighty a few months later, bronzed and with my, er... horizons... broadened, *Hatful of Hollow* had been released. I took to my mattress for a fortnight. I was right back where I started, though this time in a squat in South London.

I tried going cold turkey and living in the real world rather than a shell. I took a succession of jobs including: TV deliveryman, bouncer, cocktail waiter, warehouseman, double-glazing salesman, gym instructor, house painter, chauffeur, photo-love novel model (the horror!), all of which came to an abrupt end after I asked myself foolish questions like: *why do I smile at people I'd much rather kick in the eye?*

I only need to mention the fatal names, *Meat is Murder*, *The Queen is Dead*, *The World Won't Listen*, *Strangeways Here We Come*, and you'll know what happened to the rest of my mid-Eighties. When The Smiths split in 1987 I was elated: I thought I might have a chance now, that I might be finally rid of this guy and his terrible illness. But then he released *Viva Hate* and some of the highest charting, most intoxicating singles of his career. In the early Nineties, desperate now, aware that my youth was already slipping out of sight like a boat on the Manchester Ship Canal, I tried running away again, this time to the the West Coast of the US where I thought I'd be safe. And I was doing OK, really I was, until someone put on a copy of *Louder Than Bombs*. The cloudless Californian sky immediately turned leaden and I was back in the UK inside a week.

On my return I drove five hours non-stop and flat out in a borrowed ten-year-old Renault 5 automatic, shredding the transmission on the Pennines, just to get to see him perform in Glasgow. I had to see my dealer. Of course, the bastard stood me up. The concert was cancelled – due to 'ill health'. A bitter, Morrisseyan joke.

When I got to hear *Kill Uncle* things began to look up. I felt optimistic about the future at last. I thought that we were finally through, that I was over him, that he'd finally returned the ring. But then in 1992 he made *Your Arsenal*. And followed it up in 1994 with *Vauxhall & I*.

I abandoned all hope. And of course did what anyone would do in those circumstances: I became a writer.

Then, just when I'd reconciled myself both to the fact I'd never be rid of him and the incurable, terminal nature of the dose of melanalgia he'd given me back in 1983, Morrissey himself moved to the West Coast in the late Nineties, and it looked as if he was on the verge of retirement. His 'difficult' 1995 album *Southpaw* and lack-lustre 1997 album *Maladjusted* were poorly received and he was promptly dropped by his record company. In other words: Just when I'd begun to 'come to terms' with him and what he'd done to me and was finally willing to talk about it the fucker had walked out on me!

To make matters worse it looked as if he might actually be having *quite a nice time* in Los Angeles, that he might be *getting out and about* and actually be *having a life*.

This was intolerable. So I resolved to expose him. To write a book about him. Or rather, to write a book about what he did to me and millions of others. With words. It was to be my revenge. Paragraphs taking on blank verse, prose assaulting bloody poetry. Pathetic and hopeless, I know, but satisfaction of a kind – the only kind available to me.

Of course, by the time I'd found a publisher willing to be an accessory to this vendetta, Morrissey was back in Britain with a record deal and was on everyone's lips again. Now my revenge merely seems like tribute. But then, just like the bitterness and sweetness, euphoria and nostalgia, melodiousness and melancholia of pop music — and Mozza's voice — there's maybe not so much between them.

you are your mother's only son

A person is not born a genius or normal. He becomes one or the other, according to the accidents of his history and to his own reaction to these accidents. I maintain that genius is . . . an outlet that a child discovers when he is suffocating.

JEAN-PAUL SARTRE, SAINT GENET

I had the upbringing a nun would envy . . . Until I was fifteen I was more familiar with Africa than I was with my own body.

JOE ORTON, ENTERTAINING MR SLOANE

3

Steven Patrick Morrissey was born in Manchester, England on 22nd of May, 1959. For most people, their birthday is a date they never forget. For Morrissey, it was a day he would never forgive.

> *Where and when were you happiest?*
> May 21, 1959
>
> MORRISSEY

Angry, petulant children, unable to answer their parents' arguments as to why they should do or endure something they don't want to often exclaim, 'I didn't ask to be born!' Steven Morrissey may or may not have used this complaint when he was a child, but he would spend the rest of his life saying it over and over, in as many — or more — words.

Life, to paraphrase Shelagh Delaney, is thrust upon us without so much as a please or thank you or even a light ale and bag of chips. A little bit of love, a little bit more lust, and there you are. The childish complaint 'I didn't ask to be born!' is a futile attempt to tear up a contract that we had no part in drafting, which was in place long before we were slapped into life or even a twinkle in someone's sty; an attempt to assert our uniqueness and our own authorship in the teeth of all the dreary, mundane evidence to the contrary. An attempt to establish our genius.

Life, much more than death (which is just the final sub clause of life), is an implacable, immovable fact that we are supposed to get used to – or, to be more precise, abandon ourselves to. We are expected to 'pull ourselves together' when it was not our idea, or our congress which put us together in the first place. But not little Steven. Instead, he resolved, with all the fury, malice, resentment and heroism of a small but very, very sharp child (which is rather a lot of fury, malice, resentment and heroism), that he would not resign himself. He would not forgive his parents, Nature or Fate the outrageous demands they had made of him. He would not, in other words, grow up.

Most of us learn to stop making the complaint about our non-consensual origins, not because we change our minds and suddenly decide that life is a 'great gift' (one, mysteriously, that you never find in Grattan's Xmas mail order catalogue), but simply because nobody will listen to us. We discover very quickly that this whinge does not get us what we want and try to forget about it; the lucky, 'vital' ones amongst us succeed. An artist – especially one who craves fame – however, is someone who doesn't forget, and instead persuades people to listen to their 'childish' complaints for the rest of their lives. That is their gift and, of course, their ultimate curse. The artistic disposition is little more than an extreme form of sulking. And Steven Morrissey was destined to sulk for England.

It is no coincidence that Steven was born into a working class, immigrant, Irish Catholic family during the Feast of Humility, a celebration of the 'life' of a thirteenth-century nun who voluntarily entombed herself, sleeping on her knees with her head resting on the wall of her bricked up cell, eating nothing but bread, water and the occasional bunch of parsley. She was sulking for Jesus. Catholicism – the Mother Church – has a masochistic relationship to the world, which turns moaning into singing, and which keys into this basic human complaint about our origins. What else could the meaning of 'original sin' be? Of course, original sin is seen by non-Romans as a cruel, sick trick to play on innocent, pink-skinned chuckley babies, but they miss the point. Infantile indoctrination is not the beginning of an unfair burden — conception is. *In the midst of life we are in debt, et cetera.*

Catholicism celebrates the lives of those who resist the way of the world, the temptations and corruptions of the flesh, those who martyr themselves for the One True Faith, who deny themselves mortal pleasures and safety for the promise of immortal bliss and protection. In this fatal cosmology where the veil of flesh we are born into is our prison-guard our torturer and our executioner we are all spawned as monsters: *What can make GOOD all the BAD that's been done?*

Those revered as saints are usually very peculiar chaps and chapesses who succeeded in refusing life just short of actually killing themselves (which is considered cheating, and takes you straight to purgatory), or those who arranged for someone else to kill them — preferably in some theatrically gruesome manner, such as slow suffocation on a wooden cross or being torn apart by wild animals in the Coliseum. (Morrissey, in his relationship with the press and in his stage performances, was to re-enact both these scenarios repeatedly.)

Oddly enough, this life-denying strand of (Irish) Catholicism is highly compatible with the Puritan Protestant tradition of English culture, which is distrustful of pleasure, hostile to success, suspicious of riches and always expects to be punished for any happiness — a tradition otherwise known as Northerness. Manchester, the dank, damp, melancholy town of Morrissey's birth, was this tradition turned into anxious narrow streets, resentful leaden skies and gloomy terraced houses stained by soot from coal burned generations ago in other people's grates.

> People always ask me if I'm religious, I don't know why.
> *Well you were born into a Catholic household weren't you?*
> Quite vividly Catholic. Then it became vaguely Catholic.
>
> NME, 1985

Little Steven, however, was not destined to sulk for Jesus, despite his family's initial devoutness and his attendance at schools named after Catholic saints (Winifred and Mary), where he learned about hell fire and damnation. This was, after all, the Sixties, and the Catholic Church was in decline, rapidly losing its authority to science and secularism and its flock to the Sodom and Gomorrah of consumer culture. The Mother Church's incense-and-bells version of showbusiness couldn't compete with the new freedoms, sensations and escapisms proferred by the neon-lit, stereophonic Cities of the Plain (and laughable as it may sound, Manchester to an immigrant from Fifties Ireland, was Sodom and Gomorrah with knobs on). Nevertheless, while the Morrisseys like many of their immigrant generation, lost their respect for the Mother Church, they somehow managed to cling on to their repression — it was, after all, what they knew, rather more tangible than God's love, and what they had in common with the natives.

> There was no such thing as strong language or nudity. Unfortunately, I was raised with the notion that excitement and exuberance were something other people did and were not for me.
>
> DETAILS, 1994

Steven, for his part, found a route to passion and apostasy through the dizzyingly sacrilegious, concentric grooves impregnated into the vinyl of a pop record. When he was just six, he bought his first 45 — 'Come Stay With Me' by Marianne Faithful, a spooky, mysterious, enchanting record in which Marianne's neurotic yet strangely pure and soothing voice promises the listener anything they wish, and pledges, in a divinely passive-aggressive fashion, to negate all her own needs if they will only come and live with her. Steven didn't need to play his records backwards to hear Satanic messages. Marianne spoke to him directly and personally and uniquely. Pop music's wicked apostasy, its false consolations and illusions proved irresistible to a young Steven and he went to stay with Marianne and never came back.

> I lost myself in music at a very early age, and I remained there . . . I did fall in love with the voices I heard, whether they were male or female. I loved those people. I really, really did love those people. For what it was worth, I gave them my life . . . my youth. Beyond the perimeter of pop music there was a drop at the edge of the world.
>
> SELECT, JULY 1991

Pop music was to be the vinyl heart in a heartless world, the catchy sigh of the oppressed. It became a place to which Steven Morrissey escaped as his home life deteriorated and closed in on him like a trap.

His natural sulkiness was proved disastrously correct and was permanently reinforced when his parents' marriage, in a sign of their modernity and apostasy, began to fall dramatically apart, and he became not only someone who hadn't asked to be born, someone whose story had been written before they were conceived, but someone whose story was now being erased around them in the most brutal and frightening way. He was being turned into that most modern and common of jokes – the child whose reasons for existing, such as they were, had ceased to exist. Pulled apart by those who had put him together.

> It's nothing unique. Millions upon millions of people come from 'damaged backgrounds', shall we say. Mine wasn't so much damaged as merely nothing at all.
>
> *Details*, 1994

If Morrissey's disappointments were entirely modern, so was his remedy. Unlike the Virgin Mary's, Marianne Faithful's voice and love were palpable and always there, as were Cilla's, Twinkle's and Sandie's, waiting in the grooves of the record. Visions appeared to order, without the need for fasting and scourging. All that was needed to summon them and prove their fidelity was the devilish needle that he held in his hand in the besieged privacy of his own room. These were disembodied voices, spiritual not fleshly, constant not fickle, beautiful not hateful, undemanding and existing entirely for him. In Steven's life, as in more and more young people's lives (though perhaps none quite so much as his), pop culture stood in for missing or congealed human relationships. In other words, Steven was turning into the prototypical nerd, a young man with a religious, fetishistic dedication to images and sounds – to the iconography of pop – and a superstitious, self-abusing aversion to people. In the Eighties he would be transported to world fame on the dandified back of his dysfunction, becoming the symbol of what turned out to be an increasingly single society trying to come to terms with the love-shaped hole in their lives where Nietzsche would once have found a god-shaped one.

In Manchester's Stretford of the Sixties, however, there was no such thing as a 'nerd', and dandies were an endangered species. Morrissey was simply a freak. And he was about to discover the terrible truth of

Wilde's assertion that while society often forgives the criminal; it never forgives the dreamer.

> There's a famous quote which goes something like, 'You are what you are, having secretly become what you wanted to be'. Maybe there's some truth to that. We like to think that society shapes us, but I don't think that that's the way it happens.
>
> SELECT, 1991

Unfortunately for Steven, his graduation from the relative innocence of primary school to the Edenic exile of secondary school coincided with the deterioration of his parents' marriage. Secondary school, which might have rescued him from himself, offering human contact and interaction beyond the tragic histrionics of the kitchen sink drama of his home life, turned out to be the source of even more despair, instilling in him as it did every day his separation from the human race. School was also where Morrissey learned the meaning of his class: no prospects. Sent to a secondary modern meat grinder designed to produce semi-skilled, semi-literate, semi-conscious fodder for Manchester's factories, he experienced a daily crushing of the human spirit which was certainly not unusual for the time, but which he felt more intimately than most, precisely because he understood more than most the sadistic trick that society was playing on him.

'Education' is derived from the Latin verb 'educo', meaning 'I draw out'. But in Manchester in the Sixties, this education was only available for middle class kids and the handful of working class kids smart or sad enough to determine whether the next symbol in a sequence should be a shaded triangle or a stripy square and thus make it to Grammar school (public school for the lower middle classes) and escape their class sentence. For the rest, 'education' meant simply, 'I hem in', 'I stamp on', or 'I condition to expect nothing from life': *education in reverse.*

For a brilliant, extremely sensitive and self-conscious young man who happened not to be very interested in symbolic algebra (he failed his 11 plus), this kind of 'education' was little more than a daily visit to a slaughterhouse of the mind run by 'belligerent ghouls'. St Mary's Secondary Modern was Morrissey's first collision with the world and it almost destroyed him, confirming all his worst fears about the malignity of life. He discovered that if his parents had inflicted a narrative on him that he didn't want to feature in, the world had even worse in store. It's a lesson that, as usual, he never forgot or forgave.

> My education in St Mary's Secondary School in Manchester wasn't an education. It was all violence and brutality. As soon as you'd walk into the class at ten past nine, a minute later someone would be viciously beaten. And everybody would just sit there in silence. It was so abysmal — and you may snigger, you may not, I'll chance it — that I've considered actually suing the Manchester Education Committee because the education I received was so basically evil and brutal. All I learnt was to have no self-esteem and to feel ashamed without knowing why.
>
> THE IRISH TIMES, 1999

Young Morrissey's experience of the horror of school life was mostly unmitigated by the usual childish alliances and shelters against the awfulness — friendships, gangs, games and the loss of self in the crowd. He experienced it alone, apart, separate. Although his surprising prowess at athletics, an inheritance from his father that he was later to deliberately squander, meant that he wasn't bullied, and saved him perhaps from becoming a dreary cliché, he was never popular or even noticed much. He glided through his school years like a ghost. A *snooty* ghost.

> I despised practically everyone. Which does somewhat limit your weekend activities.
>
> BLITZ, 1988

Steven was already too much of a freak and, secretly, already too much in love with being a freak, to connect with the other children. It would have meant lowering himself to their level. He would have had to be phoney. He would have had to pretend to be stupid. He would have had to pretend not to be an individual. In other words, he would have had to want to be liked. Not perhaps such a great burden, since everyone wants to be liked, but Morrissey wanted to be liked so much that he couldn't bring himself to admit it. It would have meant risking everything — including what little peace and tranquillity he had managed to scrape together from books and records and a haughty distance from the world. So, not for the last time, he resolved to set himself against his own desire, and choose his own rejection.

> I think, yes, there was in some ways a wilful isolation. It was like a volunteered redundancy, in a way. Most of the teenagers that surrounded me, and the things that pleased them and interested them, well, they bored me stiff. It was like saying, 'Yes, I see that this is what all teenagers are supposed to do, but I don't want any part of this drudgery.
>
> MELODY MAKER, 1984

Mummy, as is often the case (who would be a mother?), was to 'blame'. Elizabeth or 'Betty' Morrissey the librarian, had introduced her son to the literary vice and passed on her love of books in general and Oscar Wilde in particular. It was monstrous enough to have a brain, but quite inexcusable to have a cultivated one. However, it is possible that Mrs Morrissey had passed on something even more anti-social than an interest in words and ideas. Like many mothers unhappy with their marriage, which, back then, meant their lot in life, she may have passed on her aspirations, magnified through her own frustrations, and they were aspirations that had no place in a Manchester secondary modern sink school. A clue to Betty's aspirationalism, and a portent perhaps of her later 'irreconcilable differences' with Steven's dad, appears on the infant's birth certificate: she gives her address as '17 Harper Street, Stretford'; Peter gives his address as '17 Harper St, Old Trafford'. They were inhabiting the same house but already living at different addresses (Old Trafford was the home of Manchester United Football Club and also a large, ugly industrial park; Stretford was a slightly more well-to-do, tidy and respectable working class area).

> I was born in Manchester's Central Library – the crime section.
>
> MELODY MAKER, 1984

To her great credit, and in stark contrast to Greater Manchester's school system, Betty had recognised little Steven's sensitivity, his brilliance, his enquiring mind, his facility for words, and had encouraged these traits. Morrissey was actually the 'little genius' that many mothers like to think that they have spawned when all they've really managed to produce is a failed candidate for *Countdown*. Steven was going to escape from the narrow life that she had had to lead and

'make something of himself' (and Mrs Morrissey was of a generation
— perhaps the last one — which believed that you 'made something of
yourself' by reading books). Steven and the world owe Betty Morrissey
a great debt. But Betty may also owe Steven, as her ambitions and attentions, as always in these cases, will have had a price attached. They
probably did for Steven as much as they made him, exacerbating his
alienation from other children and setting him up for a soul-destroy-
ing disappointment when he collided with Manchester schools' own
idea of 'education'.

It is clear that Morrissey never quite got over his relationship with
his mother. But then, most men never do. And Mrs Morrissey was a
mother who was more difficult to get over than most. She was pretty,
she was intelligent, she was feisty, she was well-informed and read.
And she was devoted to her son. (And apparently, she is still all of
these things.) It seems reasonable to speculate that in her heart she resigned herself to the failure of her marriage long before she and Peter
finally divorced (when Steven was seventeen), and that she turned her
spurned affections towards someone she could be more sure of, someone who needed them so much that he would never reject them.

If this is the emotional calculation that Mrs Morrissey unconsciously made, it would appear she got her sums right. Certainly, in a
Freudian sense, he has remained faithful to her: he has never married.
Such an intense filial-maternal relationship is, of course, usually seen
as pathological; Morrissey is probably imagined stalking his mother's
house after dark in her nightie, clutching a carving knife à la Anthony
Perkins. But perhaps it has to be pathologised precisely because such
a relationship is so (un)easily understood. If your mother is attractive,
intelligent and loving, and one of the few people you can have a decent conversation with, then why give up that attachment? Especially
if Dad is out of the picture. Everything else is likely to be something of
a disillusionment. More to the point, the insult 'mummy's boy', one
of the worst accusations in the English language, carries little or no
sting if you are already an outsider and have, you believe, no care for
the opinions of others.

It's a national disgrace! We know there's a shame attached to it. If you're
still living with your parents at 19 you're considered some club-footed

bespectacled monster of repressed sexuality — which is in every case absolutely true!

NME, 1986

An unusually close relationship between mother and son was the domestic dynamo that propelled some of the most creative talents in history. That good Jewish boy who loved his mommy, Freud, considered that when a son is sure of his mother's love he is given a confidence that survives setbacks and can take on the world. Moreover, language is something that most sons learn from their mothers, and those fortunate enough to be born to interested mothers will also learn to read and appreciate the arts. Another famous Irish Englishman Oscar Wilde certainly did. The arts that Mum inculcates a passion for in her offspring can be the popular ones — Elvis Presley acquired his love of singing (and dressing up) from his mother Gladys, and it was she, not Colonel Tom Parker and certainly not his loser father, who provided Elvis with his ambition and his talent. Culture, if it is passed down at all, is usually passed down the maternal line: and is no doubt the reason why Judaism, which is also passed down the maternal line, is the oldest religion in the world. Catholicism — especially Irish Catholicism — built as it is around the Divine mother-child dyad, is also passed down the maternal line (along with guilt).

Why then is so much opprobrium and ridicule heaped upon mummy's boys, especially within Protestant culture? Because the mother-son dyad is a bond to be feared and envied — separation from mummy has to be enforced and compelled because otherwise it might never happen. It is the most enduring of all relationships (not for nothing do brave men dying on the battlefield call out for their mothers), and, at least during infancy, it is the strongest and purest of any love known, hence all other relationships can seem its mere shadow. Romantic love can be an eternal disappointment after true maternal love. There is an invincible, 'hand in glove', narcissistic energy in the mother-son romance which is often reflected in the work of the artist touched by it. It is this energy which gives an artist, especially a performer, their 'radiance' or 'star quality', whether it is Elvis, John Lennon, George Michael, or the 'quivering distillation of mother love' that was Liberace. The whole world recognises it and is in awe of it. But awe is another word for terror, and in a Manchester secondary modern school playground — even a Catholic one — this ageless relationship can provoke equally primal responses.

Of course, Oedipus has to pay a price. Perhaps not in the form of literal blindness as in the myth, but certainly in a failure to be social-ised, to be integrated into the world. This is often a source of resent-ment in adult life when the cost becomes more apparent (*And you ran back to Ma/Which set the pace for the rest of your days*). For mummy's boys, the loss of the bright, massive centre of their lives can be a trauma from which they never recover, never quite finding their orbit again. Elvis famously never got over the loss of his beloved Gladys, and it was her death, not his entry into the Army, that marked the decline of his talents. With Mum gone, the cherished, prized, spoilt son, protected so long from the harshness of life, is left alone in the world with his own mortality. And his 'difference'.

> What did I want to be when I grew up? Oh, I'm afraid I always wanted to be a librarian. To me that seemed like the perfect life: solitude; absolute silence; tall, dark libraries. But then they started to become very modern, you know, these little pre-fabs and they had no romance whatsoever. So suddenly the idea had no fascination for me.
>
> STAR HITS, 1985

Mummy's boys are thought to be feminine-identified, which until quite recently was considered the most terrible tragedy which could befall a boy (nowadays, of course, it lands you your own TV series). Indeed, Young Steven appears to have made, at least for a while, a feminine identification himself. He stayed with his mother when his father moved out, and while he has often spoken of Betty, he hardly ever speaks of Peter (it seems likely his football-crazy dad was in some ways disappointed with his sensitive, bookish, only son).

Not only did Steven want for a while to follow his mother's profes-sional footsteps he was also an avid reader of feminist tracts which attacked masculinity and blamed men for the evils of the world. Even his famous decision around the time of the formation of The Smiths to drop his first name and to be known simply as the non-gender-spe-cific 'Morrissey' seems telling. Fathers often choose the first names for their first-born sons, and 'Steven' or 'Steve' sounds like the sort of name and future an Irish working class footballing father might choose for his son; it is certainly not the sort of name or future an Oscar Wilde-reading Cilla Black fan would choose for himself. He was, in other words, the son and heir of... *nothing in particular*.

However, the filial-maternal family romance can be as suffocating as it is supporting. Certainly in Morrissey's lyrics there is often a close relationship between smothering death and motherhood: *'Oh, smother me Mother . . .'* ('Rubber Ring'); *'No, Mamma, let me go!/Young bones groan and the rocks below say:/"Throw your white body down!"'* ('Shakespeare's Sister'); *'Oh Mother, I can feel the soil falling over my head'* ('I Know It's Over'). By saving her sensitive child from life, the over-protective mother runs the risk of making him fall half in love with easeful death and the tomb-womb. And the risk is even greater when the newspapers are full of extremely uneasy death.

> I happened to live on the streets where, close by, some of the victims had been picked up. Within that community, news of the crimes totally dominated all attempts at conversation for quite a few years. It was like the worst thing that had ever happened, and I was very, very aware of everything that occurred. Aware as a child who could have been a victim. All the details . . .
>
> THE FACE, 1985

Little Steven was just six when the 'Moors Murderers' Ian Brady and Myra Hindley were driving around the streets of mid-Sixties Manchester looking for their next child victim to whisk away to the foggy moors, a brutal death and a shallow, unmarked grave. Being Morrissey, he didn't miss any of the significance of these events just because he was so young. He understood them all too well. He recognised completely that it could have been him, and had none of the cosy 'it-couldn't-happen-to-me' psychological defences that less imaginative children have. He also understood what these actions said about human nature; the awful reality of deliberate human cruelty in addition to the unintentional variety he was becoming familiar with at home. What had been dragged into the world against its will could be dragged out again, just as pointlessly: *Oh John you'll never be a man....*

There was more than a little identification with the victims on young Steven's part. This can be put down to his nascent sense of drama, but was as much to do with his precocious knowledge of injustice. In a sense — the irrational, hyperbolic sense of childhood hurt and resentment — it was him that had been abducted, tortured, deprived of his innocence and ultimately his life, and dumped in a lonely shallow grave, not by Brady and Hindley, not by physical assault, but by his experience of humdrum, dysfunctional, strangulated Manchester family life. 'Suffer Little Children', one of the first lyrics Morrissey wrote for Johnny Marr, his Smiths songwriting partner, was about the moors murders. A painfully evocative lyric, it begins with Morrissey murmuring (bad) dreamily: *'Over the moors, take me to the moors/dig a shallow grave and I'll lay me down'*. Which is as powerfully, as dramatically direct an identification with the fate of these children as anyone could make. Later, he gives the still undiscovered victims of Brady and Hindley's evil a chance to rise and speak from 'the sullen misty moor' where they lie buried: *'we may be dead and we may be gone/but we will be right by your side/until the day you die/this is no easy ride . . .'*, adding, *'you might sleep/BUT YOU WILL NEVER DREAM!'*

This promise/curse seems to be addressed to Hindley and Brady, but it could also be Hindley and Brady's last words to their victims. It is also Morrissey's promise to the world in which he grew up and which deprived him of his happiness and innocence. Morrissey is casting himself as the avenger of lost childhood, a role he was to play repeatedly in his work, well into a disgraceful middle age (though of course for Morrissey childhood is lost the day you are born). 'Suffer' finishes with an eerie and ambiguous refrain which again blurs and smudges the bloody line between the murderers and adult society in general, and between Morrissey and the murderer's victims, implying that Morrissey sees himself, like the windswept 'sullen misty' moors that loom over Manchester, forever separate, brooding, hostile, abandoned: *'Oh Manchester, so much to answer for/Over the moor, I'm on the moor/the child is on the moor.'*

Brady and Hindley were, after all, the most terrible, but also, perhaps because they were so terrible, the most glamorous thing that had ever happened to Manchester. Brady and Hindley's crimes were unspeakable, but nobody could stop talking about them. Their cold-blooded, casual but calculated destruction of other people's children struck at the very heart of Manchester society by assaulting the twin consoling myths of childhood innocence and the unassailable goodness of the family. They were like a film negative of what a couple should be — their highly erotic, perverse passion for one another, reducing the population instead of adding to it, destroying other people's families instead of raising their own, *taking not giving*. They represented passion, sadism, sex, rebellion — the spiciest elements of the popular culture which was luring more and more young people into its car and whisking them away from their families and familiar surroundings to an unknown fate. While the children were quickly forgotten by the media, Myra ('society owes me a living') and Brady's arrogant, black and white mug shots — especially Myra's — stared out coolly from television sets and newspapers like the latest monarchs of the Sixties' hit parade. (Even forty years on Myra is still an icon — a giant reproduction of her mug shot, composed of the handprints of children, was the controversial centrepiece of the famous BritArt exhibition in the late Nineties).

Although Myra hadn't carried out the actual physical torture or taken the children's lives herself, she was generally considered to be much guiltier than Brady. If Brady was unfathomably sick; Myra, as the Christian-name familiarity suggests, stuck closer in the public mind and was decried as an obscene insult to her sex and to Nature Herself. It was her fully complicit presence which made the abductions possible, fatally reassuring the young victims. With her natty clothes, with-it perm and her (initial) gritty determination to tough it out rather than resort to the evasions of the 'weaker' sex ('whatever Ian has done, I have done'), Myra was a very up-to-date young woman. She was monstrous but also modern, in the sense that she rebelled against her anatomy, her class and her social role. She was proudly hedonistic and shamelessly sexual; the Sixties was, after all, the decade when abortion was legalised and the Pill became widely available. Four years before Gore Vidal's Ms Breckinridge, Myra was the monstrous, 'murderous' 'mannish' modern woman that all women guiltily feared might lurk inside them.

To young Steven, who increasingly felt himself to be something of a monster, oppressed and deformed by society's expectations and prejudices, Myra the Bad Mother, Myra the self-confessed harbinger of death and pain, Myra the malicious outsider, must have been a terrifying but compelling figure. Especially to a boy more than usually dependent on his Good Mother.

Most of all, Myra showed him that in a world of wickedness, infamy was almost as good as fame.

> You see it was all so evil: it was, if you can understand this, ungraspably evil. When something reaches that level it becomes almost . . . almost absurd really. I remember it at times like I was living in a soap opera . . .
>
> THE FACE, 1985

dump her on the doorstep, girl

The Northern Woman, she's like the Galapagos Turtle. She's an entirely different species.

ALAN BENNETT

Morrissey is a woman trapped inside a man's body.

TONY WILSON

Tony Wilson is a man trapped inside a pig's body.

MORRISSEY

There isn't another man like me anywhere. I'm one on his own.

SHELAGH DELANEY, *A Taste of Honey*

4

The most arresting thing about Morrissey's work, the thing that grabs you like a particularly overzealous store detective, is *that* voice. It's a voice which drives some to distraction and others to infatuation. Love it or loathe it, it is a voice on its own. In an industry full of stars who started out by imitating their predecessors so badly that they were mistaken for original talent, Morrissey's voice seems utterly, *shockingly* unique. Aurally *and* authorally.

That oddly affective/effective self-possessed wobbliness, which disgruntled parents, rightly worried that their daughter or son is listening to something deeply unhealthy and unhygienic, have described in irate letters to the star as the sound of a man 'having his legs sawn off', is the signature of someone who is determined to sing, but at the same time half-reluctant, driven but self-doubting, inspired but repressed. A soft boy who has made some very tough choices – a choirboy who has chosen his own damnation. All underscored, comically, mockingly, by his understated-but-unmistakable hard, sharp northern vowels and softly cynical-lyrical, almost Chaucerian consonants and vowels (*and in a darkened unnderpasss I thought oh Godd my channce has cum at lasst* [phoenetically typing, that is]), delivering that native black humour ('*and if a ten ton truck kills the both of us/to die by your side/the pleasure, the privilege is mine'*), that self-promoting self-deprecation (*'Well me without clothes/a nation turns its back and gags'*), and that oddly naturalistic poetic pop vernacular (*'So stay on my arm, you little charmer'*).

In fact, the reason so many people hate Morrissey's voice is precisely because it is so dramatically *personal*, confiding in their ear that he is not just another jobbing popster or busking entertainer, thank you very much. The forthrightness and candour of his voice is an instantly recognisable challenge that its melodiousness merely makes more pronounced; it demands that you listen to it, really listen to it instead of merely hearing it, at the same time conveying the impression that if you don't like it, well, you can bloody well lump it. If you happen to be too stupid or too Southern to get the joke it is always telling against itself, there is nothing more abrasive and offensive and than Morrissey's voice.

In a (regional) sense, of course, Morrissey's 'voice' is not really so unique. In fact, it's rather common — as common as you can get, according to some Southern snobs. Morrissey's 'voice', you see, is that of the Northern Woman.

However common the Northern Woman might be, she is still a very special creature, thriving only in damp, cool, slightly backward climes where people actually talk to one another at bus stops and check-out queues, and where you're never more than a ten-minute walk from a good fish and chip shop. She has a certain intensity mixed with a certain breeziness, a certain desperation mixed with a lot of self-irony — perhaps the product of her awareness of her contradictions. She doesn't suffer fools gladly, but she doesn't always make sense herself. She is direct, but frequently overdone. She is a survivor, but strangely tragic. She is strong, but touchingly vulnerable. She is all woman, but sometimes there seems to be more than a little man in her. She's a bit of a queer fish is the Northern Woman, and she is Morrissey.

> I have a talent for eavesdropping and it's amazing what you learn while waiting to pay for your fruit juice.
>
> MELODY MAKER, 1987

Yes, of course, she's quite 'camp' too, although the word has been so abused of late that it seems almost worthless now. In this context, it might mean that she's 'larger than life', but also larger than conventional ideas of femininity. The sharp-eyed social comedians Alan Bennett and Victoria Wood, from the northern counties of Yorkshire and Lancashire respectively – and much admired by Morrissey – made impressive careers in the Eighties out of recognising the comic potential of the Northern Woman and her lovable, minor monstrousness and modest madness (qualities which were taken to their hilarious extreme in the Nineties and Noughties in *Mrs Merton* and *The Royle Family* by working class Mancunian comedienne Caroline Aherne). Like Morrissey, Wood and Bennett are northern artists who did something very few other writers bothered to do before them: they listened to the way northern women talk. Morrissey's achievement, however, was the incorporation of that voice into Eighties pop music, introducing the Northern Woman to millions of young people around the world who had never heard of her before. And even if they had, the last thing they expected was for her to speak to them through the skinny body of a be-quiffed, be-jeaned, James Dean impersonator.

However, the Northern Woman had made it into the British pop charts before – way back in the Sixties. And Morrissey had bought all her records. He spent his childhood adoring Northern girls who had grabbed the limelight; women such as Cilla Black, the little Liverpool lass with the big voice, big ambition, big teeth and the even bigger nose who sang in a Northern accent complete with working men's club cabaret ('*Sumthing tells me sumthing's gonna happen to-ni-i-i-i-i-i-ght . . .*'). Or Lulu, the raucous redhead who exhorted '*everybody shout now!*', who was so Northern she was actually Scottish.

> [Lulu's 'The Boat That I Row'] has nothing to do with a boat – I'm sure you've guessed. She's more or less saying to the world, 'You're not going to change me. This is me, take me as I am.' . . . There's always more to these things than meets the eye.
>
> BRIT GIRLS, CHANNEL 4, 1997

Or Viv Nicholson, the Lancashire lass from a mining town who didn't cut a record, but whose spectacular pools win in 1961 represented the same kind of disposable success as a Top Twenty hit – and had the same giddily transforming effect. Viv bought her way into a realm of bad taste so extreme that it took her back into penury but gained her fame, turning her into a folk hero, immortalised in her warts-and-all autobiography (now a West End stage show), *Spend Spend Spend*. She was accorded the exceedingly rare and prestigious honour of gracing not one but *two* Smiths record sleeves ('Heaven Knows I'm Miserable Now' and 'Barbarism Begins at Home').

The Sixties in Britain was an era of social mobility, or at least the promise of it. The rise of consumer culture was fuelled by wage increases to the working classes, which meant that for the first time they could afford to buy some of the things they made, and that kids like Steven had pocket money to spend on Cilla Black records and other faddish nonsense. This new spending power and the explosion of pop culture it provoked gave working-class status a new sexiness and fashionability. It was seen as an antidote to stuffed-shirt, stiff-lipped (Southern) British bourgeoisdom. Culturally, big-heartedness was gaining the upper hand over small-mindedness, and the common people were now hip and in the charts. And in Britain the most common people were Northerners, which was precisely why they had been derided and pitied for so long — and why the northern voice began to be heard loud enough to wake the deaf bat next door in British popular culture in the Sixties.

'Northerness' in British culture has faint echoes of 'blackness' in American culture. It was the Sixties which saw the first real advance of 'coloreds' in the US: 'vital', 'soulful' black music from the booming 'Motortown' of Detroit was crossing over into the mainstream, that is white, market (and finding its way into the record collection of young Steven, who was a fan of Motown). Ironically, many northern working-class British female singers in the Sixties sang songs that had originally been written for black artists in the US, but whose blackness was considered uncommercial in Britain. Cilla 'Black', for example, built her career out of covering Dionne Warwick hits (much to Dionne's distress, apparently). Even her pals, the Beatles, from Cilla's home-town of Liverpool, and of mainly Irish immigrant descent, began as Chuck Berry impersonators, and later included on their records songs originally performed by black girl groups. In Britain, to be northern, working class and Irish, as Steven Patrick Morrissey knew only too well, was the next best worst thing to being a nigger. Not for nothing did his skinny spiritual antecedent, the southern Anglo-Irish malcontent John Lydon title his autobiography after a notice which was a common sight in the windows of London rooming houses in the Fifties: 'No Irish, No Blacks, No Dogs' (it wasn't necessary to add 'No Northerners' as a strictly controlled internal passport system meant that until the Sixties northerners weren't permitted south of Newport Pagnell).

Is God alive?
I'm far too provincial to answer that question.

Rolling Stone, 1999

Mind you, just as 'blackness' turned out to be a quality not entirely exclusive to blacks, 'northerness' wasn't exclusive to the North of Britain. Since the Northern Woman was an archetype, she didn't actually have to be from the North geographically – just emotionally. For young Steven, London's Dusty Springfield, aka Mary O'Brien, with her soulful singing style, beehive, extravagant eye shadow and not entirely convincing/over convincing femininity, qualified immediately.

But standing head and rather broad-shouldered above them all, was Sandie Shaw, née Sandra Goodrich, 'the princess of Britpop', who hailed from Dagenham, a dour-but-doughty working-class 'motortown' downwind and downriver of London. Steven fell swooningly in love with Sandie (eventually consummating his passion in 1984 when he persuaded and cajoled her out of retirement to cover his beloved 'Hand in Glove', the song that Sandie had being trying to sing all her life).

It's fantastic working with Sandie Shaw – it's like meeting myself in a former life.

Morrissey, 1984

Sandie was not just any old pop singer, but a true star in the sense that she embodied all sorts of contradictions. Her voice was strong but soft, giving it unusual depth, and her big hit songs conveyed a happy melancholia, hinting at a psychological complexity beneath their apparent straightforwardness. Songs such as the poignant urban hymn '(There's) Always Something There To Remind Me' (probably responsible for Steven's later weakness for overlong single titles), the extravagantly bitter-sweet 'Girl Don't Come', the clearly influential 'Heaven Knows I'm Missing Him Now', and the paradoxically self-pitying 'Stop Feeling Sorry for Yourself' (*don't sit there on the shelf/get out, stop feeling sorry for yourself today*'), a song which dispenses wise advice but somehow only encourages you to ignore it, and which was obviously written specially for Steven. Even her exuberant smash hit 'Long Live Love' (*'Venus must have heard my plea/she has sent someone along for me'*) seems to have a kind of implicit ironic pessimism to its very naïvety. The dark side even makes itself felt in her 1967 Eurovision winner 'Puppet on a String', which for all the lyric's grating shallowness, and the mechanical Euroompapa orchestration, Sandie manages to somehow suggest it might be a reference to toy execution.

> I liked '(There's) Always Something There To Remind Me' because it sounded as if she'd just walked in off the street and begun to sing, and strolled back home and bought some chips. Good old Essex.
> BRIT GIRLS, CHANNEL 4, 1997

Nor was Sandie an unambiguous figure herself. She was not exactly the shape that a girl was supposed to be: tall, big-boned. Worse, she had a reputation for being somewhat strong-headed and didn't appear much bothered with pretending to be ladylike. She also had ideas that a girl wasn't supposed to have, taking an interest in left-wing politics and feminism — probably part of the reason she came to loathe 'Puppet' with its vacuously submissive if not downright masochistic refrain.

> We don't talk about that ['Puppet on a String']. Not round here.
> BRIT GIRLS, CHANNEL 4, 1997

Through the alchemy of Sixties pop music and thanks to the rising tide of androgyny, Sandie became loved, prized, beautiful; she became a star. And apparently on her own terms. Shucking her shoes off on *Ready Steady Go* was a sexy gesture of liberation from restrictive definitions of femininity which Steven recognised completely (more substantively, perhaps, behind the scenes she also retained tight artistic control and was producer of most of her music, a fact that went publicly unacknowledged for more than twenty years). Although her songs were often sad, and about suffering at the hands of men, Sandie, by dint of her personality and that belting voice, came to represent a new feminine independence and optimism.

There were other, more native Northern Women who made it on to Steven's TV screen in the Sixties. Granada TV's *Coronation Street*, Britain's first soap opera, was full of them. Set in a cobbled street of terraced houses in Manchester and centred on the corner pub, The Rover's Return, *Coronation Street* managed to capture (and fetishize) working class life at the very moment that it was changing for ever, as a result of the rise of consumer and pop culture which the show itself symbolised (it was paid for by advertising).

Coronation Street was first broadcast on ITV, Britain's only commercial channel at the time, in 1960 and rapidly became a big hit nationwide, still dominating the ratings today and also an institution of Manchester life. The characters — and they really were characters — soon took on a life of their own and 'Corrors' as it was known locally became more Manchester than Manchester, something that Mancunians had to watch or else miss out on what it meant to be Mancunian. 'Corrors' gave the residents of this 'backward' Northern mill town, including young Steven Morrissey, some early lessons in post-modernism and irony — and how life can be made to imitate art.

> Usually North Country people are shown as gormless whereas in actual fact they are very alive and cynical.
>
> SHELAGH DELANEY

Like most soap operas, *Coronation Street* was aimed largely at women, and tended to portray them as very much in control, tough, wise and self-reliant, but also vulnerable and often tragicomic creatures forever being let down by the fickleness of foolish men whenever they made the fatal mistake of not treating them like aberrant little boys or mental retards — men whose masculinity always proves sadly lacking next to their own. As one Eighties character, Susie, a young, dodgy strumpet-type bestowed with great psychological insight memorably remarked, 'Men! They're all limp lettuces aren't they Gail?' This was partly flattery of the show's core audience and partly social verity — the north is a devoutly matriarchal culture. However, the 'Corrors' girls' battery of caustic put downs, tart common sense, and fondness for gallows humour barely disguised a deeply romantic worldview; one that had been disappointed time and time again in its contact with the world in general and men in particular, but often took a perverse, I-told-me-so consolation from that disappointment. The credo of pop culture, in other words — or at least of the kind of pop culture Steven was devoted to.

To Steven, *Coronation Street* was not a TV programme but nothing less than Utopia in a cathode ray tube. It featured characters that were entirely familiar to him — were him, to some degree, and were certainly family — but the like of which had never been seen or even acknowledged before on television (with the possible exception of afternoon re-runs of Bette Davis movies, America's own, aristocratic version of the especially impossible Northern Woman). For a boy rapidly retreating into the wasteland of his head, it was a world that he could be part of from the comfort and safety of his own (matriarchal) home. Most enticingly of all, 'Corrors' offered Steven some hope — if *Coronation Street* could be a hit, perhaps there might be a place in the world of pop culture for a mummy's boy from the streets of Stretford. He bombarded Granada TV with scripts and storylines, all of which were politely declined, perhaps because the producers suspected that Steven was pitching for more than a writer's credit; that really he was asking to be allowed to live on Coronation Street, probably with Elsie Tanner, played by that 'force of nature' Pat Phoenix (who would later be officially canonised through her appearance on the sleeve of 'Shakespeare's Sister').

> Oh she [Pat Phoenix] was simply a blizzard of professionalism — of goodwill, of warmth — she was like a hurricane. She just simply exploded into the room and I was quite taken aback by this. You simply wanted to rush towards her bosom, and — you know — remain there forever.
>
> RECORD MIRROR, 1985

Fortunately, Steven didn't go to live with Elsie Tanner (or disappear into her bosom). Instead, he went to live with a dreamy, gawky girl called Jo, in her dilapidated bedsit in Salford. Jo was the creation of Shelagh Delaney in her winsome play A *Taste of Honey* written in 1956 and made into a film in 1961 by Tony Richardson, now seen as one of the best examples of the short-lived New Realism movement in British cinema, before the escapism, materialism — and commercial success — of US-targeted Bond movies sidelined kitchen-sink drama to the small screen. Morrissey's voice may be that of the Northern Woman, but it is supremely the voice of one Northern Woman in particular: Shelagh. Such was the influence of this one, in some ways rather slight, but in other ways extraordinary play on Morrissey that

55

references to it run through his entire oeuvre like the lettering in a stick of Blackpool rock. Sandie may have been the love of his pre-teen years, but Shelagh was the love of his adolescence, reaching him in a way that no one else had done before: emotionally and intellectually.

Jo: You've got terrible tendencies, haven't you?
Geof: How do you mean?
Jo: You like everything to be just that little bit out of date, don't you? Clothes, books, women.

SHELAGH DELANEY, A TASTE OF HONEY

Shelagh was swallowed whole by a ravenously lonely boy and eagerly incorporated into his world. In fact, A *Taste of Honey* became his world, in much the same way that, years later, Morrissey's own work would provide an alternative, symbolically rich landscape for millions of other lonely kids to inhabit/moon about in. Just as his words were to provide a generation with its inspiration, so Shelagh's provided him with his own.

Shelagh isn't the only writer whose words have been taken on loan by Morrissey — the Big Nosed roll of honour includes Dorothy Parker, Elizabeth Smart, Joe Orton, Dame Edith Sitwell, Leonard Cohen, James Dean, Oscar Wilde, Noel Coward, Richard Allen and Jack Kerouac, to name just a privileged few. However, none of these, not even Oscar Wilde, provided Morrissey with the lyrical 'inspiration' that Shelagh did. The list of cribs from A *Taste of Honey* alone is so impressive it is worth setting out (more or less) in full:

'Hand in Glove': *And I'll probably never see you again* ('I'll probably never see you again. I know it!')

'Reel Around the Fountain': *I dreamt about you last night/and I fell out of bed twice* ('I dreamt about you last night. Fell out of bed twice'.); *You're the bees knees/but so am I* ('You're the bees knees, but so am I'.)

'You've Got Everything Now': *As merry as the days were long* ('As merry as the day is long'.)

'Shoplifters of the World Unite': *Six months is a long time* ('It's a long time, six months'.)

'I Don't Owe You Anything': ('I don't owe you anything'.)

'Alma Matters': *It's my life/to ruin/my own way*
('Anyway, it's your life, ruin it your own way'.)

'This Night Has Opened My Eyes', an exquisitely mournful track, even by Morrissey's moody standard, from the second album *Hatful of Hollow*, in which his voice hovers behind Marr's lilting, stone-kicking, shoulder-shrugging riffs like a haunting painful-pleasurable memory. It's also an intense, distilled, three-and-a-half-minute version of the play, where the 'lifts' come thick and fast: *Wrap her up in the News of the World/dump her on a doorstep, girl* ('You can't just wrap it up in a bundle of newspaper . . . and dump it on a doorstep.'). Characteristically, Morrissey improves the line by changing 'newspaper' to *News of the World* a Sunday scandal sheet otherwise known as *News of the Screws* — an ironic comment on an unwanted baby's first contact with the harsh realities of life. *In a river the colour of lead* (That river, it's the colour of lead.'); *I'm not happy and I'm not sad* ('I'm not sorry and I'm not glad.'); and, most famously, *The dream has gone but the baby is real* ('Oh well, the dream's gone but the baby's real enough.')

Even I — even I — went a bit too far with *A Taste of Honey*.

Q, 1994

Years later Morrissey was to accuse Suede's Brett Anderson, someone who has clearly assembled himself from leftover bits of Seventies David Bowie frocks and spare Morrissey lyrics, of having reference points so close together that there was no space between them. An unkind and unenlightened person might have said the same about Morrissey's early work. But these are more than simple 'cribs'. As the man himself is fond of quoting: talent borrows; genius steals. Morrissey was no petty thief; he was much more professional than that. He turned up in a removal van outside Shelagh Delaney's house in broad daylight, instinctively knowing which plant-pot she'd hidden her keys under and brazenly emptied her house of its contents. (The neighbours didn't call the police because he looked the sort that Shelagh would hang around with.)

Morrissey took much more than mere words from *A Taste of Honey*; he took its world, its language and its voice, made them his own and in the process fashioned something new and yet timeless.

You're nothing to me. I'm everything to myself.

SHELAGH DELANEY, *A TASTE OF HONEY*

It isn't too difficult to see why *A Taste of Honey* would have such an impact on a teenage Steven buried (half-alive) in his bedroom, hunched alternatively over a book or the manual typewriter his mother had bought him, trying to master the world through words. Written by Anglo-Irish Shelagh when she was just eighteen and set in her home town of Manchester, it is a bitter-sweet story of Jo (played in the film by a captivatingly goggle-eyed, slightly boyish Rita Tushingham), a misfit, bastard teenage girl struggling not to be a victim of fate, whether in the form of her sex, her class or her origins. She is the unwanted but not unloved product of her sluttish mother's 'little love affair that lasted five minutes' with a 'retarded' man Jo never met (Jo's 'brass' mother is played by the redoubtable Dora Brien in an extraordinary semi-comedy performance that is one of the great supporting roles of British cinema). Exemplifying the awful injustice of original sin, Jo's own birth ended her mother's marriage, ensuring she never had a father and distancing her mother from her, and, to boot, may also have bestowed upon her a genetic predisposition to madness, a concern which preoccupies her throughout the play. Like all of us to some degree, and Morrissey more than most, Jo is an embarrassed, neurotic product of dissipated passion – it just so happens that the passion that produced her dissipated sooner than is usual in polite society.

> I'm afraid that they [the British Sixties new realism films he loves] probably remind me of my childhood because I lived in lots of those circumstances and I also think that . . . I gaze upon them fondly because it was the first time in the entire history of film where regional dialects were allowed to come to the fore and people were allowed to talk about squalor and general depression and it wasn't necessarily a shameful thing. It was quite positive . . . people were allowed to be real instead of being glamorous and Hollywoodian, if that is a word, and I sincerely hope it isn't.
>
> MORRISSEY ON AUSTRALIAN RADIO, 1985

In an attempt to break away from her mother's well-meaning if dissolute and distracted influence and taste what little sweetness life has to offer, Jo has an affair with a black sailor, another outsider in Fifties Manchester.

He asks if she's worried about being seen with him; she replies that she 'doesn't care'. 'You mean it too,' he says, impressed. 'You're the first girl I've met who really didn't care.' Jo, like our Steven, is already outside of society, so she really doesn't care; she has nothing to lose (*And if the people stare then the people stare/I really don't know and I really don't care*). However, she knows — and perhaps half hopes — that despite the ring he's given her and the way he is dreaming big dreams and planning big plans, 'I'll probably never see you again'. She's proved right and discovers that she, like her mother and a billion other women before her, is pregnant with spent affection: 'the dream has gone, but the baby is real enough'.

Having, half-gratifyingly, discovered love to be just a miserable lie, and reconciled herself to a single life, Jo embarks on a platonic romance, unlike any other love, with an effeminate homosexual art student who wants to mother her (and practically give birth to her baby himself) while she wears the trousers — two misfit bastards (Geof as 'one of them' is illegitimate by default), victims of and rebels against Nature, clinging, hand-in-glove together, refusing to be downtrodden, the sun shining out of their behinds. There is a slight, eerie premonition of Myra and Brady in this odd, outsider relationship, but with pathos instead of bloodlust, impossible desire instead of evil.

> I'll bash its brains out. I'll kill it. I don't want his baby, Geof. I don't want to be a mother. I don't want to be a woman.
>
> SHELAGH DELANEY, A TASTE OF HONEY

Taste is arrestingly realistic and matter-of-fact yet has a dream-like quality to it, something more pronounced in the film, which, even in 1961, seems to be already nostalgic for a disappearing Manchester; the black and white cinematography of cobbled streets and factory chimneys, together with the poignant use of light and dark, sunshine and gloom, lends an aesthetic reverie to the gritty documentary feel, especially when backed by the strangely bitter-sweet sound of children laughing and playing in the streets and continuously, endlessly, effortlessly singing hypnotic nursery rhymes (lyrically underscoring the pre-pop music context of Jo's world, but also an echo to Morrissey of his own, solitary investment in singing to himself, something he spent much of his childhood doing).

59

There's even a day trip for Jo and Geof to the moors outside Manchester, affording a distant, aerial view of the narrow streets (a sunlit, carefree visit now inevitably contrasted with the 'sullen misty' moors of Myra and Ian). Most of all, the film is steeped in the sense of disappointed desire, of happiness just out of reach, forever slipping away in plain view, like Jo's sailor smiling and waving to her from the deck of his boat as he disappears down the Manchester Ship Canal, off on the 'alley-alley-o', taking his lying promise with him. In other words, *Taste* is the landscape, the mother country, the heart of much of Morrissey's work, especially his Smiths period; it is a lyrical play whose affecting but plain-speaking poetry proceeds from ordinary people showing their extraordinary side, the ordinariness of extraordinariness. Likewise, it exists narcissistically in a world of its own, where it is everything to itself: the drama and all the characters seem to proceed from Jo's adolescent imagination; they are merely aspects of her own predicament, conversations between her emotions. This is not so much a weakness as a strength and the source of the play's – and Morrissey's – mesmerising charm.

> Women never have young minds. They are born three thousand years old.
>
> SHELAGH DELANEY, *A TASTE OF HONEY*

Unlike the other works by Fifties (usually northern) working class authors that were turned into films in the early Sixties, such as *Saturday Night, Sunday Morning, Billy Liar*, and *Room at the Top, Taste* was written from a female perspective, or rather *intro*-spective. Unashamedly self-absorbed, it manages to be genuinely 'shocking' and contemporary in its subject matter: adultery, promiscuity, teenage pregnancy, maternal irresponsibility, abortion, miscegenation, homosexuality, congenital madness . . . (if this list reads like an episode of *Brookside*, perhaps this is why, in the late Eighties, Morrissey made an appearance in a spin-off of that show called *South*). However, *Taste* managed to cover all these themes without being sensationalist, refusing to hide behind pompous gestures and pseudo politics. It isn't a play about an angry young man, but a vaguely anxious young girl – a much more 'universal' subject, since most of us are vaguely anxious young girls at some point in our lives. And all of these characteristics – poetic naturalism, shocking without sensationalism, refusal of pompous gestures, dreamy introspection, a freshly feminine perspective — were to be features of Morrissey's own work.

It has been pointed out that the 'Sheila' in The Smiths' infectiously exuberant single 'Sheila Take a Bow' is probably Shelagh Delaney. The song certainly sounds like a tribute, but one which recognises the trap of self-sufficiency and isolation that lures those unruly boys and unruly girls who will not settle down — a trap which Morrissey can't escape from. Like Jo, he's speaking-singing to himself as much as anyone else, telling himself not to stay at home (not that he's going to pay any heed, mind): *'Is it wrong to want to live on your own?/No, it's not wrong — but I must know/How can someone so young sing words so sad?'*

Sheila/Shelagh/Jo/Morrissey/the listener is invited to take a bow and *'boot the grime of this world in the crotch, dear,'* asserting her independence, her strength, her purity, but at the same time, in typical push-me-pull-me fashion, she's told to come out *'and find the one that you love and who loves you'*, which is, in practise, as we all know, the ultimate compromise.

Morrissey is the one doing the singing, and it is he who tends to choose 'sad' words, yet in a sense, it is Shelagh's voice that he sings in: *boot the grime of this world in the crotch, dear.* Taking his identification with the Northern Woman to its ultimate conclusion, and tallying with the picture of Candy Darling, the Warhol transsexual and inspiration for Lou Reed's 'Walk on the Wild Side' on the single's sleeve, Morrissey is clearly also the 'Sheila' of the song (perhaps this is partly why 'Sheila' is bowing rather than curtseying). In this way he's just being true to Delaney's own message. The gender roles within Geof and Jo's relationship in *Taste* are very mixed up and unclear; it's what makes their odd affair of two single people being single together seem so exciting, liberating, fresh — and ultimately doomed. It's what makes it seem so genuinely touching — in places where you haven't been touched before. Hence in 'Sheila' the identity and gender of the narrator, as in so many of Morrissey's songs, is not so much unclear as *transcended*, providing both the male and female listener with multiple points of identification (the key to the subtle, fecund richness of so many Morrissey lyrics; even subject and object naughtily refuse to follow convention and switch positions frequently, sometimes playing top, sometimes bottom).

61

A little later, both the song's and Morrissey's own deliberately, exuberantly confused 'transsexuality' is spelt out in an invigoratingly casual fashion: *You're a girl and I'm a boy/La la, la-la, la-la/Take my hand and off we stride/La la la, la-la la-la, la/You're a boy and I'm a girl/La la, la-la la-la.*

It's the childish, infectious, taunting, carelessness — wordlessness — of the '*La la la, la-la la-la la*' which stays with the listener, haunting them long after the last chord dies away, like the sound of the children playing happily in the streets in *A Taste of Honey*. It's a lyrical raspberry blown to the world and the destiny which it decrees is anatomy, a brazen, laughing, giggling, brawling challenge to convention and normality — a challenge which Morrissey, hand in hand with his inner 'Sheila', from 'Girl Afraid' to 'Alma Matters', was to continue delivering like an insult wrapped in a kiss for the rest of his career.

Did you hear TATU's version of 'How Soon is Now'?
Yes, it was magnificent. Absolutely. Again, I don't know much about them.
They're the teenage Russian lesbians.
Well, aren't we all?

WORD, 2003

Jo should have been a pop star, but she appears to live in a world where pop music hasn't been invented yet — at least for girls like her. Her 'madness' is the protest of someone suffocating, gasping, drowning — a child born prematurely but somehow still alive.

Morrissey would change all that. Morrissey, the ultimate, if highly unnatural evolution of Northern Woman made his masculine body the instrument of Jo's frustrated, premature aspirations. He took her tough vulnerability, her girlish resolve, her proud awkwardness, her endearing neuroses, her dreamy realism, her Lancastrian scorn, and hand in hand with his own perversity he strode off with them into posterity, far surpassing the artistic achievements of all the Northern Woman pop stars of the Sixties he adored.

But all this was to come later. In the meantime, teenage Steven was to be abducted by a trans-sexuality much more overt and extreme than anything Delaney had ever come up with.

It was called the Seventies.

i need advice

To be natural is such a very difficult pose to keep up.

OSCAR WILDE

All truly beautiful things are a mixture of masculine and feminine.

SUSAN SONTAG

Beauty is nothing else but a promise of happiness.

STENDHAL

5

Glam rock saved Morrissey, at the same time damning him forever.

In 1971 Steven attended a Marc Bolan gig at Manchester's Apollo Theatre. He was just twelve years old. Like his attendance at a gig by The Sex Pistols when he was sweet sixteen, it was a rendezvous with fate. His tickets to these events were couriered to him by Lucifer himself. In fact, it could almost be said that glam and punk only happened so that nice boy Steven could be exposed to them and led gloriously astray. If these cacophonous movements hadn't produced a single record worth listening to thirty years on, they would still have proved themselves more than worthwhile just by what they did to this quiet little Sandie Shaw fan. Steven was directly and intimately exposed to the most corrupting influences of the decade. Fortunately, he took copious notes.

Glam rock was the crowning glory of pop, and it was perched on Marc's pretty, perm-curled head. Glam rock was the strutting, preening realisation of the transformative, terrifying potential of pop culture. Glam rock was a second chance at the Fifties for the British, who had been too strangulated by class and convention (and the memory of rationing) to really enjoy it the first time around. Glam rock told those who once had nothing that they could now have everything. If Sixties pop had told them that they could have fun and sex, and maybe even be rich (one day), the Seventies were telling them that they could be something much more valuable — that they could be beautiful. That they could be noticed, they could be loved — and more than a little feared. Glam rock said that proletarians were the new aristocracy.

Such captivating creatures that they could become the centre of their own universe, sufficient unto themselves, not beholden to parents, convention, class, or even gender. The glam rock pop star was the symbol of pop culture's supremacy, living out the fantasies of his frustrated fans with increasingly psychotic determination. As a badge worn proudly, arrogantly on school blazer lapels at the time announced, half ironically, half threateningly: 'Marc Bolan Rules, OK!'

A ruthless, wilful, seductive and entirely self-conscious childishness was at the irresponsible, glittery heart of glam. Freud once mockingly dubbed the infant tyrant who has no interest in anything except the immediate satisfaction of his own needs 'His Majesty the Baby'. In the age of vulgar aristocracy that glam heralded, His Majesty the Baby was not to be mocked but emulated. Infantilism was the very essence of 'star quality' — a calculating wonderment and fierce innocence. 'Nothing more resembles what we call inspiration than the delight with which a child absorbs from colour. . .,' wrote Baudelaire. 'Genius is nothing more nor less than childhood recovered at will.' And just as it is difficult to imagine childhood or royalty without the luxury and sensation of colour, so it is difficult to imagine glam rock without *colour television*, which, typically, arrived in Britain much later than in the US, not reaching working class homes until the early Seventies. Pretty much the whole of the 'Swinging' Sixties had been witnessed by the Brits in monochrome in their front rooms.

Then, suddenly, in the early Seventies, thanks to the 'white heat of technology' and hire purchase, *Top of the Pops* was a Technicolor dream, a land of Oz to which the twister of pop music could snatch away any young person trapped in one of those grey, ugly new houses in the suburbs.

To me popular music is still the voice of the working class, collective rage in a way, though seldom angst ridden. But it does really seem like the one sole opportunity for someone from a working class background to step forwards and have their say. It's really the last refuge for articulate but penniless humans

NME, 1984

Really, if the lower orders don't set us a good example, what on earth is the use of them?

OSCAR WILDE, *THE IMPORTANCE OF BEING EARNEST*, 1895

However, the rising aspirations of consumer culture only turned up the contrast on the monochrome reality of British working class life in the early Seventies. Since there was little or no chance, post-Sixties, of changing the world, the only option was to have your own personal coup d'état and aestheticise yourself: the 'children of the Revolution' weren't fools, but they didn't mind dressing like gorgeous ones. The instruments of vibrant transformation were within the reach of eve-ryone: tubes of glitter, satin, itchy man-made fibres, platform shoes and, most important of all, cheap hair dye. Millions of kids undertook this solemn bathroom ritual, often with disastrous results – and not just for their mum's best towels and the bathroom carpet. Horrifically, their hair frequently turned a peasant, muddy green colour instead of the divine gold they were aiming for. Bathroom-sink dramas hit both Steven and that other sharp-tongued second-generation Anglo-Irish dandy misanthrope John Lydon. John, who was also moping around his parents' council home in Finsbury Park, North London, a couple of hundred miles south of Steven nursing a grudge against life, would have his own moment of revenge on the world seven years before Morrissey, in a movement whose hairstyles seem to have been inspired by those earlier glam bathroom-sink disasters and which was, in many ways, glam with the lining turned inside-out: *'We're so pretty, oh-so pretty . . . And we don't care!'*

I was born into a working class family in Manchester at the right time. I was overwhelmed by British pop culture as it was conquering the world. And I started to get involved when punk music arrived. So that was per-fect. It would have been a fate worse than death if I was born in 1974. But I would also have hated to be born in 1930 . . . and believe me, I have spent much time thinking about this dilemma.

POP, 1998

The exasperating reality of working-class life in the Seventies and the frustrated creativity of the vandalism wreaked by bored, angry kids, that only made the landscape they were condemned to more depressing, was captured most evocatively — so evocatively they made it sound defiantly beautiful — by New Wave mod band The Jam in 'That's Entertainment': urban boredom and frustration, the 'smash of glass and a rumble of boots', vandalised phone booths, watching television and 'thinking about your holidays'. Appropriately enough, the track was later covered by Morrissey himself (sounding to paraphrase David Bowie commenting on a Moz cover of one of his records, like Morrissey doing Paul Weller doing Morrissey). Glam rock was not Entertainment. Glam rock was the end of Entertainment. Glam rock refused the adult division of the world into work and play, pleasure and pain, a life ordered around bells, factory hooters, electric train schedules and regimented bank holidays. Instead of industry it advanced idleness, instead of repression it advanced... a better dressed kind of repression. Glam rock called for and, for a brief moment, seemed to actually offer escape from the humdrum by becoming your own special creation. It was a glamorous glue giving off fumes of excitement, adrenaline, fear; it was life as funfair. A call, orchestrated through the apparatus of pop music, for the childish mob nationwide to rise up, mobilise, take to the streets in an ominous clatter of platform shoes and flutter of fake silk scarves and demand, right here and now. . . beauty: *Panic on the streets of London/Panic on the streets of Birmingham/I wonder to myself/Could life ever be the same again.*

According to Johnny Marr, 'Panic' (one of The Smiths' biggest chart successes, reaching Number 10 in 1986) was written at a time when Morrissey was especially obsessed with Marc Bolan, and he exhorted Marr to copy the chugging rhythm of Bolan's 'Metal Guru' to the point where they were 'almost the same song'. 'Panic' was officially an attack on the pap pop music of Eighties BBC Radio 1 (which banned Smiths songs), prompted after the station's most popular and most loathsome DJ, who also happened to be the most implacable enemy of The Smiths, played, completely unsullied by any irony whatsoever, Wham!'s vacuously sunny 'I'm Your Man' following a news item reporting the explosion at the Chernobyl nuclear reactor. But even here, in one of The Smith's more overtly 'political' songs, one ostensibly concerned with Morrissey's pet cause of environmentalism, the Chernobyl explosion ends up being really just a faint and somewhat delayed echo of the emotional explosion from his childhood that Morrissey is much more fascinated with (with an admixture of Morrissey's own apocalyptic fantasies). 'Panic' captures perfectly the danger, hysteria and revolt of a youth cult like glam, and how, like nuclear fallout, there was no escape from it once it was in the air, causing Panic on '*the streets of Carlisle, Dublin, Dundee, Humberside*'.

Not for nothing does the list of provincial towns in uproar sound like a list of tour dates; Morrissey saw The Smiths as seditionaries, spreading aesthetic, lyrical rebellion across the glummest, most despairing – and yet for all that, most oddly attractive – parts of England. 'Panic' builds and builds into a repeated catchy refrain which sounds like a cross between a football chant, a revolutionary slogan and a nursery rhyme – just like glam, in other words. One which however makes explicit, albeit ironically, the threat of political violence in glam: '*HANG THE DJ, HANG THE DJ, HANG THE DJ*'.

As much if not more as it is about crass indifference to environmental disaster, 'Panic' is about Morrissey's vengeful hopes of a day of reckoning for the collaborators with blandness who have betrayed the incomparable legacy of British youth culture and bowdlerised their only hope – pop music. The masterly touch of children's voices backing the baying for blood recalls both the radical childishness of glam and the purity and naturalness of its hatred (and also the street kids of *A Taste of Honey*).

It's difficult to appreciate the wickedness of glam unless you understand something about the nature of the British class system. Until the mass de-industrialisation and unemployment followed by lifestyle consumerism of the Eighties and Nineties (a poor, stunted descendent of glam) effectively destroyed it, working class identity was based entirely on the idea of work. What you did was who you were, even if it was the most boring, mindless work imaginable. If you didn't work you were literally nobody. A waster. A bum. Invisible. Idleness was unthinkable, chosen idleness unimaginable.

> My mother always supported me in an artistic sense, when many people around her said she was entirely insane for allowing me to stay in and write. It's this working class idea that one is born simply to work, so if you don't you must be of no value to the human race. Because I didn't work, it was a cardinal sin.
>
> THE FACE, 1984

Working class men in particular were supposed to make themselves *useful*, they were to work with their hands, not manicure them. Thus the sissy, effeminate or simply unmanly boy was an embarrassment in most working class families, at least to their father. Fairy boys – for that's what they were, regardless of their sexual orientation – were worse than useless, and frequently less loved than runt puppies. Their only hope was to run away to London and become hairdressers. Or pop stars. 'Nature's cruellest trick' was to put a sensitive, dreamy boy in the body of a working class lad. And Nature played its trick on Morrissey as cruelly as she could.

Above all, the working class man was supposed to work on some-thing – usually something that belonged to someone else. This was his lot in life and he was supposed to lump it; whingeing and whining was definitely not permitted. His labour, his feelings and ultimately his life were alienated from him before he was even born. Glam opposed that. Glam said you were your own boss and encouraged working class boys to work on something they did own – themselves. It proved to be the only job that Steven was qualified for.

> I remember buying David Bowie's 'Starman' when it was No. 42 in the charts and that was a truly extraordinary time for me. I was falling in love with the potency of the pop moment. That's why I'm here. That's why I'm involved in music, because the pop moment in my life was the only thing that ever spoke to me.
>
> THE IRISH TIMES, 1999

Steven was taken to the mountaintop by the Men Who Fell To Earth – Marc, David and Bryan (the Geordie coalminer's son turned cool miner) – and shown the kingdoms of an alternative, lazy kind of world, a world where people like him would be revered as royalty instead of treated like freaks, followed as leaders rather than chased down the street. But the world turned, and Lucifer, the brightest evening star, began to wax, wane and set over the horizon. Marc faltered, Ziggy returned to Mars, and Bryan went to LA. Steven was forced to look to the New World to keep the faith.

* * *

In 1973 he saw a kooky, anarchic underground US glam band called the New York Dolls on a late-night TV rock programme and quickly became their biggest UK fan — even more devoted than he had been to Marc. Bolan had been too commonly adored, too successful, while the obscure, foreign, self-destructing Dolls were all Steven's. Throughout the Seventies he held up a lone lighter flame for them in the auditorium of pop fandom until his gas ran out, editing a breathless fanzine/scrapbook about them and penning fervid letters to music papers and even TV producers extolling the East Village junkies' limitless merits and damning their critics to eternal perdition (though there weren't too many critics — most were simply oblivious). Characteristically, Steven had chosen to worship a pop band that wasn't very popular, ensuring that there was little chance of finding himself in a social milieu as a result of his new obsession. His fascination with pop culture wasn't to give him something to chat about down the pub; it was a way of making himself even more inaccessible. His pop interests led him not out of his bedroom into a world of laughing, smiling, dancing, drunken young people, but further into the recesses of his own unhealthy mind. Glam rock and rebellion was all very well, but you mustn't let it become too *democratic*.

> I don't know where the New York Dolls obsession came from . . . I went to all the right gigs in Manchester in the 70s. I was there at the age of 12, I was there at the age of 15. I may have gone to these events totally alone but I stood there and I saw everybody, so cross-breeding this with understanding words and enjoying Joyce Grenfell is . . . well what is it? It's made me what I am today.
>
> *NME, 1989*

In choosing to support the Dolls, Steven had, as ever, demonstrated impeccable taste. But the point of taste is to distinguish yourself from hoi polloi — especially when it is the culture of hoi polloi you are consuming and enthusing about. When, around 1976, Steven began to realise that his only hope — in fact his only option — lay in somehow turning himself into one of those professionally idle creatures known as pop stars, he began advertising in the music press for other band members. Of course, he stipulated that they must be 'New York Dolls/ Patti Smith fans' (the strung-out, stormy, tortured New York songwriter and poet was the kind of woman on the inside that The Dolls tried to be on the outside; she may even have provided the patronym for Morrissey and Marr's 'marriage'). There were no replies. Which must have been saddening and gratifying all at once. As was often to be the case in Steven's life, disappointment was its own consolation.

However, young Steven wasn't quite the only person in the UK to see the potential of the New York Dolls. The London-based Manchester Poly educated fashion designer, situationist spiv and Fagin-wannabe Malcolm McClaren was also a fan of the band accorded the singular honour of being voted the Best and also the Worst Band of 1973 by US magazine *Creem*. Hence the Dolls ended up being the strumpet American progenitors of that other seventies pop revolution, a transatlantic bridge of pink pantyhose between glam and punk over which Malcolm McClaren, who 'managed' the New York Dolls for a mad moment before they finally imploded (a sticky end he hastened by dressing them in red patent leather and hanging hammer and sickles behind them onstage), was eventually to lead John Lydon and the swaying Sex Pistols, a group who took the 'street' and 'hustler' part of their street trannie on the game look but discarded the rest, (Steven was to complain vociferously in letters to the British music press about the Pistols bad clothes.)

For their part, the Dolls seemed to base their striking look, and quite a bit of their driving sound, on the Rolling Stones circa their 1966 hit single 'Have You Seen Your Mother, Baby, Standing in the Shadows?'; in the promotional film the Stones dressed in disturbingly sexy 1940s drag.

Arthur Kane on bass for the Dolls wore laddered tights and black sequinned hot pants, guitarist Johnny Thunders wore leather pants and a mini skirt, Sylvain Sylvain (such a good name, such a pretty name, he used it twice), Jerry Nolan sported big, teased perms and David Johansen wore little more than a pair of pouting lips. Theirs was a glam look crazily cranked up (literally — the Dolls had a reputation for serious drug abuse) until it was precariously close to out-and-out drag.

However, what made the New York Dolls special, and what endeared them so much to a certain fourteen-year-old increasingly obsessed with the tyranny of gender roles, was the fact that their 'drag' was not terribly authentic, but instead was terribly, provocatively 'half-cocked'. It was neither one thing nor t'other — neither Arthur nor Martha. Moreover, their playing style was extremely tough, aggressive and hard. They were androgynous but they weren't eunuchs. These were rowdy trannies, the kind that were more likely to roll you in the alleyway than kiss you. If all beautiful things really are a mixture of masculine and feminine, then perhaps it's also true that all truly terrifying things are also a mixture of masculine and feminine.

The crossed cross-dressing of the New York Dolls, which was probably basically heterosexual (whatever that might mean), had parallels with the 'rad-drag' of gay liberationist street activists who were very visible in Manhattan's Village in the early Seventies (before gay lib was taken over by the disco-dancing Marlboro Man). In an attempt to theatricalise and expose what they saw as the absurdity of gender conformity in general and masculinity in particular, these street activists would take 'cross-dressing' at its word: wearing female clothes but being careful not to shave; or shaving and wearing fussy wigs and pancake make-up, but pulling on a pair of men's trousers and not bothering with underwear. The effect was intended to frighten the horses, and frequently did.

The fuck-you gender fuck of the New York Dolls, years before the antics of Kiss and other heavy metallers rendered them a cliché (and, it goes without saying, massively popular in a way that the Dolls had never been), was even more troubling and transgressive, precisely because it wasn't neatly explained in either a commercial or a political fashion. The Dolls dressed the way they did because they wanted to. It was by drawing on the spirit of this almost forgotten tradition, rather than on the obvious campy panto drag of the New Romantics, that Morrissey's understated, casual androgyny of women's shirts, men's jeans and cheap plastic jewellery seemed so fresh when it arrived on the pop scene in 1983, rendering the 'outrageous' frocks of the 'gender benders' passé overnight (with the honourable exception of Pete Burns, of course, who was practically the sixth, Scouse member of the NY Dolls; not so much gender bender as gender *mugger*).

Gender bending/gender fuck was already well underway in Western culture in the Seventies, and both glam rock and gay lib were as much expressions of this as causes of it. The rise of feminism in the Seventies, which Steven was to support as fiercely as he had supported glam, and the arrival of women in public life and the workplace, had already messed around with gender roles and flipped male supremacy the bird (quite literally, in the case of a leathered-up feisty female glam rocker like Suzi Quatro). Militancy was 'in' and slogans such as 'the personal is political' and 'our bodies ourselves' filled the air. Glam interpreted these currents in its own vain, selfish, largely male fashion. Though glam rock didn't see itself as part of an assault on 'patriarchy', even in its bruising, bricklaying Sweet/Slade incarnation it represented the most blatant expression so far of the unspoken but universal wish among young men on which pop (and rock) music was built: Please God, don't let me grow up to be like my dad. If long hair pissed dads off in the Sixties, platform shoes and make-up were bound to give long-haired dads in the Seventies a stroke; an outcome that a fourteen-year-old Steven trying (not very hard) to negotiate his Oedipus complex and his father's indifference/absence must have found not entirely unappealing.

> There's a perverse and bitter joy in feeling unique, but you pay dearly.
>
> MORRISSEY

Self-invention as a mantra, androgyny as evangelism, sexual ambiguousness as a style, narcissism as a religion, self-cultivation as a way of life — this was the credo of glam rock which Steven Morrissey enthusiastically intoned, confirming those elements of his own personality that he had already developed as a strategy of psychic self-preservation (and, ultimately, retribution). Of course, practically speaking, they weren't the best lessons an unpopular, sensitive boy trying to survive a sink-hole Manchester secondary modern in the Seventies could learn. Dyeing your hair, wearing eyeliner and carrying a handbag made from the seat of a pair of old jeans was not going to make you Captain of Games. Fortunately, Steven, despite his sporting prowess, wasn't terribly interested in being Captain of Games (even if he may have sometimes enjoyed watching him from the touchline).

He told himself that he wasn't interested in being popular, either — and ended up almost believing it. And for the first time in his life he was being noticed — or looked at twice. Steven was beginning to openly advertise his uniqueness; he didn't want his appearance to declare anything but his genius.

others conquered love

I had a very small bedroom and I remember going through periods when I was 18 and 19 where I literally would not leave it for three to four weeks.... I'd be sitting there in near darkness alone with the typewriter and surrounded by masses of paper. The walls were totally bespattered with James Dean, almost to the point of claustrophobia and I remember little bits of paper pinned everywhere with profound comments . . . newspaper clippings like 'Fish Eats Man'. Probably the most important quote was from Goethe: 'Art and Life are different, that's why one is called Art and one is called Life.'

MORRISSEY

It is through Art, and through Art only, that we can realise our perfection; through Art, and through Art only, that we can shield ourselves from the sordid perils of actual existence.

OSCAR WILDE

6

Life for Steven failed to begin when he left school at the age of sixteen, armed with three 'O' Levels in English Literature, Sociology and the General Paper. All fairly useless qualifications in the worldly scheme of things, but quite sufficient for someone destined only to be the greatest lyricist and pop star of his generation.

In fact, apart from the occasional call of nature and plate of baked beans on toast, he now had no reason to leave his bedroom at all. He did make some brief, half-hearted attempts at living in what passes for the real world, working as a clerk for the Civil Service and later for the Inland Revenue — typical bureaucratic Government jobs for a literate secondary modern school leaver in the pre-Information Technology and Mrs T. Seventies; 'It's secure and has prospects,' the school Careers Officer would say, trying to accentuate the positive aspects of being buried alive — completely wrongly as it turned out. But by the time he was eighteen Steven found himself bored before he even began, and so drew the curtains on the world, signed on the dole and off the human race, and spent the rest of his adolescence living in a shell. Like all dreamers, Steven mistook disenchantment for truth.

I was never young. This idea of fun: cars, girls, Saturday night, bottle of wine . . . to me, those things are morbid. I was always attracted to people with the same problems as me. It doesn't help when most of them are dead.

MORRISSEY

Life may not have begun when he left school, but at least his education did. While his contemporaries were satisfying themselves of their own identity and destiny by exploring oral cavities other than their own and taking their clothes off in company, Steven set out to discover himself and his future through reading forgotten books and watching old movies. While others practised the tricky business of walking down the street arm in arm, Steven was courting famous corpses such as Oscar Wilde and James Dean. While others heavy-petted in the park, he was conducting a spot of cultural grave-robbing to further his fiendish experiments in self-invention. While they worried about unwanted pregnancies and whether it really was safe to shag a girl standing up, he was feverishly fathering himself in the form of the literary-inseminated monster, 'Morrissey'.

> I read so much that I tried to give it up because I wasn't actually living. I was just creased up in a chair 20 hours of every single day . . . I tried to be a journalist, but failed miserably. I used to write songs but with only nebulous tunes because I couldn't play an instrument.

AUSTRALIAN RADIO, 1985

Steven was determined to make something of himself by way of the most difficult route imaginable: mastering those impotent, worthless, fickle things called words. The desperate pathetic fool was determined to become that most absurd of creatures — *a writer*. He lived for the written word and people came second or possibly third. The very intellectualism, the very self-reflexiveness, the very illness which had ravaged and ruined his life and set him apart from the human race was, he thought, going to set him free. He was determined to make sense of himself, the world and his place in it by . . . typing. It was, needless to say, a ridiculous enough project in itself. Yet, Steven's nuttiness went further. He harboured the loony, laughable notion that words might one day help him to conquer something as defiantly illiterate as pop music.

Of all the silly scribblers that Steven cavorted with in his bedroom, Wilde was quite the silliest, and hence the one who aroused him most. His style was irredeemable and his way with words quite fatal. Wilde of course was a poet of foolishness, a spinner of oddly convincing sophistry who managed to bring the world to its knees before it came to its senses instead and sent him to rot in Reading Gaol.

> I've read practically everything (by and about him) and I have a vast collection of first editions. Although he was the most intelligent he simplified everything, therefore practically anybody could read Oscar Wilde and understand. He wasn't complicated yet he still left you lying on the bed panting because it was so real and truthful.
>
> *NME, 1988*

A piece of pop trivia which would have appeared anything but trivial to Steven: The New York Dolls gave a performance in 1972 at The Mercer Arts Centre in New York in a room named after the effeminate Irish dandy who entertained, anatomised, shocked and finally provoked respectable British society to strike him down. It was an entirely apt venue — as has been pointed out Oscar Wilde was, after all, the leader of the Nineteenth-Century Glam Rock Movement (though back then it was known as The Aesthetic Movement). This relatively vulgar upstart full of gentle rage set about assaulting English bourgeois mores with relentless zeal, but more importantly — and this was something which both disarmed and embittered the English — with wit. No wonder Steven was obsessed with Oscar.

Moreover, Oscar was that very rare kind of writer, one that appealed to the heart and the head simultaneously (an even rarer gift among lyricists until Morrissey). By sheer force of will and the meticulous cultivation of his personality, Oscar succeeded in making himself a pop star without learning to play an instrument, forming a band, or signing to a record label, long before pop music had even been invented. His epigrams were 45rpm singles *avant la lettre*: beautiful, poisonous, brilliant little flashes of lyrical egotism and vanity that proved instantly catchy, zooming to the top of the social hit parade and played over and over again at parties.

Wilde was entirely artificial, but frequently succeeded in being more direct and honest than anyone else. He was a creature of culture, but managed to appear completely natural. His style allowed him to step outside of himself and social expectations into something much more truthful and fearless than any man had a right to.

Oscar's whole life was a work of art, which is to say that he was entirely doomed. He was both enthusiastically perverse and a keen invert, which means he gleefully turned conventional wisdom upside down and knavishly assaulted traditional attitudes, something any star worth his twinkle wants to do.

> *What do you consider the most overrated virtue?*
> Common sense.
>
> KILL UNCLE TOUR BOOK, 1991

These were reasons enough for Steven to want Oscar as his spiritual father. But there was more. Oscar was a mummy's boy, but, like many over-talented mummy's boys, including Steven, he was the author of his own personality; more his own man than any daddy's boy could ever be, or want to be. Oscar was Irish but, like many other Irish émigrés to England, he became more English than the English. Oscar became more aristocratic than the aristocracy, who were already beginning the undignified scramble to become middle class. Despite this, or perhaps because of this, he succeeded in appealing to all social classes — even Americans. Best of all, he embodied and lived his own creative contradictions: he championed idleness, but was at least intermittently prolific; he was an idealist, but was the Queen of Cynics; he was a romantic, but was frighteningly realistic; he was a moralist, but completely dissolute (Morrissey of course is an immoralist who is scandalously virtuous).

> Do you want to know the great drama of my life? It's that I have put my genius into my life; all I've put into my works is my talent.
>
> WILDE QUOTED IN ANDRE GIDE'S OSCAR WILDE

Oscar's life was of a piece with his work, and ended up transcending his art. Sexual scandal involving rent boys made this aesthete and all that he stood for synonymous with the 'filthiest' and 'ugliest' of crimes, provoking national disgust, anger and hysteria on such a scale that it lasted well into the next century; the merest mention of his accursed name was sufficient to drive some men into apoplexy. However, by the Sixties and Seventies it was precisely his indecent acts and scandalous reputation that had made him the hippest dead poet in town. The symbol of aberration had become a symbol of liberation. In 1967, in the wake of one of their drug scandals (by this time drugs were the new degenerate threat to British life), The Rolling Stones single 'We Love You' was promoted with a short film in which they re-enacted Oscar's trial: Mick Jagger, of course, was the poet in the dock, complete with green carnation — symbol of the aesthetic movement. It was a slightly impertinent gesture: after all, despite what might be described as Mr Jagger's 'cocksucking lips' a claim to Wilde's corrupting-inspiring mantle by a pop star wasn't fully justified until two decades later, when Morrissey covered the stage and his audience with flowers and petal-jism during a performance of 'This Charming Man'.

> I hope you have not been leading a double life, pretending to be wicked and being really good all the time. That would be hypocrisy.
>
> OSCAR WILDE, *THE IMPORTANCE OF BEING EARNEST*

Today, in a world that has been conquered by rock and pop, or at least by its most vulgar representatives, and where everything has been aestheticised and 'madeover', the rehabilitation of Oscar Wilde is horribly complete. He is now the Queen Mother of New Labour, the loved by everyone, a threat to no one. Tacky statues to him are unveiled by government ministers and glossy feature films are made portraying him as a harmless poof with some good one-liners and tasty waistcoats, the hapless victim of other people's nasty, outdated, unfashionable, chintzy bigotry. In fact, today Wilde's greatest misfortune you might be forgiven for thinking was that he was born too soon to be a presenter on *Changing Rooms*. Wilde, who once existed outside of society to bring it to account, now exists for it, to tell us how with-it we are; how tolerant, how groovy, how good-humoured, how tasteful, how relaxed.

> *Gerald:* I suppose society is wonderfully delightful!
> *Lord Illingworth:* To be in it is merely a bore. But to be out of it simply a tragedy.
>
> OSCAR WILDE, *A WOMAN OF NO IMPORTANCE*

To be sure, the real Wilde was an outsider who wanted to be an insider, but only the better to spike the city's drinking water. Oscar has been done to death by his fans, even more than Reading Gaol.

Of course, this assimilated, emasculated, populist Wilde bears no relation to the wicked Wilde that Steven worshipped, emulated and relentlessly rehearsed in his bedroom. There were probably always two Wildes — Steven's Wilde and Stephen's Wilde. But just as it was Morrissey's skinny, malcontent Wilde that was the only version worth remembering and imitating, it was perhaps inevitable that it was Fry's flabby social-climbing *Wilde* that the world would ultimately take to its bosom. (It is equally inevitable that even before the first clod of earth hits his coffin, Morrissey will himself be rehabilitated too — miraculously cured of his scorn and self-destructiveness he will be remembered as a lovable 'eccentric', a singing Grinch with a touching tendency to become mildly distracted at the plight of small furry animals and small furry orphans; in his biopic he will be played by Gareth Gates wearing a hearing aid).

Mind you, the worship of a fan like Steven is a very dangerous thing; much more dangerous than the worship of a Stephen. Whilst most who emulate their heroes (quite deliberately) never come close to matching their achievements let alone surpassing them, Steven was to match Wilde's achievements and quickly overhaul them — after all, how many times was Oscar hugged and kissed onstage? How many times did he throw his sweat-drenched silk shirt into the crowd and witness it torn to shreds? How many times did he get on *Top of the Pops*? How many millions of adolescent bedrooms was he entertained in? Oscar may have scandalised and corrupted Nineteenth Century polite English society (and a few rent boys who didn't exactly need much corrupting) but Steven was to corrupt a whole generation — in their parents' homes. And pay *him* for it.

Young Steven wasn't entirely monogamous in his affections however. He kept in his room another famously cool corpse, one younger and fitter than Wilde, but even more pernicious. If Wilde had tainted the golden age of English bourgeois culture, this one had almost single-handedly spoiled the American Fifties, depriving it of its innocence and white-picket fence Mom & Pop blandness. Even better, he had

81

died before his twenty-fifth birthday, just at the moment when his corrupting influence on American/Western youth was about to provoke
an unstoppable chain reaction, and just before the world could exact
its usual price for his fame. By impaling his young body on his Porsche
Spyder's steering wheel he reneged on his Faustian deal and managed
to cheat the world of its revenge; he didn't end up in Reading Gaol or
Bel Air. He didn't just leave behind a beautiful — if somewhat worse-
for-wear — corpse, he left behind a reputation unscathed.

> I would like to go to Indiana and mess with his soil, but so many oth-
> ers have done it. They've taken away the monument, they've taken away
> the stone and they've taken away the grass. People have been so greedy.
> What's left for me?
>
> NME, 1985

His name, of course, was James Byron Dean. And his image covered the walls of Steven's adolescent bedroom prison, as if he wanted
to replace the dreary limits of his Manchester existence with Dean's
beauty. And why not? Jimmy symbolised success, fame, glamour, origi-
nality, integrity, immortality. *Handsomeness*; such heartbreaking, hurt-
ful handsomeness.

> He had that strange quality that he could look good anywhere, in anything.
>
> THE HOT PRESS, 1984

Dean was the epitome of Steven's life-long obsession with men
whose looks bring them popularity, smooth their passage through life,
and appear, rightly or wrongly, to be an index of their ease in their
bodies and the world. Their happiness. Like many outsiders, Steven
felt himself to be essentially unlovable. To feel simply ugly would have
been a relief; instead he felt *monstrous*. Like most who stand apart,
Steven had exiled himself with his own inferiority-superiority complex. Learning that Dean was also insecure and unhappy only made
the actor's handsomeness all the more astonishing and alluring.

> Send me anything that Jimmy touched.
>
> JAMES DEAN IS NOT DEAD, 1983

By pasting his bedroom walls with countless images of Jimmy, he
turned his prison tower into a fantasy mirror in which he saw himself

reflected back as he would like to see himself: a creature who may have been tortured and full of self-doubt but always managed to look comfortable in his skin and radiate an animal magnetism. Steven may have wanted Wilde's mind, but he wanted Dean's body. In an attempt to get under Dean's skin, and to combine two of his obsessions — words and beauty — he wrote an essay about Dean, in which he described himself as a 'James Dean fan and devotee'. Essentially, it was an act of literary resurrection; reading it you can feel Steven trying to breathe life into Dean's broken body with his feverish words. Called *James Dean Is Not Dead*, the subtitle might have been: 'He's Just Sleeping Under My Bed'.

> You can look into a mirror and wonder — where have I seen that person before? And then you remember. It was at a neighbour's funeral, and it was the corpse.
>
> BLITZ, APRIL, 1988

Steven's identification with Jimmy was intense, possibly sexual, and certainly sick and ill: But then, so was the interest that most young men had in Jimmy. Steven's peculiar perversion was to apply his intellect to what was, essentially, a splendidly stupid phenomenon. But to lonely, misanthropic Steven, hiding from the world in his bedroom in his mother's council house in Manchester, it must have appeared perfectly natural — or the least unnatural thing in his life. Jimmy was, after all, the most hopeful dead body Steven had in his bedroom — an unpopular loner who achieved world fame and worship from teenagers of both sexes on a scale never seen before. He was a mummy's boy who was masculine. He had been rejected by his father but he had become his own man. He was masochistic, but fearless. He was a complete twat, but he was cool. He was bisexual, but all-American. He was that most cosseted of creatures, a Hollywood actor, but he took terrible risks. He was a total fuck-up, but achieved astounding success. He was famous, but — and this is a trick that few mortals ever manage to pull off (today's generation of pliant young Hollywood stars don't even bother to try) — *on his own terms*.

Above all, he was a freak, *but he was desirable*. James Dean was the latter-day Narcissus, in love with the reflection of himself in the silver screen. Jimmy had given a face and a name to a romantically depraved male vanity and made it not just acceptable, but hip. Steven wanted that face. Fortunately for him, it was for sale.

If Wilde was 'the first pop star', then Jimmy was the first pop star you'd want to shag (Frank or Bing *sans* cardie and slacks anyone?), the first pop star whose body, whose desirability was completely commodified. The public queued up, in a (strange) manner of speaking, to sniff his underwear. This was the nature of the pervy deal that pop culture offered — in exchange for your dough you were given the chance to possess a commodity that was a fetish or Holy Relic standing in for the star: the film (the residue of his aura); the poster (the imprint of his halo); the blue jeans (the nearest thing to his skin — and talent); and above all, the single (the magical piece of vinyl which captured his soul). But, of course, there weren't any singles, since Dean happened to be a pop star who didn't make records just movies (it would take Colonel Tom Parker to work out what the world needed and produce a singing hillbilly Dean).

I gotta know who I am. I gotta know!

JAMES DEAN IN *EAST OF EDEN*.

Perhaps this was why, after Dean's death at the age of twenty-four in 1955, the very year in which the pop star and pop music were definitively brought together in the person of Elvis - who actually wanted to be a film star like Dean — the teenage public went crazy for him. Now he was gone, they couldn't get enough. *I am so sickened now.*

Death was undoubtedly more than half hinted at in his self-absorption, particularly in *Rebel*, released eerily after he was already six feet under and food for worms, but death at *high speed* (in his own 'chicken run' with a black and white sedan driven by a rustically oblivious Mr Turnupseed on Highway 46) was the perfect ending for Dean, containing as it did the elements of both activity and passivity that marked his on-screen persona and which made him so desirable (and which Morrissey was to incorporate into his own persona). Death rendered him entirely prone, subject to complete possession by his audience, as commodified as the hamburger and ice-cream cone which his hometown of Fairmount, Indiana, also bequeathed a lipsmacking world.

But the manner of his death, its impetuousness, preserved his dangerous boyish masculinity, at the same time guaranteeing that he would 'never be a man' — or become Dad. Hence Jimmy was the first pop star that lived forever.

Steven, whose own fame would not begin until he was the age at which Dean died, was awed by Jimmy's Oedipal Houdini act, but resolved that he would improve on Dean's achievement by pulling off this feat of famous frozen adolescence without having to resort to the inconvenience of actually dying (much of his carefully assembled iconography and album covers have the whiff of Holy Relics about them).

As Steven described breathlessly in *James Dean Is Not Dead*, 2,000 letters arrived at Dean's studio every week addressed to a man who was famously deceased (obviously they thought Hollywood would have a forwarding address for him — or else thought Hollywood was actually Heaven). Others bought rings which claimed to contain chips from his tombstone, or paid to sit in the Porsche Spyder next to the buckled steering wheel which tore his chest open, and touch his dried blood. *East of Eden* director Elia Kazan pointed out that James Dean was a 'sick kid' — but pop culture was far sicker. Morrissey himself would later be accused of having a morbid and unnatural interest in death and suicide and fetishism, to which charge he is entirely guilty, but it was the James Dean cult that had taught him that death, suicide and morbid fetishism were what pop culture was all about — lessons which would ensure that he would end up a pop star adored as much by his fans alive as Dean was after his death. (A point ironically underlined by the scene in the promotional video for the 1988 single 'Suedehead' in which he 'messes with the soil' of James Dean's grave in Fairmount — an act of homage and also perhaps a kind of desecration: *why do you come here when you know it makes things hard for me?*)

But there was something more to Dean's fatal narcissism, something more unyielding and lasting than all the diamonds that Hollywood pay-packets could buy. Something with which Steven passionately identified: Dean was a Beautiful Bastard. A traitor not just to his own father and friends but to his trade, he was determined to betray all its values, transgress all its fond nostrums and proud traditions for the sake of a much higher cause: *himself*.

> Acting is just interpretation. I want to create myself.
>
> JAMES DEAN

In contrast to Brando and Clift, the actors with whom Dean is usually compared and who were consummate professionals, able to immerse themselves chameleon-like in their roles, Dean was never very interested in his characters, or what he could tell us about them. He was only interested in them in terms of what they could tell him about himself, and what he could tell us about himself through them. Dean had little or no technique, only style. Like Wilde he pursued a more authentic version of himself through artifice – his style was the truest expression of himself. He habitually changed lines, dropped them, or omitted whole speeches, and frequently eased himself into the director's chair (Nicholas Ray allowed Dean unprecedented input during the making of *Rebel*). He abused his profession in the most appalling fashion, had no respect for it or for the film industry, or for that matter for the Fifties, and consequently transformed it beyond recognition and assured his greatness. This was the pattern that Morrissey was to repeat faithfully in his own career.

> It's not his acting, actually I think he was a bit of a ham. I get quite embarrassed when I see those films. But I'm fascinated by the way he seemed to represent his time and his generation.
>
> HOT PRESS, 1984

In his single-minded, selfish, slightly psychotic self-creation through pop culture, Dean the Beautiful Bastard became an inspiration for millions of young malcontents who, like Steven, were unhappy with the role or script that their agent Dame Fate had landed them. He was to become an inspirational Oedipus for the illegitimate children of junk culture, a boy determined not so much to kill his father as cut him off from his destiny by simply refusing to reproduce him, and instead choose his own antecedents, taken from pop culture (Dean hero worshipped Brando as much and as embarrassingly as Steven later worshipped Dean).

In *Rebel*, his compromising, complacent, uncool father who attempts to ingratiate policemen by offering them cigars, who allows himself to be hen-pecked by his harridan wife, who can never say what he thinks or feels, is clearly not worthy of being Jim Stark's/James Dean's father (though, in deference to Fifties gender politics and a fashionable paranoia about 'Mom-ism', Jim Stark is portrayed as driven to rebellion by his pinny-wearing father's emasculation; by contrast, Steven's and Jimmy's problem appears to have been a conventionally masculine and distant Fifties father who never wore a pinny). In *Rebel*, Jim/Dean's delinquency is a refusal to be a product of his parent's dysfunctional narrative which deprives him of his own identity: *"You're tear-ring me a-part!"* He, on the other hand, is putting himself *together*. He wants to tell his story, not repeat theirs. The Beautiful Bastard is a rebel with a cause — a psychopathic determination to be unique.

Of course, there is another 'bastard' in *Rebel*, one that Steven probably recognised only too well. Plato, played by a brooding, sullen Sal Mineo, is from a broken home. Abandoned by his father, he lives with his overprotective mother. He has a soft focus publicity picture of Alan Ladd, a potential Smiths cover star, pinned on the inside of his school locker where he should have a picture of Jayne Mansfield or a faceless baseball star. Clearly with an eye for the iconic, he dotes on Jim/Dean with big, black, upraised cow eyes from almost the moment he meets him (in the police station, appropriately enough). For a brief moment in the final reel, Plato becomes Dean's barely platonic, mildly incestuous 'son' (Dean lets him wear his soon-to-be-famous and much-copied windcheater, something which clearly causes Plato more than a frisson of pleasure), with Natalie Wood as his strangely indulgent mother, playing peculiar happy families in a condemned building.

Rebel was released the year before A *Taste of Honey*, another parable of alternative families blooming and withering in a derelict landscape, was first performed. Of course, Hollywood organised a much tidier and more humane ending than *Taste*: where Geof mooches off into the night, Plato is helpfully gunned down by the cops (when Jim sees the dead body he zips up the windcheater Plato is still wearing, in a fetishistic gesture of consummation which millions of young men around the world were to repeat after Dean's own death.)

Not surprisingly, Steven didn't want to be Plato. Truth be told, this failed school-leaver and wannabe delinquent was fed up with *being* Plato. He didn't want to be a victim. He wanted to be a new kind of hero. One with great hair. Steven was determined that the world would one day look up to him with the same, wide, greedy eyes as Plato, and he would see reflected in them... Jim Stark.

The problem was, he had no idea how he was going to bring this about.

And time was against him now.

stay on my arm you little charmer

I just opened the door one day and there he was, exactly how he found me he hasn't made clear. He just appeared at my door one day. It sounds really fanciful, but that's exactly how it happened. He said 'Would you like to write, and form a group?'

MORRISSEY

The lunatic, the lover, and the poet,
Are of imagination all compact: . . .
Such tricks hath strong imagination,
That, if it would but apprehend some joy,
It comprehends some bringer of that joy.

WILLIAM SHAKESPEARE, A MIDSUMMER NIGHT'S DREAM

7

After 'Morrissey', Johnny Marr was Steven's greatest inspiration. So no wonder he loved him.

Marr, like anyone meshed in the web of someone else's desire, like any beloved trapped in the amber of the lover's imagination, laboured under the extravagant delusion that he was his *own* idea. He even thought that meeting Steven that fateful day in 1982 and proposing they form a band was something he had dreamt up himself. He was gravely mistaken. All these things came from Steven, and Steven's exceedingly uncharacteristic decision to answer the doorbell — if only because the idea of Morrissey, assembled in Steven's bedroom over a thousand years, was so intense and had a gravitational attraction so strong, so irresistible, so evil, that it was bound to make a satellite of anyone foolish enough to fly anywhere near him.

Marr the beloved had to love Morrissey back for reasons that no mortal could argue with: Because Morrissey wrote at the drop of a hat the kind of lines that other lyricists strive for over a lifetime. Because he sang to Marr's music like his life depended on it (which of course it did). Because Morrissey, for all his heinous faults and failure to mix at parties, had the most beautiful soul in the world (in the right light). Which he proceeded to pour all over Marr.

It was perhaps understandable that Johnny should have entertained such notions about his own authorship and agency. Even though he was, chronologically speaking, four years younger than Steven, he was the worldly-wise one. He was a ladies' man, a wide boy, a charmer, and a virtuoso guitarist whose riffs were the envy of his mates. Steven, on the other hand, was just a loser — a skinny, celibate vegetarian who couldn't play a note on a Vibraphone and could barely even leave his room in his mother's house; Steven was seven going on seventy. He had no friends to speak of. He certainly had no lover. He had no job. He had no life. Johnny, of course, had everything and anything he didn't have he knew how to get. And Steven wanted to be tied to the back of his car.

> I lead a saintly life, he lives a devilish life. And the combination is wonderful. Perfect.
>
> *NME*, 1983

In other words, Steven was a dreamer and Johnny was a man of the world. But men of the world and all their enviable practical qualities are invented by dreamers, because men of the world are necessary for dreamers to do what all dreamers want to do; what all dreamers have to do: inflict their dreams on the rest of us.

Naturally, the world and men of the world (and more often than not even dreamers themselves) don't want to see it that way. They want to think that activity controls and shapes passivity, when in fact passivity always encloses activity, using it for its own ends.

> Johnny, Mike and Andy played their instruments in a very aggressive way. The feeling of power was just like having a vacuum cleaner shoved up your blazer.
>
> *NME*, 1990

According to the legend, Johnny was the gallant Prince Charming to Steven's sulking beauty. Johnny's arrival on Steven's doorstep cut a swathe through the enchanted forest that imprisoned Steven in Stretford; the romantic proposal to 'write and form a band' was the awakening kiss that liberated him from his womb-tomb bedroom and let him loose on the world. However, the script and even the gender roles in this production were not what they appeared. As it said on the sleeves, the words were by Morrissey the music was by Marr. Since it was written by Steven the story was more *Rebel Without A Cause*, and Johnny Marr was more

Natalie Wood than Jimmy Dean (certainly Johnny's unfortunate haircut on the sleeve of *Hatful of Hollow* bears this out). Jimmy was, after all, the tortured, introverted loner that Natalie, outgoing, popular and a bit of a tom-boy, introduces to 'the kids'. Jimmy, the passive/impassive boy stands apart, as distinct and scornful as Steven's Deansian quiff.

> Johnny had grasped the thread of all that was relevant and yet he was – and remains – a very happy-go-lucky, optimistic person who was interested in doing it now. Not tomorrow, but right now! Also he appeared at a time when I was deeper than the depths, if you like. And he provided me with this massive energy boost. I could feel Johnny's energy just seething inside of me.
>
> THE FACE, 1985

Perhaps Marr's decision five years later in 1987 to break up the family and leave Morrissey and The Smiths was prompted by the realisation that he was more Morrissey's fancy than his own man. A decision which may have devastated many fans, including of course Morrissey, and which may have been a mistake professionally speaking – the world was at their feet in 1987 – but one which nobody, not even Morrissey, could really hold against Marr. Johnny, in addition to being by all accounts a likeable, modest guy, is a great, dazzlingly original and bafflingly talented musician and composer, who has been rightfully guaranteed a place in the pop pantheon. Nevertheless, Johnny the Charmer's greatest and most serious contribution to pop/criminal history was to galvanise Morrissey into action, to bring levity into a world of depression, and, most of all, to provide him with the means by which he could impose his wonderfully warped reality on the world – to be the catchy vector by which the Moz virus could infect and ruin millions of lives.

For Steven, as for any hermit prophet whose wish comes true and the mountain comes visiting, meeting Marr was literally fatal. Just as he had hoped and willed and dreamt and prayed, (chaste – the only kind really) love and salvation had come to him through the medium of pop music. He had been vindicated in his misanthropy and malcontent. Now that he was actually going to become a pop star and was, moreover, to have company along the way, there was no need to ever become socialised, no need to grow up, no need to ever enter into the world of people or compromise. *No need to ever become a human being.*

Oscar Wilde had a few words to say, of which you should take careful note: 'When the Gods wish to punish us, they answer our prayers.'

THE FACE, 1984

We had no row during the entire existence of The Smiths. For a long time Johnny and I were intertwined — and that's unusual in pop music — in his life and certainly in mine.

GUARDIAN, 1997

This was an odd, fateful marriage between Beautiful Bastards, it was Jimmy and Natalie, Jo and Geof together against the world (though, like Jo, Steven was already pregnant before he met Marr). Together they set up their own alternative family called 'The Smiths', a name which, like most of the Mancunian misanthrope's art, is both a deliberate parody of average normality and a wistful homage to it. This 'family' which emerged from the derelict, condemned post-industrial landscape of early Eighties Manchester, included not only the lost boys Mike Joyce on drums and Andy Rourke on bass, but later all their fans — an extended family of Beautiful Bastards. And, like a traditional girl getting married and starting a family, Steven changed his name. Steven, the poor twisted child was gone, banished. Now there was only the iconic 'Morrissey'.

The wedding music was not traditional, however. The first single, 'Hand in Glove', released in May 1983, an ominous day in the history of pop music, contains lyrics which appear to be as much a declaration of Morrissey's love for Marr as a declaration of The Smiths' manifesto, since the two are, of course, the same thing. It is, simply put, a declaration of war on the world. This is in fact the hidden agenda of all great love affairs, from Anthony and Cleopatra to Romeo and Juliet to Alexander and Hephaeston to Wilde and Bosie — to Jo and Geof. All lovers are haters, haters of that which is unfortunate enough to be not them.

Geof: We're unique!
Jo: Young.
Geof: Unrivalled!
Jo: Smashing!
Geof: We're bloody marvellous!

SHELAGH DELANEY, A TASTE OF HONEY

The adolescent arrogance of this love affair, its impish mooning at the world, is somehow all the more poignant for its ancient-as-the-hills irony: *no it's not like any other love/this one is different – because it's us*. Like any love worth mentioning, this love's greatest strength and its greatest delusion is its pathological self-sufficiency: *and everything depends upon how near you stand to me.*

This is a love-hate so strong that it will succeed in sweeping away the empty-headed glamour and shoulder-padded power worship of the early Eighties and, in fact, the Eighties themselves: *The Good People laugh/yes, we may be hidden by rags/but we have something they'll never have.* That 'something' is integrity. Honesty. Intelligence. Wit. Total fanaticism. Genius. Scary stage movements. Otherwise known as Morrissey. Hand in glove he stakes his claim, *I'll fight to the last breath/If they dare touch a hair on your head/I'll fight to the last breath.*

These are the words of a man taking on the world and relishing it. Marr can't have been listening too closely, otherwise he would have split much sooner. What Morrissey was promising was the loneliest of musical partnerships (well, lonely for Marr; for Morrissey it was positively crowded compared to his adolescent exile). The Smiths was to be a vast, noble, windswept mountain on top of which Morrissey and Marr would live alone, breathing in thin, cold air and surviving on a diet of lichen and snow, Joyce and Rourke biding their time thousands of feet below them at base camp. From their glassy eyrie, Morrissey and Marr would cast down their bouquets and bolts of lightning and watch them awe and stun the ants below. No manager, no record label, no business or professional imperatives – no reality – would be allowed to touch a hair on the head of The Smiths. Morrissey did not see Marr and The Smiths as a way to open a door on to the world, but a way of *kicking in* the door of the world. Like all lovers, dangerous idealists and teenagers, Morrissey would broach no compromise, he wanted nothing less than the imposition of his reality on the world. He wanted revenge, and he wanted it NOW.

> I won't rest until that song is in the heart of everything. It was so URGENT – to me, it was a complete cry in every direction. It really was a landmark. There is every grain of emotion – that has to be injected into all the songs and it worked perfectly with 'Hand In Glove'. It was as if these four people had to play that song – it was so essential. Those words had to be sung.
>
> JAMMING, 1984

Listening to this first single, Morrissey's brilliant, barmy, agenda is all too apparent. It is Morrissey's voice and vision which stands out. While Joyce on rhythm is crashing around like his punk idols, Rourke the disco fan is funking on bass guitar, and Marr is indulging in a nearly-embarrassing spot of Beatles 'Love Me Do' *homage*-hubris on his harmonica. But Morrissey already sounds completely confident, fully-formed and utterly, terrifyingly original. Yes, his sources are worn on his sleeve, but his conjunction of them is truly inspired. After all, a bloke who looks like an anorexic James Dean singing words steeped in Shelagh Delaney and Oscar Wilde in the style of Sandie Shaw crossed with The New York Dolls in a Mancunian accent is original enough for anyone.

In fact, Morrissey sounds like nothing ever heard before, yet entirely familiar all at once. Unearthly yet disarmingly real, a voice beyond tears and laughter, he sounds assured that this is it, this is his chance for a taste of the honey, and no one and — after all these years of hiding in his room and not answering the doorbell — no inhibition, no care for what society or *Jukebox Jury* thinks, is going to stop him. 'Hand in Glove' is pop song-ness distilled so strongly and sweetly that it threatens to make any that come after it sound weak, foolish, second-hand and second-rate. There's an urgency and directness in Morrissey's voice that will brook no delay, no argument, no excuse. When he growls and groans between lines, like a wounded animal with perfect pitch, or (as in later songs, such as 'Barbarism Begins at Home', 'The Boy With a Thorn in his Side' and 'Last of the Famous International Playboys') allows his words to sublimate themselves into a divine, demented yodelling, he transmits a passion that is all the more eloquent in its wordlessness, coming as it does from someone so supernaturally articulate.

In 'Hand' Morrissey sounds exactly like what he is: a Northern librarian with a frightening but spellbinding beautiful grudge against the world let out of the damaged books store-room where he's been locked up for a month of endless Sundays, but sounding disarmingly fresh where he should be dusty. It's a grudge enacted through words but distilled into something much more dangerous and debilitating through the heat of his own passion — into something truly melodious. It's a grudge, in other words, the listener can't resist, can't help but ending up sharing. However, like Jo, Morrissey is aware that this union will be fleeting, he knows his luck 'too well' '*And I'll probably never see you again*'.

There is something in the third repeat of that last line and its drawn-out delivery that is sad and pensive, but also celebratory: *I'll prob-ly ne-ver see you-ou a-gain* . . . It's partly the bitter wisdom of inexperience, something that you can collect duffel bags of if you spend your teenage years indoors reading too many books, but it's also a sentimental greediness, an inability to resist savouring the sadness of something gained and then lost before it's lost, or even just slightly misplaced. That this is the closing line of the song, providing a pessimistic counterpoint to the opening insolent optimism makes it quite clear that it is the prospect of losing what has been gained which is already preoccupying Morrissey. In turn, this implies that the whole point of possessing someone in the first place is so that you can lose them.

This is perhaps the very essence of pop: something which at its best and most powerful is a kind of masturbatory melancholia, a kind of crying to oneself; even when it isn't explicitly about loss and pain, but appears instead to be about the 'upside' of love going right, rather than the dark downside of love going wrong, pop music is still about loss and pain. The 'ooh I really love you baby' lyric is frequently implicitly about a perspective gained in contemplation, after losing 'baby'. Pop is a murmuring, sighing attempt to master the experience of loss itself by making it something you control, making it something that makes you feel ooh-so-good-it-hurts, but also something that you secretly wished for yourself and therefore imagine that you *brought about yourself*. It's a childish game that we all play from the earliest of ages to try and master our own basic unhappiness and inability to control the world and people around us. Morrissey understands better than any other performer — no, Morrissey exemplifies the fact — that at its happy-sad heart, the magic of pop music, its dreamy narcotic effect, is precisely this bitter-sweet-sweeter blend of hope and despair; the sweetness of happiness and the even sweeter sadness that lies behind happiness.

For Marr, alas, it is also proof that even during the triumph of their very first single — a triumph singularly unhampered, it has to be said, by chart success – Morrissey had already had the idea of Marr leaving The Smiths for him. It is Morrissey's hand in the glove.

a murderous desire

I repeat, the only thing to be in 1983 is handsome!

MORRISSEY

8

In 1987 a distressed young man in Denver, Colorado, held his local radio station hostage insisting, at gunpoint, they play nothing but Smiths records. This they did — for four hours — inflicting Morrissey on the good Christian people of Colorado, who up until that point had been for the most part blissfully unaware of his existence. Eventually, the police besieging the building persuaded the unhappy young man to give himself up.

This was both an unhinged, impotent romantic gesture and a dangerous, revolutionary act. If any music ever had a chance of changing the world, or at least giving it some seriously bad dreams, it was the music of The Smiths. The fervent zeal of this mad lad who forced the Denver radio station to saturate the airwaves of his hometown with records by this obscure, depraved British band was, in its own casualty-free way more 'murderous' and ambitious than the rage of the two young shallow nihilists who went on a shooting spree many years later in their High School in Littleton, also in Colorado.

The Smiths were relentlessly opposed to the world as no other band had been before, including even those priceless sneering anti-heroes of the Seventies, the Sex Pistols. Unlike the Pistols who often bluffed it, or struck antagonistic poses for their own sake, The Smiths — or rather,

Morrissey — really did appear to hate everything; or at least, everything young people were force-fed as 'normal'. His lyrics assaulted the education system, the family, marriage, adulthood, gender, the Church, meat-eating, money, governments, royalty, discos, fame, relationships, the music business and, in fact, the whole of the Eighties. Morrissey was the real mad lad holding the world hostage at the point of a pop single.

> *When did it dawn on you it would work?*
> Instantly, really . . . because it did happen very quickly, even if we're just talking about the first few Smiths gigs. It was more than I expected. There were lots and lots of people ready to identify with what I was feeling. Hatred! Hating everything, but not being offensively hateful. It was like hate from quite gentle people.
>
> MORRISSEY

When, after the frustrating failure of 'Hand in Glove', The Smiths' second single 'This Charming Man' charted in the Top Thirty in November 1983 and they were finally, (and one hopes) reluctantly invited on BBC TV's *Top of the Pops*, the excitement of Andy, Mike and Marr put together did not even equal the excitement of the plastic beads around Morrissey's neck. *Top of the Pops* the loved-and-hated tacky TV chart show institution where he had seen so many of his heroes, Sandie, Bowie, Bolan, Sparks. The hopeless, helpless fan(atic) had finally become a *star*. His strange whooping, whirling, lunging movements that evening on the BBC stage that so alarmed the schoolgirls bussed in from Basingstoke may have formed the dance of the damned, but the damned who know they are not going to hell alone any more. Like a genie released from a bottle with no intention of granting any wishes except his own (after all, he had released himself), he taunted the world which had stoppered him up for so long. He was going to make sure that people not only noticed him but *experienced* him. Like the romantic terrorist in Colorado, he was committing the most violent, most terrifying act of all — *making people feel what he felt.*

> The Smiths do tease people, making them laugh, then making them cry — operating at opposite ends of the emotional scale. What we're ultimately hoping to do is make them laugh and cry at the same time.
>
> *MELODY MAKER*, 1986

Perhaps because it was sincere, Morrissey's hatred was *sensual*. Unlike the oddly asexual Rotten persona, which understandably eschewed romantic lyrics, Morrissey's aura of hatred was openly corporeal. It was a decidedly *handsome* hatred. Instead of theatrical violence he offered a poisonously sensitive lyricism; instead of gesture politics he traded in the most powerful and distilled language of hate – love. Instead of nihilism, he offered romanticism. In order achieve these ends he committed the supreme act of terrorism: he tried to reinvent sex.

> Every song is about sex. I'm very interested in gender. I feel I'm a kind of a prophet for the fourth sex. The third sex, even that has been done and it's failed. All that Marc Almond bit is pathetic . . . I'm bored with men and I'm bored with women. All this sexual segregation that goes on, even in rock 'n' roll, I really despise it . . .
>
> SOUNDS, 1983

Morrissey the self-styled 'prophet of the fourth sex' was intimately committed to destroying the affective world that most people inhabited, but from which he had been excluded, or had excluded himself from. His erotic terrorism consisted of nothing more than speaking the 'truth' of desire – naked (if somewhat neurotic) lust unclothed by fond clichés about gender and warm prejudices about sexuality. In the sweaty handful of first Smiths singles, the seedy-chaste first album *The Smiths* and its bountiful overspill *Hatful of Hollow*, Morrissey ejaculated a completely careless desire into the face of the world. A desire that was outside – outside of marriage, outside of the family, outside of convention, outside of romance, outside of sexuality. As the definitive outsider, excommunicated from even the brief satisfaction of frustration and alienation offered by 'normal' or even conventionally 'abnormal' sex, Morrissey understood perfectly that desire is always outside – outside the institutions with which society tries to civilise it and force it to speak in more hopeful, house-trained, certain terms than it can or should. A desire which is, finally, outside of *us*, and therefore ultimately unknowable. Love may well be Natural and Real, but never for *us*.

True to his doomed devotion to the revolutionary truth of desire, sex in Morrissey's work is almost always anticipated, frustrated, averted or disappointed rather than consummated: '*And Sorrow's Native Son/he will not rise for any one . . .*' ('Pretty Girls Make Graves'); '*I grabbed you by the gilded beams/and that's what Tradition means/and I doused another venture/ with a gesture/that was . . . absolutely vile'* ('I Started Something I Couldn't Finish'). When sex actually does manage to raise its sorry head it is almost always in lonely public places — literally 'outside': *'On a hillside desolate . . .'* ('This Charming Man'); *'Under the iron bridge we kissed'* ('Still Ill'); *'shove me on the patio/I'll take it slowly'* ('Reel Around the Fountain'); *'But I don't want a lover/I just want to be tied to the back of your car'* ('You've Got Everything Now'); *'I know a place where we can go/Where we are not known'* ('These Things Take Time'); *'If you ever need self-validation/just meet me in the alley by the railway station'* ('I Want the One I Can't Have'); *'On a groundsheet, under canvas/your tent flaps open wide . . ./on a forecourt . . ./on a desk is where I want you'* ('Alsatian Cousin'); *'And I know a place/where no one is likely to pass'* ('Jack the Ripper').

Morrissey's devotion to the undomesticable truth of desire has nothing in common with the mainstream tendency of pop to validate 'sex' as good in and of itself, exemplified in its relentless empty pursuit of 'sexiness' (which in any case is just about selling — which is not actually very sexy at all). Morrissey's vision of desire is utterly pessimistic, but strangely liberating for that.

> *Pick five words that describe yourself.*
> Loving, lovable, lovely, lovelorn, loveless.
>
> Q, 1995

This outsider 'love', which represented a rejection of everything society called 'decent' (in other words what everyone knows is false) is the very heart not only of Morrissey's rebelliousness but also his directness. The unpretentiousness of The Smiths, their plain name, appearance, lack of marketing and sweetly simple guitar arrangements was not only a reaction to the pomposity of New Romantic excess, but also a way of driving home the naked truth of Morrissey's words; a constant reminder that The Smiths were not about showbusiness, they were not about entertainment, they were not about packaged escapism, they were not about cheap shock tactics. They were not, in other words, about pop music or sex in the way that most people understood these things. Instead, Morrissey sang sincerely and frankly from his own bitter experience of frustration, in such a way that neither pop music — nor sex — could ever be the same again.

101

While the early Morrissey cultivated a certain understated androgyny in his appearance, sometimes looking like a lesbian attempting a half-hearted gesture at femininity for her visiting parents, it was so subtle, especially in the context of the strumpet world of early Eighties pop, that it represented a rejection of tired ideas about what was unconventional. Instead of the exterior androgyny of glam rock which had been resurrected by the New Romantics and 'gender benders', Morrissey was really offering an exploration of *interior* androgyny, where handsomeness supplanted glamorousness. In place of the explicit, sensationalist yet oddly didactic lessons in 'sexuality' offered by bands like Frankie Goes To Hollywood and Bronski Beat, Morrissey offered an implicit, innocent seediness — a depiction of desire which may be outside but is not Other, since we all know what it is to be born seedy and innocent, even those of us who are not fortunate enough to be Catholics. Marc Almond, who publicly proclaimed his 'bisexuality', did offer a seediness that was more satisfying than most, but compared to Morrissey's it was rather suburban and, truth be told, *showbiz* (despite all the Jean Genet references he was to employ later in his career).

The famous ambiguity of Morrissey's lyrics is often cited as an example of his cleverness in appealing to as many people as possible, and his ability to hide or at least submerge his own preferences behind a smokescreen of words. This is utterly mistaken. In his terms, Morrissey's lyrics are not in the least ambiguous and speak of desire entirely as he has experienced it himself. The songs may often be deliciously vague in terms of the gender of the subject and object of desire, and Morrissey may love code and obliquery, but this is not an evasion or a cynical 'confusion'. This is in some senses actually a *clarification*, since it is desire which by its very arbitrary, capricious nature that tends to cause confusion — confusion of gender and subjectivity and identity in a way which our prudish social expectations won't allow us to articulate. When Morrissey does, it is explosively funny and poignant all at once: *She wants it Now/and she will not wait/but she's too rough/ and I'm too delicate* ('Pretty Girls Make Graves').

Sex for Morrissey — and for anyone foolish enough to think about it — is an insoluble problem which gender, viewed through either a hetero- or a homo-sexual lens, in fact the lens of 'sexuality', doesn't come close to making sense of. The 'transsexualism' of songs such as 'Half a Person' (*I booked myself in at the Y . . . WCA*' — itself an inverted play on the line from Elvis Presley's 'Guitar Man': '*I hitchhiked down to Memphis, got a room at the YMCA . . .*'), 'Sheila Take a Bow', and 'Vicar in a Tutu' ('*the fabric of a tu-tu/any man could get used to/and I am a living sign*') are not about desire to become a woman, but about the essential absurdity of gender itself — of 'men' and 'women'. In 'Girl Afraid' (*Hatful of Hollow*) Morrissey perfectly encapsulates — from a safe distance — the preposterousness of 'masculine' and 'feminine' and the social comedy these necessary fictions produce, in which a girl 'in the room downstairs' sits and stares worrying about her boyfriend's 'intentions' and then whether he has any at all; while he 'sits and stares' worrying that 'prudence never pays' and besides 'everything she wants costs money'. Comically, tragically, they both resolve '*I'll never make that mistake again!*'

Despite being of 'opposite' sexes and despite articulating their frustrations according to the clichés of their gender, they both end up in the same place but alone, the same 'room downstairs' (a typically tongue-in-cheek Morrisseyan suggestion of genitalia and desire) but bereft, where they 'sit and stare' — in other words, the one thing men and women share and inhabit together is the same despair.

The real joke is that most of us go on making that 'mistake' over and over again — most of us except Morrissey that is, who is having his celibate, bitter revenge. Again. Most people discover themselves as freaks when confronted with the frightening and alienating nature of their relationship to desire, especially the young, who haven't yet learnt to lie to themselves half convincingly-conveniently in the way that adults do. Which is precisely why Morrissey's handsome terrorism immediately recruited so many fanatical young followers — particularly amongst young men.

Do you consider yourself to be an ordinary or an extraordinary person?
I'm probably extraordinary.
And yet a lot of ordinary people can feel great affinity with things that you write.
That's because probably everybody's extraordinary and the minority of people in this world are very ordinary.

MELODY MAKER, 1985

103

In keeping with his campaign of handsome terrorism, he deployed images of naked male passivity, desirability and flagrant narcissism — 'deviant' masculine qualities which when added together denote 'homoeroticism' — on the sleeves of the first vinyl salvos he fired at the world. Not because these qualities were shocking (although in early Eighties, pre-Levis Laundrette male striptease Britain where the male body existed only to make war, make it to the office/factory, or make women pregnant they most decidedly were) but because the desire they spoke of was as real, as natural and as commonplace as it was unspoken. Hence when used in Smiths propaganda they succeeded in making Morrissey's voice a thousand times louder.

The appeal of these images was also cross-gendered — young men responded to the freedom the rebellious new sensuality promised them; young women to the opportunity to escape airless conventions about desire which proclaimed that femininity always mapped on to passivity. Anticipating and far exceeding the way in which advertising in the Eighties would later exploit these very same 'inverted' male qualities to invoke mass desire for commodities much less durable and infinitely less valuable than Smiths songs, Morrissey inverted the usual rock and roll depiction of the female form and mined a vein of masculine longing that had actually informed pop culture since James Dean, but which had never been properly acknowledged before, not even by Ziggy and the glam boys, who were perhaps too distracted by the glitter and tinsel (on the female groupies).

Hence the 'soft' porn of 'Hand in Glove': a naked, smooth young man who could be straight out of the 1950s *Athletic Model Guild* glimpsed from behind, leaning against a wall showing off his eye-catching arse in a pose that could be one of touching vulnerability or cunning calculation; hence the hustler chic of *The Smiths*: a still from Paul Morrissey's *Flesh* depicting the casually muscled torso of a naked Joe Dallesandro, head bowed in dopey submissiveness; hence the indecent narcissism of 'This Charming Man': a prostrate and criminally handsome Fifties Jean Marais trying to embrace his own reflection in a pool of water. This was a trick Morrissey would try to pull off himself, arguably with greater success; first in the countless lascivious *N(ew)M(orrissey)Express* covers he posed for — he sold more copies to its overwhelmingly (hetero) male readership than any other cover star, male or female, especially when he had his blouse off – and then, after the demise of The Smiths, on his own record sleeves. Of course, his female cover stars, from Pat Phoenix to Viv Nicholson, tended to be as strong and feisty (if glamorous and tragic) as his male stars were vain and submissive (if brawny and 'tasty' looking).

> The sexes have been too easily defined. People are so rigidly locked into these two little categories. I don't know anybody who is absolutely, exclusively heterosexual.
>
> MELODY MAKER, 1987

Dr Freud, who is nowadays accused daily of sexist/heterosexist crimes against humanity, would obviously have found Mr Morrissey a fascinating case-study – but also a stimulating colleague. Freud often commented that wherever he went on his journeys into the human psyche he discovered that poets had been there first. Moreover, in his own way, Dr Freud, nominally a staunch defender of the family and normality, was in some ways the Morrissey of turn of the Century Vienna. He found 'masculine' and 'feminine' to be highly dubious terms (if indispensable), and took great pleasure in saying repeatedly that he hadn't come across a single 'normal' person in which homosexual attraction did not play as important a role as heterosexual attraction. In fact, by most people's standards, Dr Freud did not really believe there was such a thing as a normal person at all (his biggest hit was a book with the Morrisseyean title *The Psychopathology of Everyday Life*)

And in the sense which most people understand heterosexuality today, Freud, who is most associated with setting its normative psychological standards, simply did not believe in it. He was a lonely (and celibate) figure for much of his life, even though, or perhaps because, he was a married family man. He also conducted a passionate pen-pal romance with a rhinologist by the name of Wilhelm Fleiss. One of his letters may even have begun: 'Wilhelm, it was really nothing.'

Back in the late Twentieth Century however, neither the glam rockers' sequins, nor the gender benders' frocks, neither Frankie's leather whips, nor Marc Almond's mascara had actually spoken the ordinary, prosaic, *universal* language of same-sex attraction. Precisely because it is so universal and perfectly understandable, it had to be presented as something bizarre and exclusive, the special sensibility of an odd, minority species — when in fact it was at the very heart of pop.

It was left to Morrissey to represent a 'homoeroticism' which was not 'camp' or 'cross-dressed', 'congenital' or, for that matter, 'homo'. It was simply *handsome*. This was the supreme subversiveness of Morrissey's erotic project — to use ordinary language and feelings to convey what were supposed to be extraordinary conditions (after all, as he has pointed out, no one talks about 'heteroeroticism', instead they talk about 'eroticism'). It was also the key to his artistic masterstroke: since (homo)eroticism was simultaneously universal but still beyond the pale, it offered Morrissey an entirely fresh, unadulterated and vibrant vocabulary for his depiction of human desire — and weakness. When Morrissey sang about longing it would sound as if he were the first person in the world to ever speak of it.

While the songs are steeped in 'homoerotics', and connote all kinds of queerness, they never *denote* 'gayness' and therefore never exclude those who have not made that identification — which, of course, is almost everyone. It is easy to collect a list of 'incriminating' Morrissey lyrics: '*When in this charming car/this charming man*' ('This Charming Man') '*All men have secrets and here is mine*' ('What Difference Does it Make') '*you can pin and mount me like a butterfly*' ('Reel Around the Fountain') '*But I don't want a lover/I just want to be tied to the back of your car*' ('You've Got Everything Now') '*I could have been wild and I could have been free/but Nature played this trick on me*' ('Pretty Girls Make Graves') '*How can you stay with a fat girl who'll say:/"Would you like to marry me/ and if you like you can buy the ring"*' ('William, It Was Really Nothing') '*how can they see the Love in our eyes/and still they don't believe us?*' ('The Boy With a Thorn in His Side'). Some might even be inclined replace the 'shop' in 'Shoplifters of the World Unite' with 'shirt'. (This 1987 single may have been partly provoked by the then Tory Government's moves to make illegal any attempt by local authorities to engage in 'the promotion of homosexuality' in schools or present it as a 'pretended family relationship', later known as Section 28. After all, not only was Morrissey, from certain people's perspective, 'promoting homosexuality' to young people, 'pretended family relationships' were something he, with his Jimmy-Natalie, Jo-Geof fixation appeared to want to replace the more usual variety with; The Smiths were the most gloriously pretended, usurping family relationship of all).

> I think that 'This Charming Man' was the most revolutionary single in popular music in that area — I'm quite convinced of it, because it was all just completely natural, about male relationships; it was nice and natural but it wasn't banal.
>
> SQUARE PEG, 1984

However, such a project of 'outing' Morrissey's lyrics is finally rather 'fruitless' — and slightly misses the point. All Morrissey's lyrics and songs resolutely refuse a 'sexuality', it's what makes them heroically handsome. As 'Hand in Glove', insists, valiantly: *'No, it's NOT like any other love/this one is different because it's us!'* Morrissey adamantly and adeptly refuses the identity with which society would quarantine and enclose such 'outside' love with: *'And if the people stare/then the people stare/I really don't know/and I really don't care'*.

All the same, as the song 'Handsome Devil' (the 'B'-side to 1983's 'Hand in Glove') demonstrates to an alarming and hilarious degree, the handsomeness which Morrissey espouses is avowedly not platonic or bookish — it is very definitely hand-some, to the point of being rapacious. The streets are *'crammed with things/eager to be held'* and *'I know what hands are for/and I'd like to help myself'*

In a characteristic Morrisseyan sleight of hand, 'be held' is also the logical development of 'beheld' — looked at. Male tartiness does rather imply that young men are 'asking for it': *'and I would like to give you/what I think you're asking for'*. Exhibitionism may just be exhibitionism, but Morrissey deliberately refuses to respect the 'look don't touch' rule in this song, precisely because he follows it so obediently in his own life.

Once again, the subjectivity of the song is anything but clear-cut, which is to say conventional — in fact the most disturbing and exciting thing about the song is its *flux*, something conveyed by Marr's rambunctiously fast guitar sound which sounds like an over-excited pulse. The dirty joke in the line, *'a boy in the bush is worth two in the hand/I think I can help you get through your exams'*, seems to depend on the narrator being female, or at least having a 'bush', while the line, *'And when we're in your scholarly room/who will swallow whom?'* implies that both parties have swallowable bits (i.e. external genitalia); but on the other 'hand', Morrissey's women do tend to be sexually assertive and we already know about his anxieties regarding female 'voraciousness'.

Explaining a Morrissey song, like explaining a joke, is probably the definition of 'self-defeating', but if we really want to, we can take this further. *'Let me get my hands/on your mammary glands'* also suggests that the 'victim' is actually female – after all, 'handsome' is not an adjective which is exclusive to males, especially given Morrissey's taste in ladies. And so on.

So much for the 'gay' nature of Morrissey's lyrics. 'Handsome Devil', which seems at first glance like one of the most 'obvious' and 'explicit' 'gay' songs of Morrissey's oeuvre, has a subjectivity that would have most gays running for the hills.

There appears to be, it must be admitted here, an almost fetishistic interest in mostly male 'hands' on the part of this singer from a working class background: 'Hand in Glove'; 'The Hand That Rocks the Cradle'; his sweaty attachment to the word 'handsome'; the strong interest he developed later in his career in men who live by the handy art of boxing. Then there are the manual-oriented lyrics to songs such as 'Boy Racer' where a lad at the urinal *'thinks he's got the whole world in his hands'*; 'Shoplifters of the World Unite' containing the refrain *'Hand it over'* and the lines *'A heartless hand on my shoulder/A push – and it's over'*, which leads us by the hand to his interest in being pushed and shoved in 'Reel Around the Fountain': *'Shove me on the patio'*.

For its part, the tabloid press took its prejudices in both hands and unambiguously denounced 'Handsome Devil' as a song promoting (homosexual) paedophilia, giving The Smiths one of their first major pieces of – not very helpful – publicity. While it could be argued that the song does seem to be giving controversy the glad eye, if not actually rummaging around in its short trousers, it should be remembered that the subject of this song is a boy (or girl) who is at least old enough to sit their O-Levels (*'I think I can help you get through your exams'*) but more probably their A-Levels or degree ('scholarly room'). After all, it is about someone who has mistaken books for life. Someone, in other words, like Morrissey. As much as it is about anything, 'Handsome Devil' is about Morrissey's *own* desire as an adolescent to be grabbed by some lustful hands and saved from his scholarly room. (Of course, if the song had been unambiguously about a teenage school*girl* the tabloids would probably have described the song as 'raunchy' instead of 'sick' and run a Page Three topless schoolgirl 'Handsome Devil' special).

What is not in doubt, however, is that paedophilia is 'outside' — in fact, the most 'outside' kind of desire of all (so 'outside' that it can land you a long stretch 'inside'). Despite Morrissey's own passionate personal abhorrence for child abuse, it is perhaps the ultimate metaphor for the collision of seediness and innocence, virtue and lust, purity and worldliness, which informs his artistic outlook — and which in fact informs the human experience.

Perhaps this is why, on the debut album, there are no less than three songs which could be construed as touching on child abuse: 'Reel Around the Fountain' (*'It's time the tale were told/of how you took a child/and you made him old'*), 'Suffer Little Children' and 'The Hand That Rocks the Cradle', a shiveringly, shudderingly beautiful song which almost seems to suggest, via a kind of regression by Marr-ish musical hypnosis, a non-specific recovered lyrical memory/fantasy of paternal abuse. It appears to be a father singing a lullaby to his child, asking it not to cry because *'the ghost and the storm outside'* will not *'invade this sacred shrine/or infiltrate your mind'*. But it's a lullaby which is as disturbing as it is soothing: the father seems to get carried away with the threatening images he invokes even as he promises protection from them. *'my life down I shall lie/if the bogey-man should try/to play tricks on your sacred mind/to tease torment and tantalise'*.

'Tease, torment and tantalise' is tongued alliteration which sounds inviting and threatening at the same time — and this is in fact exactly what the father is doing in this song. The 'ise' of 'tantalise' is a corrupted rhyme and spooky echo of the earlier ('I shall') 'lie'. It is clear that dad is himself the seductive bogey-man (he goes on to summon up the image of a piano playing in an empty room and asserts 'there'll be blood on the cleaver tonight', an extremely ambiguous reassurance here — even without Morrissey's vegetarian principles). 'Cradle' ends with a couple of lines from Jolson's 1928 tear-jerker 'Sonny Boy': *'Climb up on my knee Sonny Boy/Although you're only three, sonny boy...'*.

These lines from a song in which a father struggles to express his love for his dying son, fighting back the tears, are given new layers of meaning by Morrissey's extraordinarily empathetic, intimate voice which promises-threatens so much and adds reassuringly-ominously: '*You're mine... and your mother she just never knew*':

Despite his critique of the family and normality, Morrissey is also very capable of understanding the irresistible pull of the family romance, the original and most powerful — and dramatic — of all love affairs. After all, it pulled him into the world and then pulled him apart. The 'abuse' that this bastardised boy is drawing attention to here with his hints at a warped paternalism is not the specific, exceptional abuse of paedophilia and incest but the 'healthy' sexual abuse of bringing a child into the world (full of ghosts and storms and torment) for your own selfish reasons — which are, of course, the only kind of reasons that anyone has for having children. Morrissey's lyrics, backed by Marr's languidly caressing, swaying melody, deliberately smear the already indistinct line between legitimate paternal impulses and the illegitimate variety, between what is 'inside' and what is 'outside', in order to draw attention to the potential deviance of something which is considered so normal and good: *climb up on my knee, sonny boy* . . .

Morrissey is not content to point out the naturalness of the 'unnatural', as in 'This Charming Man' or 'Hand in Glove'; in 'The Hand That Rocks the Cradle' he also spotlights the 'unnaturalness' of the natural — the 'outside' love that is inside all of us, bound up inextricably with our origins, like original sin. By way of illustration perhaps, there is even a lyrical echo of the 'wrong' love of the first 'Hand' song: he sings of words as 'old as sin' fitting him 'like a glove'. 'The Hand That Rocks the Cradle' is a song, like so many of Morrissey's songs, about the monstrousness of desire (the 'bogey-man outside' who is in fact inside.) Especially the desire which we think of as most familiar, fond and homely (even down to 'kitchen aromas', which according to 'Meat is Murder', are really the 'unholy stench of murder').

Nor is the family romance he invokes a one-way seamy street. 'The Hand That Rocks the Cradle' also hints at the child's desire for the father to the exclusion of the mother ('your mother...she never knew'), the so-called negative Oedipus complex which Dr Freud identified as affecting male children as universally as the more familiar love for mummy and desire to kill daddy (but which his prudish followers hastily brushed under the couch after his death). The hand that rocks the cradle may rule the world but it isn't always mummy's hand doing the rocking: *'There never need be longing in your eyes/as long as the hand that rocks the cradle is mine'*

Unlike that of the mother, the warm, protective, seductive promise of this paternal love is of course never properly realised – can never be realised – particularly not, we can be sure, in incest. All boys grow into men with the lonely knowledge of this disappointment. Some feel it rather more than others; many spend their adult lives pursuing its impossible satisfaction, either by having sons of their own (and, inevitably, repeating the pattern), or by hanging around in leather bars (a refusal to repeat which ironically results in *constant* repetition). Or by becoming pop stars. Morrissey himself was sired and brought into the world by a father whose distance and then actual absence seems to have characterised much of his later ambivalent 'longing'.

It was precisely this wounded, lost-boy quality in Morrissey which appealed to the growing ranks of other wounded lost boys. By the early Eighties the break-up of the family, which meant in fact the increasing obsolescence of the institution of fatherhood, was well under way (particularly in working class families). Since women almost always gain custody, divorce is effectively a ritualised, finalised elaboration of paternal disappointment and separation.

The extended family of Beautiful Bastards, which Morrissey had imagined in his room for all those years, had turned out to be palpably real. And, with the shining eyes that Plato offered Jim in *Rebel*, they eagerly looked to Morrissey, a very alternative masculine role model, to rock their cradle. *Where is the man you respect?/And where is the woman you love?* The answer of course, is Morrissey.

It is a measure of Morrissey's greatness and his unhappiness that having reinvented/abolished sex, he has managed to reproduce himself asexually through the narcissistic voodoo of pop music. Squinting out from the stage through the dazzling spotlights at his audience, he is greeted by the sight of thousands of young Moz clones, male and female, complete with dyed black quiffs and eyebrows, eagerly trying

to catch the eye of their 'pretended' 'perverted' pop cultural 'parent'
— whom many probably wouldn't mind swallowing in their scholarly
rooms.

> A lot of male followers are, as far as the eye can see, natural specimens
> who have very anguished and devilishly rabid desires in my direction.
> And I find that quite historic.
>
> *DETAILS*, 1991

Like all great pop stars, from Wilde to Bowie, Dean to Bolan,
Morrissey was clearly a flaunting 'pervert' in the sense of (ostentatious-
ly) straying from the 'natural' course — that is, convention. Calling
himself the prophet of the fourth sex was not just an extravagant claim
which made good copy, but also a sober acknowledgement of his his-
torical role. The pop star is an ambitious outsider, a pied piper, luring
young people away from their parents and their known destiny to a
completely unknown one, if they're at all original. In other words, just
like desire itself.

   Though, of course, desire more often than not is something which
is supposed to stitch us into a familiarly-unfamiliar world of compulso-
rily shared values and repetition. The family has been called the cradle
of fanaticism, a folie à deux into which the child is introduced and immediately abused by the alien, ever-so-slightly psychotic consciousness
into which he or she has been unwittingly and unwillingly immersed.
In other words, from birth the child is forced at parental gunpoint to
listen endlessly to a playlist they did not choose until they mistake it
for their own fave raves. Pop, a gasp for air amidst the family's incestuous ideological smothering, is a product of fanaticism and a protest
against it. At its best it's a form of revenge and (self-)hatred as much as
a statement of identity. The fan is always impelled by their handsome
hatred of what they are and where they come from as much as they are
by their murderous desire for the pop star who tells them please don't
cry, but makes them cry rivers.

   And no one understood or represented this sadistic law of desire
better than the gawky fan Steven turned criminally handsome pop star
Morrissey.

celibate cries

You see, it's not the marrying love between us, thank God.

SHELAGH DELANEY, *A TASTE OF HONEY*

Morrissey's just an old closet queen.

BOY GEORGE

Whatever people say I am, I'm not. God knows what I am.

ALBERT FINNEY, *SATURDAY NIGHT AND SUNDAY MORNING*

9

The early, frenzied brandishing of gladioli apart, Morrissey is perhaps best known for not doing the nasty. His abstinence is seen as both symbol, proof and cause of his eccentricity. After all, in an age utterly obsessed with and possessed by SEX, such party-pooping is inconsiderate, anti-democratic, downright unhealthy, and, well, positively sinful. And in a pop star who hasn't been knighted and whose main audience isn't grandmums, it's actually *heretical*.

As Oscar Wilde put it, celibacy is the only real perversion; and in Mozza's eyes, this was a good enough argument for practising it. Like any form of Utopianism, reinventing sex requires you to renounce the thing you want to reinvent. Paradoxically, although celibacy is perhaps the least innocent sexual option — renouncing sex makes everything sexual — publicly it provided Morrissey with the innocence he needed to carry off his seductive-seditious project. Celibacy, like the gladiolus, is after all a sweet, delicate flower with a rather well-developed phallus at its heart.

In order to be above sexuality, the prophet of the fourth sex had to be above sex. And in a world which can only, on a good day, conceive of two and a half sexes, the prophet of the fourth had to 'take the vows' (and marry not Jesus but himself) to avoid being enmeshed in a dreary, mundane, mind-numbing parochialness. Whatever he did, whatever the mechanics and topography of his nakedness with another person, and the all-important, all-consuming details of whether their genitalia were internal or external, would be taken as the complete explanation of Morrissey himself — what he was, how he wore his hair, how he tied his shoelaces and, of course, the rationale behind his whole *oeuvre*. He would, in other words, lose control of his own narrative, surrender his own authorship. He would cease to be his own special creation and become instead someone else's dirty joke.

What do you like in your music?
I can't forgive anybody a bad lyric really. I like to think a singer is singing with a sense of immediate death. The Gallows Humour, lah de dah. That it's the last song I'll ever sing, quite literally. I like singers to sing with desperation.
Humour?
Well you know, desperation, humour, what's the difference?
Sex?
Well, yes, humour; we've mentioned sex.

NME, 1989

Celibacy massively enhanced Morrissey's stardom by turning him into a conundrum, a puzzle which had to be solved. As a highly sexual pop star who renounced sex, he made himself the Rosetta Stone of sex itself and found himself interrogated about his 'sex life' like no other pop star had ever been before. (By way of contrast, Boy George's infamous 'I prefer a cup of tea' remark was rather too eagerly believed.)

Where does the anguish and the hate come from?
As with most things, I'm still trying to find out.
Why can you fall in love so easily with images, but not with people?
I'm still trying to find out.

BLITZ, 1988

In an age fascinated with telling the secret of sex, over and over again, Morrissey had to be made to talk. In interview after interview the celibate star would be pushed up against the wall, bright lights shone into his eyes, and made to explain his alibi over and over again in the hope of catching him out. Tricks mixed with threats mixed with wheedling pleadings in an attempt to get this most uncooperative of witnesses to turn Queen's Evidence.

You must get a few propositions these days . . .
Not many! The shock of the whole thing to me is that not many situations do arise. I thought literally queues upon queues would form, but it's not the case. After the end of a sizzling performance, where people are simply eating each other to get close to the stage, I find myself back at the hotel with Scrabble and an orange. It's all very curious.

JAMMING, 1984

What is your ideal sexual experience?
I don't have a vision of it at all. Why do people ask me questions like this?
Because you ask for it. You're the only person who can seriously be asked those questions.
Oh, come now.
Is there any sex in Morrissey?
None whatsoever. Which in itself is quite sexy.

BLITZ, 1988

Well, I don't believe you haven't ever gone out with anyone, Stephen [sic].
Well, I haven't, so put that in your Sony cassette and . . . [laughs sharply] I really haven't.
But you're a human being.
You've no evidence of that. Artists aren't really people. And I'm actually 40 percent papier maché.

MELODY MAKER, 1997

One biographer even announced that he was writing a book about Morrissey's 'love life', an exceptional, if slightly disturbing, accolade (though, oddly, years later, there's still no sign of it). Clearly, by making his private life a tabula rasa, Morrissey succeeded in provoking everyone to write all over it.

What is the greatest myth about fame?
That someone somewhere consequently wants to sleep with you.

MORRISSEY

116

Interviewers frequently asked him point blank if he was gay. When this got nowhere, in their terms, some would resort to cutting out the question altogether and just going straight to the answer they wanted. One grilling him for an American rock magazine in the early Eighties announced: 'Morrissey is a man who says he's gay' — without providing any quotes to back the statement up. As a consequence of this, Morrissey and The Smiths were perceived in the US almost from the beginning as a 'gay act', something which did not exactly help them, but rather more importantly it simply wasn't true. This journalist was merely doing his job, however. He was just simplifying things for his readers, just filling in the gaps, just helping Morrissey 'out' — as more and more people have been inclined to do as Morrissey's career has progressed. Since Morrissey was openly admitting, nay flaunting — in his work — the fact that he wasn't 'straight', he must, therefore be 'gay'. Stands to reason, dunnit?

What these very helpful, very kind people forgot, however, was that the law 'what's not one thing must be t'other', absolutely correct and inviolable as it is, is a law which *only applies to stupid people*. And journalists.

Are you gay?
I feel that I am quite vulnerable and that's quite good enough because I wouldn't want to be thought of as Tarzan or Jane. . .. I don't recognise such terms as heterosexual, homosexual, bisexual and I think it's important that there's someone in pop music who's like that. These words do great damage, they confuse people and they make people feel unhappy so I want to do away with them.

STAR HITS, 1985

There was that quote in...
Here we go, here we go . . .
that you were gay or something like that.
Yes I know.
How do you view that?
Well, I just think it's all so untrue and I think it's so unfair, I mean, obviously, any kind of a tag I'll dodge. I'll really dodge any kind of a tag, whatever it is . . . I'm not embarrassed about the word 'gay' but it's not in the least bit relevant. I'm beyond that frankly.

AUSTRALIAN RADIO, 1985

You write a lot about the homosexual experience . . .
Well . . . not a lot.
OK, you write a lot about homosexual 'longing'.
I've always said I leave things very open and that I sing about people. Without limitation. And I don't think that automatically makes me a homosexual.
You've always taken offence at that word.
Because it's limiting and restrictive.

THE FACE, 1990

What about camp flirting?
I never do that.
You do!
I knew you'd stray. I knew as soon as I mentioned 'camp' you'd stray from the real meaning of the word. I knew you'd suddenly think of feathers and things like that. No, I don't flirt. You were there at Wolverhampton, you could see the steam, there was aggression.

NME, 1989

Some have pointed to the fact that Morrissey has admitted to both male and female (rather unsatisfactory) encounters in his life and wondered why he didn't simply announce that he was 'bisexual'. Well, perhaps because bisexuality isn't an escape from sexuality at all, it's *two* sexualities. Moreover, it suggests twice the opportunity instead of merely twice the frustration. Yes, Morrissey's struggle to resist the iron law of 'sexuality' which most of the rest of us have to submit to was always flagrantly self-important and lofty. Teenage even. But isn't that what artists and stars — rather than common-or-garden celebrities — are for? Morrissey's ambition, his perversity, his *sensibility* was far too large, too talented, too vicious to be fitted into this harmless, silly, precious, sequinned little word 'gay'. (He would assert repeatedly that he had nothing against 'g' people themselves, but then who could blame him if he did?)

Have you got a love life?
I'm not answering that question.
Why not?
Because you're just too nosey, you don't deserve to know.

ON THE JANICE LONG SHOW ON BBC RADIO 2, 2002

Throughout his career the pressure on him to 'come out' (with his hands up) increased. This capitulation was allegedly for 'Morrissey's own good', a contemporary version of that line from old cop shows: 'make it easy on yourself, kid'. The skinny spectre of the camp *Carry On* star Kenneth Williams, who claimed not to be interested in sex but admired workmen's oiled bodies in his private diary, was invoked rather too facilely. Besides, it wasn't as if Kenneth Williams was someone whose existential problems and narcissistic erotic attachment to his own sexual repression and isolation would have been solved by an appearance on *Gaytime TV*, a cocktail kiss from Serena McKellan and a bottle of poppers. (Well, maybe the *poppers* might have helped.) People nowadays seem to imagine that 'sexual identity' is a place where people find themselves and true love, rather than the place where they lose all hope.

> *Is celibacy really a victory of guilt over lust?*
> I wish it was, I wouldn't feel so badly about it then. In fact, I wish it had any purpose whatsoever. It certainly wasn't something I ever tried to instil on the public at large — I never expected a massive movement of celibates storming down Whitehall — it was just something that slipped out really. In a manner of speaking.
>
> MELODY MAKER, 1987

By the late Nineties the fashion for 'coming out' had reached a feverish pitch; people who had once been happy to hear as little as possible about gayness began to outpace even gayists in their dogmatic insistence on the need for 'honesty'. A married British MP caught visiting a male pick-up area was clapped in the stocks by the press, tabloid and 'quality', not because of the homosexual dimension, they claimed, but for his 'hypocrisy' and 'denial' about his sexuality (he refused to 'confess' that he was gay). Even the President of the United States faced impeachment for not coming out about his extra-marital (non-penile vaginal and therefore, under the law of many US States, 'sodomitical') 'sex' life. And in 1998 that other sexually ambiguous British pop performer, George Michael, whose shuttle-cock-stuffed shrink-to-fit perma-crotch was launched on the world around the same time as Morrissey's shrub-stuffed baggy-arsed jeans, was caught 'performing' in a public toilet — in a painful pincer movement involving the British tabloid press and the Beverly Hills Police Department.

Sex is a waste of batteries.

MELODY MAKER, 1986

The refusal up until this time of the 'elusive' Mr Michael to make a public announcement about his private life (despite having all but announced his orientation in his more recent work and interviews) apparently amounted to a crime of global proportions. Realising the game was up, and ever the consummate showman, he responded by giving the public what they wanted – he out-tabbed the tabloids, and confessed all in televised interviews in the US and the UK. By co-operating fully with the authorities – and the public – in regard to his sexuality, he was able to avoid having to express any shame about the arrest, and instead was actually able to go on the offensive and allege he was the victim of police entrapment. He even released an hilariously vengeful single and video called 'Outside' which turned his arrest into a celebration of 'sexuality' and 'public sex'.

Ironically though, the brightly-lit, out-and-proud undeniably catchy 'Outside' was so concerned with sunny self-justification and literally shame-less self-promotion it failed to capture anything 'out-side' at all, and said much less about the real, shadowy nature of de-sire and compulsions than his 'in-the-closet' songs such as 'Fastlove' or 'Spinning The Wheel'. Or – it goes without saying – any of Morrissey's criminally ambiguous and evasive 'outside' songs. In truth, 'Outside' effectively marked the end of George Michael's ca-reer as a serious artist. Not because 'coming out' turned the straight world against him, but because, paradoxically, it meant that he could no longer write about 'inside' feelings honestly. He could only be a spokesperson.

Were you being slightly flippant when you said your love songs were written from total guesswork?
No, I was being absolutely serious. Which isn't really funny.

MELODY MAKER, 1985

Perhaps, as many people appear to be convinced, Morrissey is simply lying. Perhaps secretly he is the life and soul of Elton John's hot-tub parties, has his own booth at Heaven nightclub, possesses Europe's largest collection of peaked caps, and has a live-in boyfriend who is Kylie Minogue's personal stylist and colonic-irrigationist. (Funnily enough, no one ever seems to think that Morrissey's 'really' covering up a life of secret heterosexual bliss, even though being outed as straight, i.e. post-Seventies Bowie, would probably be much more embarrassing for him).

But if Morrissey is just fooling us, just 'living a lie', how do you explain his *work*? How do you explain the obvious, undeniable, massive, throbbing sublimation not just of eros but *life* into his songs? Why, in other words, would this pathologically, paralytically, criminally shy creature *bother* to get up on the stage and sing at all?

Despite an acknowledgement of sorts in 1997 that he had finally succumbed, albeit briefly, to some kind of relationship with a young Cockney boxer (and, in all honesty, who wouldn't?), and heavy hints that celibacy and he had parted company, Morrissey resolutely refused the blandishments of the press and refused to kiss and tell and show the home video — except in his 'enigmatic' songs — and the gossip and speculation continued. Perhaps because he was not vulgarly famous enough to warrant the kind of media gang-bang at gunpoint which Mr Michael endured, perhaps because he was not quite as reckless, or perhaps simply because he still didn't really have much of a 'sex life' at all, Morrissey was able to continue protecting and preserving the virtue of his private life — such as it is.

Many of Morrissey's fans however recognise his celibacy as a saintly gesture and continue to believe in it rather like Catholics believe in the virgin birth (which is to say: 'I know very well that . . ., nevertheless . . .'). For most of his career it had proved the seriousness of his commitment, even if it was to his own misery. He might perform before a crowd of thousands, he might be mobbed by ecstatic, sweating fans, male and female, eager to hug and kiss him until they were finally dragged away by bouncers, but he returned to an empty bed every night — the perfect vantage-point from which to observe other people's messy love lives.

> I find that people who are knee-deep in emotion and physical commit-
> ment with human beings, I find they're often totally empty of any real
> passion . . . I mean, if we look back on the history of literature, it's always
> these really creased, repressed hysterics, if you like, who are enchained
> in these squalor-ridden rooms, who say the most poetic things about the
> human race.
>
> MELODY MAKER, 1984

Celibacy, which as has been pointed out by others, actually, pedan-
tically means a refusal to get married, crystallised Morrissey's image
as the loneliest man in the world, and only enhanced his appeal to
those proceeding through the loneliest time of life — adolescence.
It is a period which is often — even in this day and age when sex is
more compulsory than taxes — excruciatingly characterised in the
relationship department by lots of thought but little action; a pecu-
liarly pleasurable pain which Morrissey vocalises as no other has. In
publicly eschewing the consolations of coupledom, perhaps the only
remaining religious faith in the Western world, he once again displays
his genius for turning a powerless, frustrating situation (rejection) into
an extremely powerful and satisfying one (*rejecting*) — again, something
which powerless, frustrated adolescents under an entirely inhuman
pressure to couple/conform could relate to.

> I constantly spectate upon people who are entwined and frankly I'm look-
> ing upon souls in agony. I can't think of one relationship in the world
> which has been harmonious. It just doesn't happen.
>
> NME, 1984

Morrissey's refusal to cop off was not a cop-out but an extremely
brave avowal of his understanding of human relations and the futility,
as he saw it, of intimacy; his life was the theory and his work was the
practice, not the other way round. Pop music was his exhibitionistic
route to a virtual, ironic intimacy — which in some ways has turned
out to be rather more successful, and certainly longer-lasting, than the
usual, 'real' variety. When, during a particularly extravagant performance of 'William, It Was Really Nothing' on *Top of the Pops* in 1984,
he tore off his shirt to show the family audience tucking into their tea
the words MARRY ME scrawled in magic marker across his scrawny
chest, he was making a proposition to everyone in general and no

one in particular — or was it vice versa? Whatever, his proposal was accepted wholeheartedly by millions, many of whom, twenty years on, still remain faithful; countless actual, living human beings have come and gone out of their lives and have been forgotten. But not Morrissey. Even those who think they're over him, who think they walked out on him or that he walked out on them years ago, know deep down, in those really squidgy bits they don't let anyone else see, that they'll never ever be rid of him. The more they ignore him, the closer he gets.

> I've still yet to touch perfection . . . I'll know it when I do it, and I think it will be totally enchanting to affect other people's lives with a form of perfection. It will be like marriage!
>
> MORRISSEY, BLITZ, 1988

Crucially, Morrissey's terminal singleness meant that the fans could possess him through his work — which was full of him and his eroticism in a way that his life wasn't — reassured in the knowledge that there was no one else, no shameless groupie nor jammy live-in-lover who could possess him more fully, more authentically, than they. Morrissey's work and his public performance was, in effect, his 'private life'. His songs offered an intimacy which most people wouldn't inflict on their life-long lovers. Morrissey was a fan who had crossed the bedsit Rubicon and became a star, but he had somehow retained the fan's greatest defining feature: frustration. He did not act out his fans' unfulfilled fantasies so much as embody them. His famous celibacy told his fans that he was still one of them, still lying alone on the floor of his bedroom listening to records and moaning mother me smother me — just as they were, even and especially those clever swine who had grown up and got married.

> I'm just simply inches away from a monastery and I feel that perhaps if I wasn't doing this that I probably would be in one . . . which of course is a frightening thing to dwell upon.
>
> PICTURE DISK, 1984

Morrissey has no need of sex with people so long as he continues to have it with his audience. Each stage performance is so obviously a sexual release — one of the things which makes his concerts so memorable and so sublimely, indecently unprofessional. If the yelps and yowls and the desperate, ecstatic falsettos on tracks such as 'This Charming Man', 'Barbarism Begins at Home' or 'Maladjusted' hint powerfully at an orgasmic release, onstage they turn into a form of musical pole dancing — a protruding, curling fleshy tongue, a salacious smile, a sadistic whipping of his mike cable, a coquettish swing of those magnificently inhibited hips, a tempting spasm of his shiftless body, a golden sparkly shirt torn from his back and flung into an audience which, as one, pounces on it and renders it to the tiniest, dampest, most fragrant fragments, while the curious love-object himself lies on the stage writhing around in ecstasy-agony or on his back, legs akimbo airborne or draped over a monitor in an obliging gesture towards his audience. A Morrissey gig is an extraordinary, epic, religious prick-tease. But then, this is the self-conscious nature of his relationship with his audience: *'Tell me tell me that you love me/oh, I know you don't mean it'*. ('Tomorrow')

> *Do you ever go out dancing, stuff like that?*
> Heavens no! I can only do that in front of four thousand people. It's the answer to everything.
>
> MORRISSEY

Morrissey's celibacy is the symbol of his central contradiction. For all his bravura posturing as the loneliest monk, he can't quite make up his mind whether he is rejected or rejecting, which is itself the basic and irresolvable problem of self-consciousness. He keeps people at a distance because he feels too good for the world and the people in it, and because he feels he isn't nearly good enough for the world or the people in it. 'I Know It's Over', an emotionally exhausting, scourging track on *The Queen is Dead*, begins with the immortal, self-immolating lines: *'Oh Mother, I can feel the soil falling over my head/and as I climb into an empty bed/Oh well, Enough said'*. Climbing into an empty bed is compared, typically, to a kind of burial; at the same time it expresses the worry that he might go from the womb to the tomb without ever encountering any other kind of intimacy.

> Desire is excruciating to me, and as far as I know that's all there is. I can't imagine response, and I can't imagine being loved by somebody whom one loves.
>
> *DETAILS*, 1992

The joke here, of course, is that for Morrissey there never is 'enough said' about the matter, as the whingeing title of the track that immediately follows this, 'Never Had No One Ever', demonstrates. However, in 'I Know It's Over', celibacy is portrayed as essentially a rejection of life — all his achievements, including his art, are just empty distractions and consolations that, in the end, merely underline even more sharply this basic failure. He taunts himself, asking if you're so terribly good looking and entertaining *'then why do you sleep alone tonight?'* the answer the voice in his head hisses is, *'because tonight is just like any other night'*. You are on your own, he tells himself, with your *'triumphs and your charms/while they are in each other's arms.'*

The question 'why are you on your own tonight?' is the essential problem of loneliness, the question which solitude asks repeatedly of itself, and which can never be satisfactorily answered, even and especially by someone who has actually chosen loneliness, or at least likes to think he has (when it suits him). It is a constant theme of Morrissey's work that he would dearly love to be normal, and sex, after all, is something that we hope will render us human.

> *Which song do you wish you had written?*
> 'Loneliness Remembers What Happiness Forgets' (Bacharach-David).
>
> *Q*, 1995

Of course, Morrissey's wish to be normal can be expressed only because there is no chance of it ever being granted; it is another, equally constant theme of his work that he's glad he *isn't* normal. For a man who is a collection of celebrated, creative pathologies and dysfunctions, normality/cure would be a kind of erasure. Morrissey is much less interested in being normal than in the gap between himself and 'normality', as it is this disunity which makes him special, defines his genius and describes the walls of his confinement (and refuge). *They* may be in each other's arms, but Morrissey is hugging himself with the lonely but strangely delicious knowledge of his difference.

What or who is the greatest love of your life?
Next door's cat.

KILL UNCLE TOUR BOOK, 1991

In 'I Know It's Over', he goes on to isolate another contradiction of his celibacy: the perverse anti-faith that a cynical person has in the institution of love, rather like the atheist has in God: '*Love is Natural and Real/but not for you, my love/not tonight my love*'.

As the capitalisation of 'Natural' and 'Real' suggest, there is an irony bordering on sarcasm attached to the delivery of these words, but this is probably just a defence-mechanism; the cynical celibate idealist invests Naturalness and Realness with more substance than anyone else, since his whole sense of self (pity) is defined by his separation from these things. Undoubtedly, Morrissey's appeal to his fans and his repulsiveness to his much larger number of detractors consists of the fact that he has made a home out of his loneliness. It isn't that Morrissey is happy to be alone but that he is ravishingly resigned to it. Worse, he has made a glamorous career out of telling and re-telling the 'secret' most people, quite rightly, do anything to avoid admitting to themselves: '*This story is old – I KNOW/but it goes on*'.

If I see a beautiful woman I can be attracted like any man. But I find it very embarrassing. It's the same whether it's an attraction to a man or a woman... Human relations don't work . . . If I see someone I find attractive, then I flee in the other direction.

LES INROCKUPTIBLES, 1995

Like a latter-day St Sebastiane, exposing his flesh perhaps a little too eagerly to the cruel arrows of outrageous fortune, Morrissey has chosen to represent in himself an unpalatable truth about the contemporary human condition – the impossibility of intimacy. Impossible, that is, except through the laughably false medium of pop music. In this way he has become a symbol of the basic paradox of post-modern life and the terrible curse of self-reflexivity; a symbol which most people would rather not read because within Morrissey's own eternally adolescent self-dramatisation is a story of their own unhappiness and separateness — a teenage unhappiness and separateness only partly submerged beneath their adult busy-ness and sophistication. For such people, understandably — commendably — determined to get on with their lives and not acknowledge the sadness in it, Morrissey is an unappealing cross between Coleridge's albatross and A.A. Milne's Eeyore the donkey: 'Oh God, Morrissey.... He's soooo depressing. Have you got any Cheeky Girls?'

However, for those damned or foolish enough to read, Morrissey achieves through his art what his lyrics say is unachievable in life: by symbolising the impossibility of intimacy, he himself becomes the only person that his fans feel a pure and genuine, 'natural' and 'real' connection with. This is the very heart of pop's evil-beautiful transcendence, how the pop star both rises above and stands in for life and love.

> You broke all our hearts and never said sorry.
> That's because I never was sorry.
> Are you a bad man?
> Only inwardly.

MELODY MAKER, 1997

Morrissey himself has few illusions about his condition. For all his determined avoidance of limiting categories and dodging of discourses, Morrissey, the hypochondriac's hypochondriac, has a keen sense of his own pathologies — diagnosing oneself is all very well, and can in fact be quite enjoyable, since it's a form of self-obsession; other people thinking they have the right to do so (or worse, write bleedin' 'psycho-bios' about you) is quite intolerable. 'Southpaw', the last track on *Southpaw Grammar* (1995) a wistful and regretful work even by Morrissey's standards, asserts that a sick boy 'should be treated' because he's 'so easily defeated' and seems to speculate whether it is an attachment to 'Ma', or at least a failure to engage with life, which has cost him the kind of 'normal' happiness and companionship that more conventionally robust boys appear to have achieved without even thinking (which is, of course, the only way to achieve anything vital and normal). 'So you ran back to Ma' he sings, audibly shaking his head, '*which set the pace for the rest of your days.*' The song ends lingeringly on a closing couplet repeated

127

over and over, like someone murmuring tunefully in their sleep, not sure whether they're having a wet or a bad dream, until it finally dissolves into wordlessness and a neck-hair bristling guitar outro: *'And now there's something that you should know/The girl of your dreams is here all alone'*

> *Have you ever met the girl of your dreams?*
> No, I've rather met the girls of my nightmares.
>
> LES INROCKUPTIBLES, 1995

it took a tattooed boy

As for me, I've chosen; I will be on the side of crime. And I'll help children not to gain entrance into your families, your factories, your laws and holy sacraments, but to violate them.

JEAN GENET

Strike them all dead! What right have they to butcher me?

FAGIN IN CHARLES DICKENS' OLIVER TWIST

10

'Does the body rule the mind, or does the mind rule the body?' I dunno, an' I don't fookin' care replies the ruffian, since he is naturally ruled by the body.

Or so we, and Morrissey like to think. And this is why Morrissey loves him. To the man ruled by neuroses, this kind of brutish subjection actually represents a sort of release. The ruffian's violence is a spontaneous and authentic expression of emotion — an outlet Morrissey was deprived of at an early age by his fate, by his family and by his intellect. His emotions had to be suffocated, suppressed, bundled up in old newspapers and carefully hidden away under the bed of his airless room.

Morrissey loves the ruffian because the ruffian, from the point of view of the honest intellectual rather than the disingenuously spiteful one who never got over being bullied at school for wearing glasses, is free. The ruffian is working class, but escapes the class system (for a while) by being lawless. The ruffian is male, but evades the responsibilities of his sex — marriage, fatherhood, family life and a fat arse — by being delinquent. The ruffian is independent, but gives loneliness the slip by belonging to the brotherhood of rogues everywhere and kicking with the fray.

To a boy brought up to be 'nice', and wrestling with the consequences of 'nice' people's terrible lies, the ruffian represented something pure, something unattainable, something completely undomesticated; something Mum would never have in her house. And therefore something actually worthy of Morrissey's stoppered, stupendous desire. He wanted the one he couldn't have.

As a result, the ruffian and his unattainable state of grace is at the very heart of Morrissey's art — the hooligan is his masculine muse. In a sense, the whole point of becoming a pop star was to bring the ruffian, the Beautiful Bastard, into his life. Marr was a lovable lout. Rourke and Joyce could, from the back of the auditorium with the house lights down, be mistaken for footpads. Smiths fans were a gang of tender hooligans. His solo band are rockabilly rascals. His cherished Jimmy Dean was a delinquent, on- and off screen. His beloved New York Dolls, the rag-tag proto-punk hell-raising transvestites with whom he shared his bedroom for most of the Seventies, were raffia ruffians, as was his Eighties hero, the Dead Or Alive front-man-and-half Pete Burns — a glorious docker in (rock 'n' roll) drag, as scary as he was beautiful.

In order to bring the ruffian into his life and thus attempt to solve the central problem of his existence — how to express feelings directly and experience 'natural emotions' (with or without jumping in the ocean) — Morrissey had to become, through the alchemy of pop music, something of a ruffian himself. Even in his supposedly pacific flower-power Smiths period, before he went all Ted on us in his later solo career, Morrissey's lyrics bleed and throb with violent images: double decker bus collisions and suicide pacts ('There is a Light That Never Goes Out'), girlfriends in mysterious comas, hatcheted ears and spattered remains ('Death at One's Elbow'), smashed teeth ('Big Mouth') and nuclear holocaust ('Everyday is Like Sunday', 'Ask')

In his interviews he wields his wit like a flick-knife, and his stage performances are as stylised and serious in their aggression as any blood sport, most obviously in the tempestuous, up-tempo interpretations of his rockier numbers, during which he throws his body around the stage and mercilessly whips his imaginary enemies and his past — and himself — with his mike cord, like a demented ringmaster or a self-scourging

131

penitent who decides he isn't so penitent after all and turns his knout on the world. Like sex, extreme emotion is something he expresses in his work so much more easily than in his life. Like his hair, his shyness is something that he has fashioned into an elegant weapon.

Less obviously 'violent', and thus more threatening, are the subtly, slyly aggressive gestures for which he is famous. This, remember, is the man who liked to perform Smiths singles on the now-let's-pretend-this-is-live *Top of the Pops* without a microphone. This is the man who, during a breezy rendition of 'Shoplifters of the World Unite' took smiling aim at the bovine *Top of The Pops* audience with his fists and smilingly pumped a clip of cheerful automatic venom into them. The man who, when performing 'Panic', swung his mike cable like a noose while delivering the decidedly non-vegetarian exhortation, '*HANG THE DJ! HANG THE DJ!*'.

Passive aggression is none the less aggressive for being passive: *sweetness, I was only joking when I said....* Being consumed with self-pity often means having none left for anyone else. At least if your name is Morrissey. In the end, however, it is to his personal cost and to our general gain that his emotions are never expressed directly, which is to say unself-consciously — or inartistically. Morrissey's 'violence' is always somewhat ironic, always something of a performance, always somewhat neurotic.

> In a sense I am delicate but in another sense I'm not and I've never been anxious to be seen as Kenneth Williams' apprentice. Although that was daubed on my back door in heavy paint which I didn't like at all . . . So, yes, I played football a few weeks ago on Sunday morning and I scored four goals. I should add the game was against Brondesbury Park ladies.
>
> Q, 1994

However, when all's said and done, it's a mystery that anyone could ever have mistaken him for an unalloyed pacifist, as some of his drippier fans have done. Even the second Smiths album, *Meat is Murder*, which takes the injustice of violence as its theme, complete with anti-war sleeve image, is a disturbingly violent work, full of the satisfying sound of settling scores. In 'The Headmaster Ritual' Morrissey subjects the belligerent fools who run Manchester's schools to a frenzied lyrical and vocal assault which, if it were conducted with his hands, would have seen him sent down for a very long stretch indeed. As he spits in stabbing staccato sibilants, *'spineless swine/cemented minds . . .'*, over Marr's bovver-boy guitar attack, it is just as if Morrissey has turned up at his old school with a gang of toughs to terrorise the staff. All we can do is cheer him on, since the violence of his revenge is as nothing compared to the stranded, lonely violence of school life as he paints it, with bully-boy teachers, thwacking, kneeing and elbowing him, leaving bruises 'bigger than dinnerplates'.

It doesn't matter whether the Bash Street Kids violence recalled here is literal or metaphorical; the sheer vividness of Morrissey's hatred makes the distinction superfluous — he clearly experienced it as assault. The violence that he is violently indicting in *Meat* is institutional violence — the lawful kind of violence practised by society in the form of 'education'; by the 'meat industry' of the family in the form of its impossible existential demands where, according to 'Barbarism Begins at Home', *'a crack on the head is what you get for asking/a crack on the head is what you get for not asking'*; and the British state in the form of the enforced, inborn inferiority and inequality it stands for: *'I'd like to drop my trousers to the Queen/every sensible child will know what this means'* ('Nowhere Fast').

The eponymous title track of *Meat is Murder*, complete with the whines of the doomed creatures, preaches vegetarianism, but more importantly and more powerfully it conveys the author's identification with the raising, slaughter and consumption of defenceless creatures by their 'superiors' — no doubt as a result of his own experience in the abattoirs of Manchester's education system, where domestically reared livestock had their brains fried and were processed into insensitive meat: 'heifer whines could be human cries'. The violence of meat-eating here is, as it often is for vegetarian-anarchists, consciously or unconsciously, an unappetising metaphor for the violence that human society wreaks: 'this beautiful creature must die'. Hence the album sleeve depicting a young American soldier in Vietnam with 'Meat is Murder' written by Morrissey on his helmet — the military being another institution of civilised barbarism, another part of the 'meat industry'.

Underlining the way in which a culture of 'meat' makes brutes of us all, and Morrissey's identification with the plight of defenceless creatures, at the end of the vocal for 'Barbarism Begins at Home', which has been concerned with violent abuse of children, it breaks into an extraordinary rendition of helpless and baffled bestial-sounding groans and screams. Institutional violence makes vegetarian-anarchists very bloodthirsty (his first solo album *Viva Hate* (1988) featured the Gandhian track 'Margaret on the Guillotine', ending with the sound of the blade falling). Moreover, behind the outrage at the banal injustice of ending life merely for the satisfaction of selfish pleasures, there is often an even greater and prior anger at the 'normal' and 'natural' selfishness which starts life for its own pleasure, and thrusts it helpless, baffled and groaning into the world. Death for no reason, as Morrissey grimly intones, may be murder, but then so can life for no reason.

> *Are you more physical than it's assumed?*
> I think it's very obvious that I am. If you've seen any of the concerts . . . well, it isn't exactly the Incredible String Band.
>
> Q, 1994

As if by way of confession that it is institutional violence that preoccupies him, the album which denounces the reduction of living things to insensitive meat with such spleen contains three consecutive songs extolling the tasty appeal of meaty delinquent boys: 'Rusholme Ruffians', a tale of the dreamy-nightmarish, but definitely sexy violence of the Manchester fairgrounds Steven couldn't stay away from in his youth; 'I Want the One I Can't Have', an hilarious but all-too convincing portrait of an obsession with a '*tough kid who sometimes swallows nails*' (director Howard Sachler described James Dean as 'a tough kid who sometimes sleeps on nails') who was 'raised on Prisoner's Aid' and '*killed a policeman when he was/thirteen/and somehow that really impressed me*'; and 'What She Said', a song about a 'girl' who thought her intellect put her above the physical world but soon found out otherwise: '*what she read/all heady books/she'd sit and prophesise/it took a tattooed boy from Birkenhead/to really, really open her eyes*'. (Only Morrissey could rhyme 'read' with 'Birkenhead'.)

> I feel very excited by Eric Cantona, as long as he doesn't say anything.
>
> Q, 1995

'Rusholme Ruffians' is both confession and exposition of Morrissey's — and pop culture's — fascination with stalwart, lawless young men. Marr's music is based on a late-Sixties hit '(Marie's the Name of) His Latest Flame' by the original pop ruffian, the rockin' hillbilly Elvis Presley, someone who was sold to the public by his ex-circus promoter manager as if he were a cross between a prize-fighter and a fairground freak. Marr adds to his chugging and jaunty chords the essence of the fairground, the spirit of waltzers, candy-floss machines and drunken laughter. For his part, Morrissey's lyrics are a thieving homage to those of one of his idols, the northern comic Victoria Wood in her song 'Sixteen Again', but transform her wry whimsy into great art; unlike her light-hearted recollection of the fairgrounds of her youth, Morrissey's account of 'fun' fairs is decidedly dark, beginning with an act of casual violence reported just as casually on '*the last night of the fair/by the big-wheel generator/a boy is stabbed/and his money is grabbed*'.

Far from disrupting the evening's festivities — or the song's reverie — we are told in the next line simply: '*And the air hangs heavy like a dulling wine*'. Morrissey's fairground is a place of excitement and fear, life and death, hope and indifferent despair: '*a schoolgirl is denied/"How quickly would I die/If I jumped from the top of the parachutes?"*'

> *Which talent would you most like to have?*
> General lawlessness.
>
> KILL UNCLE TOURBOOK, 1991

Everything is accepted at the fairground because everything is possible. The fairground was Steven Morrissey's most intense experience of popular culture's promise to the working class of escape from their narrow streets, from their repressions, from their *fate* — but also its captivating horror: Eden's dark side.

> It's a macabre and very depressing fascination. Violence isn't a hobby to me. I'd rather it disappeared entirely from my life, even if I need it for my music. To me violence is an everyday reality in human relations. People treat me as if I were abnormal, as if I weren't like them — and this is already a beginning of violence.
>
> LES INROCKUPTIBLES, 1995

135

The enormous energy required to power all this fun and reckless-ness, the 'big wheel generator', is provided by sex and violence – the two life-forces which Morrissey seems to be repeatedly either sidelined or victimised by. On the same album (if you have the US version) he complains of leaving night-clubs alone and a congenital *'shyness that is criminally vulgar'* ('How Soon is Now?'), and vows elsewhere that if the day came when he felt a 'natural emotion' he'd likely lie down *'in the middle of the street and die'* ('Nowhere Fast'). All the same, he doesn't see himself as an innocent. In 'Rusholme Ruffians' and in *Meat* as a work, Morrissey is telling us that even though he did not 'get involved', he is thoroughly implicated. He might walk home alone but 'my faith in love is still devout'. And then, *'someone falls in love/and someone's beaten up....'* Falling in love and getting beaten up are of course interchange-able, rather like his subjectivity, *'...and the senses being dulled are mine.'*

Even as a voyeur/observer, Morrissey's senses are being dulled and corrupted. He is as drunk on sex and violence, as addicted to it, as the rest of us. It's in his blood. And besides, even from a distance, even viewed from the antiseptic loneliness of Planet Morrissey, he's far from safe from it himself.

> I remember being at a fair at Stretford Road; it was very early, about 5pm, and I was just standing by the speedway. And somebody just came over to me and head-butted me. He was much older than me, and much big-ger. I was dazed for at least five minutes. What I find remarkable is the way you just accepted it. That was just the kind of thing that happened. I don't think it was even that I looked different in those days. There never needed to be a reason.
>
> MORRISSEY

Given this lesson in the way that love and hate, sex and violence, death and life blur into one intoxicating experience at the fairground, it's hardly surprising that the rough, tattooed types who worked the 'rides' themselves become a promise of excitement and that the grease in the hair *'of a speedway operator/is all a tremulous heart requires'*. Perhaps this is why, five years later, post Marr, Morrissey was to collect his own band of 'speedway operators', rockabilly pin ups, who with their slicked quiffs and tattoos – they were the greased-up boys of yes-teryear who slouched on the sleeves of his later Smiths works brought

136

back to life — coolly handled the onstage, death-defying machinery of pleasure and pain at his concerts. (And perhaps part of the reason why his most passionate solo song, co-written with Alain Whyte, the most fetching and talented of his crew of rockabilly lads, is called 'Speedway'.) 'Rusholme Ruffians' ends on a poignant image of teenage love which contains within it its own bitter-sweet combination of pleasure and pain, hope and despair, love and loss: '*Scratch my name on your arm with a fountain pen/(this means you really love me)*'.

Love and loss because, with the possible exception of 'Mum', the names of lovers engraved on a man's skin for all eternity almost always outlive to an embarrassing degree the affection which prompted them. Given their reckless defiance of the way of the world, it's no great surprise that tattoos often appear above the collar and beyond the cuff-line in Morrissey's work, for example the single 'Swallow on My Neck' (which may actually be a Morrisseyan term for love-bite) and the rear of the sleeves for 'The More You Ignore Me' and *Vauxhall & I*. And not just because tattoos are associated with roughness. Artistically speaking, Moz has always had 'l-o-v-e' tattooed on one fist and 'h-a-t-e' on the other. Tattoos, after all, are a passionate, usually doomed assertion of mastery of your own destiny, or at least a defiant embrace of one that you can't control; a self-branding of your 'meat', reclaiming the body your parents and Nature thrust upon you, and which was beaten into shape by the family/school/the children's home/borstal/prison/the army as your own. Aptly enough, tattoos have also become a sign of personal dedication on the part of the fans — during the US leg of the 1997 *Maladjusted* tour, young men frequently asked The Moz to autograph their necks, returning the next day to show his signature immortalised/mortalised in Indian ink injected beneath their skin.

If the magnificently, wittily seditious single 'Shoplifters of the World Unite' offered a glimpse of an alternative career choice for an outsider who can't actually cut it outside in the real world, whose 'only weakness is a list of crimes' and is thus headed for a long stretch inside (the prison of his own head) — perhaps it isn't so surprising that the last Smiths album should have been called *Strangeways Here We Come* (or his solo 'B'-side compilation named *My Early Burglary Years*). *Strangeways* is a notorious Victorian men's prison in Manchester, full of young ruffians with home-made tattoos in highly visible places. (The actual form of the title is probably inspired by a line from the Sixties film *Billy Liar*: 'Borstal here we come').

When Morrissey went solo the romantic appeal of those boys who decided to go to hell in their own way, rather than wait to be sent there by some posh git in a wig and stockings, only increased. One of the first singles of his solo career, the instant classic 'Last of the Famous International Playboys' (1989), has more than a hint of penal flavour. It begins with a swaggering, rollicking bass intro that is definitely looking for trouble, followed by Morrissey's plaintiff voice penning a fan letter on prison notepaper: '*Dear hero imprisoned . . .*'. Ostensibly, 'Playboys' tells the story of a young hooligan's crush on famous East End underworld bosses Ronnie and Reggie Kray, the brotherly smash-hit Sixties gangster double act whose pop career ended when the terrible twins were sent down for life for the murder of Jack 'The Hat' McVitie. Morrissey offers an explanation, of sorts, for the young man's behaviour, who claims he 'never wanted to kill' and, emphatically, that he is not 'naturally evil', putting the world and its ways in the dock, suggesting that it was because the news world hands those who kill stardom: 'and these are the ways/on which I was raised'.

Thankfully, Morrissey is doing much more here than offering a critique of 'media irresponsibility'. The bitter, relishing repetition of the lines '*and these are the ways/on which I was raised*' obviously suggest the repetition of the cycles of sin in the world, but also refer back to his childhood again, offering an explanation of his own interest in violence and viciousness; after all, he was raised when the news world was handing the Moors Murderers stardom. He certainly isn't offering an apology, however. The young hoodlum (whom you may have guessed is also Morrissey) may not be *naturally* evil, but that doesn't mean he isn't evil. Born into a world of un-freedom, choosing evil sometimes seems the nearest thing to freedom; the ineluctable concept of original sin requires that imaginative and ambitious children sin originally, or at least show initiative, even if they are somewhat derivative to begin with: '*such things I do/just to make myself/more attractive to you/HAVE I FAILED?*'

The Last of the International Playboys are Bowie, Bolan, Devoto and me.

NME, 1989

138

As with 'Shoplifters', the glam, beefy beat, rascalish riffs and singalong chorus of 'Playboy' render (or simply admit) violence and rebellion perfectly understandable and more than a little sexy, an effect which is as much enhanced by the roguish humour of the song as ironised by it. This complements a strong suggestion of another kind of deviance which violence and lawlessness often leads working class boys to, ultimately removing them as it does from female company: *'and in my cell/(well, I loved you)'*. This subtle suggestion is turned into the lyrical equivalent of a hand on the knee at scoff time or a dangled arm over the side of the top bunk at lights-out by the heartfelt plea: *'Ronnie Kray – do you know my face?/Oh, don't say you don't/please say you do, oh-oh, oh-oh . . .'*

Violence and homoerotics, always courting one another in British working class culture, finally come together in the institution of prison and in the formidable and glamorous personage of Ronnie Kray (and, of course, in Morrissey). Ronnie was doubly damned and doubly romantic: the famously queer member of the terrible twinsome reigned in two underworlds to Reggie's one. (Though after his death in 2001 it emerged that Reggie, for a long time the great straight hope of many suburban gangster groupies, had been having sex with both males and females from an early age, and that for the last thirty years of his life, courtesy of Her Majesty, he conducted cell-block romances with an apparently inexhaustible supply of adoring young male villains). The legend that Ronnie killed a man for calling him a 'fat poof' only adds to his aura – an extreme, almost 'camp' mixture of vanity and violence. Open about his interest in young men, Ronnie was nevertheless determined in his defence of his name.

> *Is it natural to hate?*
> Some people are very funny. Some people are athletic. Some people are very hateful . . . It's whatever is in the blood.
>
> BLITZ, 1988

Details of the Kray twins read like a list of Morrissey obsessions: Sixties, East End working class, violent, stylish, sadistic, famous, brutally attractive, mod mummy's boys. Much more than their muscles, knuckle-dusters and handguns, their twindom, with the narcissistic and homoerotic undertones that twindom connotes, combined with their intensely close relationship with a mother whose aspirations and determination they had inherited, gave them their strength, their independence, their untouchability, their terror, their *glamour*. The sun shone out of their behinds, they could go wherever they pleased and everything depended upon how near they stood to each other.

> I think that everything there is to be lived is hanging round the gutter somewhere. I've always believed that and still do.
>
> OBSERVER, 1995

Morrissey, like Wilde, may be in the gutter looking at the stars, but the stars he fixes his gaze on are decidedly not in the heavens (and as we know, for all his elevated ideas Wilde was not averse to a bit of rough either). Despite the 'this-filthy-song-promotes-kiddie-fiddling!' scandal in the tabloids over 'Handsome Devil' that plagued his early days in The Smiths, 'Piccadilly Palare' (1990), an upbeat, singalong Moz song which is lyrically grinning from ear to ear, openly celebrates the attractions of being a teenage rent boy 'on the game'. Rent boys were young working class males, often runaways from the North, who worked as street prostitutes (most notoriously in the Sixties and Seventies, Morrissey's favourite decades) around Piccadilly Circus in London, a giant roundabout with a statue of Eros in the centre ('erected' in memory of, god's truth, the Earl of Shaftesbury), surrounded by neon-signs advertising Coke and other tasty commodities. It was 'the big wheel generator' to end all big wheel generators; the nearest thing the English had to a monument to desire that wasn't the outline of a man with a big club on the side of chalk hill. The pick-up area in Piccadilly Circus, at one point outside the Wimpy burger bar, was known romantically to those in the trade as 'the meat rack'. (As if to remind them of their ultimate destination, the train terminus in Manchester which takes the young runaways up to the bright lights and easy money of The Big Smoke fairground is also called Piccadilly).

These 'playboys' were the subject of earnestly campaigning documentaries in the Seventies, such as *Johnny Come Home*, and also prurient tabloid 'exposés' that did their best to whip up a moral panic, in between wiping away the drool. However, Morrissey's treatment of the subject matter is quite wickedly different. Instead of portraying them as mere victims, needing pity, help and a nice understanding girlfriend to get them back on the rails, he actually glamorises their lifestyle. Or rather, he merely refuses not to see the seedy glamour which is already there. Elbowing aside paternalistic concern and shrugging off moral outrage, Morrissey pushes his way to the front of the crowd and is so impressed by the boys' wilful self-damnation that he joins them: '*Off the rails I was and/off the rails I was happy to stay/GET OUT OF MY WAY.*'

He goes on to sing of being 'on the rack' and being 'easy meat', and, with false modesty, '*a reasonably good buy*'; declaring that '*we plied an ancient trade/where we threw all life's instructions away*'. Of course, throwing life's instructions away was something that Morrissey had been doing himself from the earliest age. Little wonder then that this easy nut-cutlet who proclaims himself 'a reasonably good buy' finds it natural to marry his subjectivity to that of a rent boy, and enthuse about the camaraderie of the lost boys laughing at the world: '*Piccadilly Palare was just silly slang/between me and the boys in my gang*'.

Palare's own ancient roots probably lie with the Nineteenth Century slang Parlyaree which was used by fairground and circus people as well as other despised, outsider itinerants, such as prostitutes and thespians (this was before *The Evening Standard Awards*), and also has connections with thieves' cant, Cockney rhyming slang, and sailors argot. Of course, many of the lads who ended up plying the oldest trade were themselves from those marginal groups anyway. Palare is sometimes called 'gay language' but this is inaccurate — pre-gay language would be closer to the mark, as it is an argot of desire and community outside of convention, and, in fact, 'sexuality'. It was not an exclusive language of queers, it just so happens they were probably the last group to use it (but quickly forgot it in the years of identity politics and then assimilation following decriminalisation in 1968).

Palare, also known as Polari, allowed the 'initiated' to express in public a desire, a perspective, a brotherhood that wasn't supposed to be expressed, that wasn't supposed to exist, to mock society to its face without the 'naffs' (straights/squares) 'getting it', hearing instead 'just silly slang'. The Palare lines in the song '*So Bona to Vada . . ./Your lovely eek/and your lovely riah*' translate as 'So good looking . . ./Your lovely face and your lovely hair' ('riah' as with many Palare words, is obviously backslang, further evidence of Palare's deliberate perversity, though in Morrissey's mouth there's the added, piquant layer of irony that he seems to be saying 'your lovely rear'). Like the appeal of the rent boy life itself, conventional people just don't get it: '*You never understand/good sons like you/NEVER DO*'.

Nor, of course, do they understand Morrissey properly. The added deliberate irony here is that Morrissey's lyrical language is a kind of Palare, which can be read by anyone so inclined and glossed over by everyone else; it's a universal but secret code that speaks to outsiders and marginal types everywhere, to the boys and girls who have 'thrown life's instructions away – the Beautiful Bastards.

Despite the exceptional, often painful candour of his lyrics, and their essential appeal to universal emotions, there is sometimes a level of intriguing obscurity to Moz's songs. As with Palare, the denotation may be overlooked by the 'naffs' who lack the intimate 'underworld' knowledge to translate the references, even if they wanted to – but they aren't immune to the connotation. Palare acts like a distorting lens, not an impregnable cipher – an action which is very close to the mechanism of 'deviant' desire itself. The Sixties BBC Home Service radio comedy programme *Round the Horne*, a favourite of Morrissey's, in which *Carry On* star Kenneth Williams spouted Palare, was hugely popular not in spite of the fact that it was full of homosexual innuendo, but because of it (and in fact some blame it for killing off Palare by blowing the gaffe). It was gibberish and knowing, naughty and innocent, silly and smart, outsider and insider all at once. In other words, essentially English.

As was the rent boy. For working class boys who weren't 'good sons', keen to please their fathers and follow in their footsteps, male prostitution was a way out, and even a way to turn the tables on society. Paradoxically, by stepping outside the niceties of conventional morality and formalising society's designation of them as 'meat', they could (sometimes) literally hold the whip handle over toffs who otherwise wouldn't have given them the time of day, and get paid for it at hourly rates a lawyer might be envious of, all the while ignoring the inexorable toll of the school bell and factory horn which was supposed to measure out their lives. And without ever becoming bourgeois. Rather like a career in pop music. (Though of course today's pop artists as 'celebs' are the new bourgeois role models.)

In fact, the first young British male pop stars of the 1950s and early 1960s were often little more than rent boys given a bath, a haircut and a microphone and pimped out to the record companies and thence the public by some old queen or other (a process which continues to the present day, though in the case of some contemporary boybands, apparently without the benefit of a bath). Punk rock in general and in particular the Ramones, a Morrissey favourite, were very much associated with this tradition ('punk' being US slang for a prison male prostitute or the 'receptive' partner) – hence the holes in the knees of their jeans.

'Piccadilly Palare' archly plays on the pop star/rent boy connection in a very English fashion by including an Artful Dodger-style voiceover from Suggs, lead singer with Eighties (very working class) cheeky-chappie North London 'Nutty Boys' band Madness, scolding in a chummy, worldly-wise elder brotherly fashion: 'No, no. No. No. You can't get there that way. Follow me' (and pick pocketing, after all, is not really so different to renting – both involve rummaging around in punters' trousers and relieving them of their wads.)

As a former avid reader of feminist texts, Morrissey was perfectly well aware that many boys on the game come from a background of domestic abuse, often running away from a tyrant/pervert father, but being Morrissey, he doesn't appear to see anything remarkable in that. Instead of seeing their renting as abuse, or abuse as the cause of their renting, he sees their prostitution of themselves as merely their rational response to society's use of them – being 'on the game', within the terms of this song, is neither sad nor bad, it actually makes a lot of sense.

As a parting shot, however, Morrissey speculates pessimistically, if slightly tongue-in-cheek, on the fate of bad sons who have escaped their lot in life, who live each day as it comes, dependent on the fickle whims and peculiar tastes of complete strangers: 'It may all end tomorrow/or it could go on forever/in which case I'm doomed.'

If you do it right, success in pop music – just as in renting your arse – is the 'worst' thing that could happen to a boy. It means there is no escape, no way back home. The return ticket from Manchester Piccadilly to Piccadilly Circus is not open-ended.

* * *

Most worryingly, such a lost boy might end up making an album like the teasingly named *Your Arsenal* (1992) – the 'bad' end that Morrissey's glam rock pied piper tendencies had augured. *Your Arsenal*, which was critically well-received, marks a break with Morrissey's more effete image of the Eighties and early Nineties. He finally 'came out' . . . fighting. He emerged as, if not a bruiser exactly, then certainly something of a 'tasty geezer'. After the disaster of the previous year's anaemic *Kill Uncle* for which he received a richly deserved critical pasting, Stretford's rebel with a bookcase seemed to turn from the aesthete interested in rough lads into a rough lad interested in aestheticism (and rough lads). Musically, Morrissey emerged as the motorcycle-chain-swinging Ted that he always was under those arched eyebrows and lah-dee-dah affectations, and which the original Wilde was always threatening to become, if he could have but raised himself from his chaise longue. *Your Arsenal* triumphantly fused the childish-threatening pop sensibility of glam with the coolness and greasy testosterone of rockabilly (glam rock was anyway self-consciously Fifties in its reference points). Morrissey appears to have acknowledged here that if pretty girls make graves, then pretty boys dig their own and it was time to become, if not a *man* exactly, then something rather more than an ageing boy.

The cover image for the album, taken by his life-long friend the performance artist, sometime pop star and art photographer Linder Sterling (who seems, judging by her handsomely androgyne appearance, to have been a member of Morrissey's private James Dean fan club), depicts a very different Morrissey from the dreamy dandy on the sleeves of *Kill Uncle, Bona Drag* and *Viva Hate*. Onstage, in flagrante delecto, tongue protruding, shirt torn open revealing – gasp! – a muscular body (that paternal inheritance rediscovered), his microphone held teasingly between his legs, Morrissey is being somewhat *rock 'n' roll*. His aggression no longer appears blocked but positively broadcast. *Your Arsenal* is Morrissey's Mr Hyde to the Dr Jekyll of *Kill Uncle*

— not the acquisition of a synthetic new pop 'image', but the ecstatic liberation of something genuinely, thrillingly unpleasant that was always there. With *Your Arsenal*, and squinting only a little, Morrissey appeared to have finally become the one he can't have, or at least his best mate, and it's plainly written all over his face.

Produced by Mick 'Spiders From Mars' Ronson, and Morrissey's first proper album with his band of rockabilly toughs, *Your Arsenal*, co-written with Alain Whyte, is a work devoted almost entirely to the attraction of 'low life' and violent outsiders, albeit set very clearly, like its musical influence, in the rough-and-ready Seventies of Morrissey's childhood. In addition to being a brawlingly boisterous LP, many of the track titles — 'You're Gonna Need Someone On Your Side', 'We'll Let You Know', 'Certain People I Know' — sound like snatches of overheard conversation in a particularly dodgy East End snooker hall. The lyrics for 'Certain People I Know' in particular seem to confirm that Morrissey has indeed been hanging around such unsavoury places; he talks, tongue in cheek, about taking part in pool-room brawls with and how he trusts '*the views of certain people I know*' people who look at danger and '*LAUGH THEIR HEADS OFF*', people who 'break their necks' but '*can't afford to get them fixed*'.

Naturally, 'the views' here of certain people he knows are not so much views as instincts, the vital opposite of the intellectual and aesthetic standpoints adopted by the sort of people he was used to socialising with, hence the sarcastic delivery of the song in an affected drawing-room style. Morrissey is expressing a will-to-believe in the flawed nobility of those who express themselves spontaneously and directly, relying on their fists and fast friendships, instead of insipid, faithless, fickle words (or laws) in the way that 'nice' (i.e. lying) people do; this is the first Morrissey album not to feature a lyric sheet (tellingly, *Southpaw Grammar*, *Your Arsenal*'s younger, truant brother, is the only other Morrissey album not to sport a lyric sheet).

> I'm enormously attracted to people who can look after themselves. I'm obsessed by the physical, in the sense that it almost always works. It's a great power to be able to storm through life with swaying shoulders, instead of creeping and just simply relying on your Thesaurus. It doesn't work! I've had so many conversations with people trying to convince them of a

particular point, and although I find words central to my life . . . Nothing shifts or stirs people like a slight underhand threat. They jump.

MELODY MAKER, 1988

Later in 'Certain People I Know' our hero declares, somewhat mischievously, 'I'd hate to be like certain people I know', knowing full well how 'repellent' such thuggish, lumpen types are supposed to be to decent dinner-party bourgeois and decent, doorstep-scrubbing working class alike. In fact, *Your Arsenal* is full of discontented young men who, to quote The Jam, 'smelt of pubs and Wormwood Scrubs and too many right-wing meetings'. Morrissey isn't pretending otherwise. In 'The National Front Disco', a song which was to cause him more trouble than a lifetime of pool room brawls, he sympathetically and humorously explores – instead of merely sanctimoniously denouncing – the alienation of a young loser-outsider ('*the wind blows/bits of your life away*') who has turned his back on his parents ('*where is our boy/ah, we've lost our boy*'), drifting into a nether-land of right-wing malcontents with grudges against a world they fantasise impotently about bringing to account – by going to a *disco* organised by the National Front, '*because you want the day to come sooner.../when you settle the score*'.

The National Front was an extreme right-wing party of the Seventies which advocated the repatriation of non-white immigrants and, for a while, drew significant levels of support, especially from sections of the white working-class perhaps because, unlike the middle classes, their communities were in direct competition with immigrants for employment, housing, welfare and status. The NF split and withered in the late Seventies after the Conservative leader Margaret Thatcher broke the cosy taboo on the subject within the mainstream political parties and talked about the dangers of being 'swamped' by an 'alien' culture, promising tougher immigration policies should she be elected. (She was, in 1979 by a landslide, with record working class votes for a Tory – and promptly set about destroying the working class, whatever colour.)

'The National Front Disco' is a savvy, stinging dissection of English social history in the form of a catchy pop song, and clearly anything but a recruiting anthem for racists – the title alone is a sad joke at the expense of their racially pure delusions. As is the line '"England for the

English"' — clearly an ironic quotation of the pathetic naïvety and nostalgia of the lad who pretends to believe that all his problems and those of his community will be solved if he can only keep England white.

Of course, pathetic nostalgia is a matter very close to Little Englander Morrissey's heart — which is why 'The National Front Disco' is such a powerful song and not another self-righteous lecture from a right-on whitey about the evils of racism. He is subtly but openly delineating the line between his own ironic nostalgia for a lost England, and the cynical nostalgia proffered by racist parties; the line between his interest in rough, 'lost boys', and the interest that some rough, lost boys have in reactionary politics — exploring the possibility that such right wing lost boys are not *necessarily* 'monsters', that they might possibly be motivated by misguided love as much as mis-targeted hate.

Some might argue that this subtlety is 'dangerous' because it is too artistic and not didactic (i.e. patronising) enough; that its irony might be overlooked. And they'd be right. Morrissey's mocking heavy-hearted irony *was* overlooked. Not so much by right-wing racists, however, but by knee-jerk leftists who eagerly seized upon 'The National Front Disco' as irrefutable 'proof' of Morrissey's racism: 'Of course Morrissey's racist!' they crowed, 'He wrote a song called "The National Front Disco"! He actually sang "England for the English"!!' Many of them even reheated the old chestnut of 'Panic' as further 'proof' of his racism, because it called for the burning of discos: 'And disco is black music!' And *still* they didn't get the wry joke of the song title.

> The ones who listen to the entire song, the way I sing it, and my vocal expression know only too well that I'm no racist and glorifier of xenophobia. The phrase 'England for the English' is in quotes, so those who call the song racist are not listening. The song tells of the sadness and regret that I feel for anyone joining such a movement.
>
> LES INROCKUPTIBLES, 1993

Morrissey did however made things absurdly easy for the PC peasants coming after him with scythes and burning torches. On a warm August afternoon in 1992 in Finsbury Park, North London, he helpfully tied himself to the stake and covered himself in petrol when he appeared onstage at 'Madstock', a two-day music event organised around Madness. He appeared onstage in a glittery shirt (well, the transformation into a ruffian was never intended to be complete or unambiguous) with his rockabilly boys, performing songs from the recently released *Your Arsenal* — including 'The National Front Disco' — in front of a large backdrop depicting a classic photo of young suedeheads, a violent (mind, they were almost all violent) British youth cult from the late Sixties/early Seventies whose look was that of grown-out skinheads. For good measure, he unfurled a Union Jack and wrapped himself in it.

✳ ✳ ✳

With hindsight, it seems a shockingly reckless gesture — probably because it was. To Morrissey, however, it all made perfect sense. It was his usual form of total and merciless defiance, his fearless way of displaying artistic contempt for second-hand opinions and mealy-mouthed mores, his scorn for those half-men that sought to blackmail him with their green-inked articles into apologising for something he saw as, literally, the 'best of British'.

> Skinheads [are] an exclusively British invention. That the rest of the world around us looks upon skinheads as people who tattoo swastikas in their foreheads and throw fruit at innocent football supporters is a shame. Of course, I'm aware of the fact that there exists such 'skinheads.' But the original idea of skinheads was just about clothes and music.
>
> BLITZ, 1992

Perhaps Morrissey also saw the Madness gig as an opportunity to escape the embrace of some of the paler fans he had attracted since his split with The Smiths, and get back in closer contact with the more vital, working class skinhead/bovver-boy audience — the kind of audience that the Nutty Boys had always attracted and in fact the kind of lads they had once been themselves. An historic opportunity to forge a glam rock revival, a last, glorious stand of British youth cults, of 'skinheads in nail varnish', against creeping Americanisation (*people look to Los Angeles for the language they use*); a chance to finally realise the delinquent dream the young Steven had been corrupted by back in the early Seventies at the hands of Bowie, Bolan and the other 'playboys' who threw life's instructions away.

But it wasn't to be. Instead 'Madstock' effectively marked the end of Morrissey's pop dream of England and showed the limits of his alliance with laddism. Instead of a glam revival, he woke up to the dowdy reality that he had succeeded in offending just about everyone, and provoked an odd but perhaps not entirely unnatural alliance between the finger-wagging lefties and rabid right wingers.

While a small but very vocal group of neo-Nazi skinheads in the Finsbury Park audience, unhappy with the reappropriation/liberation of 'their' flag and 'their' iconography by this guy in a glittery shirt, booed and bottled him off the stage (an exit not entirely mourned by many of the regular Madness fans-turned-skinhead-taxi-drivers present that day), some right-on sections of the music press did their best to bottle him off the music scene altogether.

The *NME*, the most powerful organ of the British music press and effectively pop music's Vatican, seemed to have decided that by flagrantly challenging their authority as the self-anointed trendy vicars of pop morality, by refusing to pay any heed to the dire warnings, bulls and threats they had already issued over 'The National Front Disco', Morrissey was cruising for a bruising and it was now their job to give him one (for the sake of the flock, you understand). They launched their marathon 'Morrissey: Is He a Racist?' witch-hunt, a latter-day equivalent of those duckings in which if the hapless defendant floats they are guilty and sink if they are innocent.

Of course, Morrissey's guilt was confirmed by the fact that he wouldn't grant them the tearful, please-believe-me-I'm-not-a-racist-some-of-my-best-friends-are-beige 'MORRISSEY RECANTS!' exclusive they had banked on. In the face of the most damaging allegations that such a newspaper could make against a pop star at this time, Morrissey simply ignored them, and remained utterly, wickedly unbowed and apostate. In fact, the heretic excommunicated *Rome*. He was to continue snubbing the *NME* for the next ten years.

The real and serious charge against Morrissey, as ever, was daring to stand apart. Of course, this crime had once brought him adulation as well, but times change, and Morrissey was in the way of them.

One large headline famously denounced him as 'This Alarming Man' — an unintended accolade from the 'nice' boys in the (I)PC

Tower, which revealed how little they'd understood him in the first place, and also how much the 'radical' music press had bought into the new bourgeois standard of respectability, otherwise known as political correctness. Morrissey was always alarming, and if in the past they hadn't seen beyond his charm, then more fool them.

I am no longer strapped to the Women's Studies section of Waterstones on Kensington High Street night and day, as many people still seem to believe.
SELECT, 1994

There was also probably more than an element of jealousy here. Partly pent-up resentment at his unchallenged eight year reign as the pop star of a music journalist's dreams and nightmares, the prophet that merely used the NME as a giant fax machine for his edicts, and near-naked centrefolds, but mostly at what his new material suggested about his social life. Morrissey, 'that big girl's blouse' with the fey ways and a good line in self-deprecating self-pity, the eccentric male feminist viewing masculinity and rough boys from a distance, twitching the net curtains of his mothers semi-detached council house was one thing. But a Morrissey dropping, or getting past, the feminism, apparently shortening that distance on working class masculinity, and worse maybe actually getting out every now and again and *consorting* with 'low life' was another, galling thing altogether. Much too much an insult for the ceremonial eunuchs of the music press to bear. "Who does he think he is?," they fulminated. Or rather, "Who does *she* think she is!"

Predictably, in this sticky explosion of journalistic jealousy, the first casualty was their tolerance of his sexual ambiguity. Doesn't he realise, complained one scandalised and deeply 'betrayed' journalist at the end of yet another 'why-oh-why-oh-why Morrissey?' article drunk on its own indignation, that the kind of people he's flirting with don't like homosexuals? Is he identifying with the oppressor? (Leftists are often perturbed when what they perceive as their pet poofs turn out to have politics and penises of their own.)

Although Morrissey's artistic career is not directly equivalent to that of the French novelist and jailbird Jean Genet, not least in the matter of Genet's unambiguous, exclusive and self-declared/self-imposed homosexuality (though it must be said that Genet's homosexuality was entirely at odds with what is now called 'gay'), there is a parallel here with Genet's poetic perversity — his love for young toughs, his own challenge to the world to come and have a go if it thinks it's hard enough, and above all his compulsion to betray the narrative that others wanted to impose on him. When he was assigned by a leftist American magazine to report on police brutality at the Democratic Convention in Chicago in 1969 he sent back copy which, instead of lambasting the 'fascist pigs' as his commissioning editors eagerly anticipated, praised the 'strong thighs' of Chicago's finest. Genet liked nothing more than 'identifying with the oppressor', if he thought it would be fun, and cause Trouble.

Like Morrissey, Genet was an artist who willed his own destiny rather than simply accepting the one bestowed on him, and despised conventional, second-hand mores, whether of the left or right (and also had an early interest in the phallic-romantic poetry of flowers). In other words, he was completely irresponsible — to everyone except himself. He also became, like Morrissey, by dint of an almost superhuman effort of will, both what he desired and what he wasn't, or wasn't supposed to be. According to one story, Genet fell so much in love with a young boxer that he taught himself the handy art of boxing to a standard where he could actually become the boy's trainer — which he subsequently did. (The boy, regardless of his own orientation, could hardly refuse or resist such a romantic and respectful gesture and became Genet's lover.)

Morrissey, who also developed a passion for boxers, did not need to become a trainer to pursue this fancy. He had, after all, spent a long time becoming something even more arduous, dedicated and demanding, something, when done right, worthy of even more respect. A pop star.

And now, after Madstock, he was a pop star who was not just used to slogging it out alone, without even the benefit of a trainer to check his gum-guard between rounds and whisper sweet-nothings in his ear, but also no stranger to losing in front of his home crowd.

* * *

As if exhausted by the fight with his critics, and by fame itself — or simply because he had made his point — his next album *Vauxhall & I*, released in 1994 (to enormous critical and commercial success) when he had reached the ripe old age of thirty-four, and which was rumoured to be his 'retirement' album, was a much less aggressive and pugnacious effort than *Your Arsenal*. In fact, it is permeated with a gorgeous sadness and resignation extraordinary even by Morrissey's standards. Nevertheless, it carries within its introspective lyrics and (bad) dreamy, valium-esque music a tremendous strength and courage, a certain masculine assurance and presence — manhood even — as suggested by the picture on the sleeve of the brooding artist, unshaven and open-necked in a Ted frock-coat. If *Your Arsenal* represents a late, delinquent adolescence for Morrissey, the boy who refused to grow up, *Vauxhall & I* seems to represent a kind of (very) late maturity.

Even if you can't actually say that Morrissey has mellowed out, he appears to have achieved, or at least hopes to achieve, an accommodation of sorts with his past, as is suggested in the religiously uplifting opening track, 'Now My Heart is Full', which like the rest of the album appears to be suffused with a mixture of mourning for the loss of the past and a kind of relief that it is indeed past and can finally be 'let go' — even if this means reassessing everything: speculating that '*a whole house will need re-building*' and that everyone he loves '*will recline on an analyst's couch quite soon*'.

As is suggested by the song's reference to, and identification with, characters from Graham Greene's novel about East End gangsters, *Brighton Rock* ('*Dallow, Spicer, Pinkie, Cubitt/rush to danger/end up nowhere . . ./ah, but Bunnie I loved you*'), perhaps this new outlook — and the rumours of retirement — had something to do with the fact that by *Vauxhall* Morrissey seemed to finally really have the one that he couldn't have, in the form of a tattooed thirty-year-old suedehead boxer called 'Jake', who tagged along at interviews, working as his driver and live-in general factotum and who may well have really, really opened his eyes. The same Jake is credited with taking the picture on the rear of the *Vauxhall* sleeve, showing what looks like Morrissey's paws on someone's muscular back with a swallow drawn on his right hand, a doodling habit, reportedly, of Jake's (hence the single 'Swallow on My Neck' is also probably a Jake-inspired work).

Jake's inked torso is also on the rear of the single from the album, 'The More You Ignore Me', and he is offered 'very special thanks' at the end of *Vauxhall*'s credits. It's even possible that the album title is itself a reference/tribute to Jake (and also perhaps the cult odd-couple 1986 Brit movie *Withnail & I*); Vauxhall is an historic working class district of London, famous for its boxers and gangsters; in interviews Morrissey reportedly referred to the name as the birthplace of 'someone I know'). In other words, the ruffian that Morrissey had been looking for, calling for in his work all these years appeared to have finally materialised.

In keeping with the theme of analysis with which the album opened, Morrissey has some ideas about where his 'sick ways' started. The sugary but deadly track 'Used to Be a Sweet Boy' is a nostalgic parental lament about a child who used to 'make all our trials worthwhile' before 'something went wrong' — but also a head-in-the-sand parental refusal to take any responsibility: 'I can't be to blame' says the distressed, bereft parent, more hopefully than seriously.

Parental nostalgia is one thing; Morrissey's of course, is another. One of the most atmospheric tracks on the album is the quasi-erotically nostalgic 'Spring-Heeled Jim' a song about a reckless and irresistible hoodlum who '*takes life at five times your/average speed*', and who '*winks an eye/he'll "do", he'll never be "done to"*', which includes suggestive snippets of dialogue between lads discussing the exploits of various crims ('*Smithy... 'e don't look 'ard, does 'e ?*' '*Nah, 'e looks a queer, don't 'e ?*') from the famous 1959 documentary about working class South London teenagers *We Are the Lambeth Boys*, directed by Karel Reisz (who also directed another Moz fetish, *Saturday Night, Sunday Morning* the following year).

Morrissey repeatedly breaks into a heavy-hearted 'La, la, la, la-la, la . . .' eerily reminiscent of the previous decade's 'Sheila Take a Bow', this time with a gliding gloominess instead of a glad-handed optimism, a contrast that makes 'Sheila' and its ambition sound as if it was written a hundred years ago — which of course it was. Hence Morrissey's last, despairing words '*and he feels too/OLD*'. (The last sound on the track is another soundbite from one of the Fifties teenage tearaways which sounds like a comment on Morrissey's own career: '*an' they catch 'im an' they say 'e's mental.*')

153

Vauxhall & I, co-written like *Your Arsenal* with his Kentish Town Boys Boz Boorer and Alain Whyte, produced by Steven Lillywhite, is, quite simply, a masterpiece, comparable to almost any of the albums achieved during his partnership with the first ruffian in his life, J. Marr — an affair apparently paid 'handsome' tribute to in the happy-sad track 'Billy Budd' (the title is a reference to Herman Melville's novel of male camaraderie and betrayal) which seems to be a kind of forlorn companion piece to *The Queen is Dead*'s 'The Boy With a Thorn in His Side' (*'How can they see the Love in our eyes/And still they don't believe us?/And after all this time'*). It may be, as Morrissey sings, '12 years on' (they met in 1982), but when he took his job application into town *'They turned me down/Yes, and it's all because of us/Oh, and what was in our eyes'*. Morrissey finishes the song mournfully suggesting that he would willingly donate 'both of my legs' if only 'you could be free', implying that the demise of their partnership is something that he still feels personally crippled by. The track ends with a sample from David Lean's film *Oliver Twist* (1948): a very young Anthony Newley as the Artful Dodger implores in an echoing, reedy, Cockernee sparra voice, *'Don't leave us in the dark!'*.

∗ ∗ ∗

The final track, 'Speedway', a shiveringly beautiful let-he-who-is-without-sin rebuke to his accusers who *'slam down the hammer'* (*'can you see it in your heart?'*), which begins with what sounds like a chainsaw revving (eat your heart out Slim Shady-come-lately), and continues almost a capella over the rolling, ominous sound of drums, also offers a show-stopping confession about *'all the rumours keeping me grounded'*. It turns out that they *'weren't completely unfounded'*.

Is he referring to the rumours that he's a 'closet queen'? The accusations of secret racism? Or just the common perception that he's mad, bad and dangerous to know? All of these things or none of them? Whom is he addressing when he sings, *'I could have mentioned your name'* and provoked *'guilt by association?'* A lover? His audience? The God he doesn't believe in? The questions are left deliberately, powerfully, provocatively — and characteristically — unanswered.

Hanging.

As the song reaches its dramatic, chest-heaving climax over drums that now sound more like a final, capital, drum roll, it begins to dawn that Morrissey has placed himself on the scaffold the press has constructed for him, that the courageous resignation of *Vauxhall* is the courage of a condemned man, and these, sardonically, sighingly sung last lines are his 'last words', addressed to his audience, to his lover, to his dead God, but mostly to himself: '*I've always been true to you/in my own sick way/I'll always be true to you*'.

And the final, harsh snared drum-beat is really the sound of a trap-door opening and a neck snapping.

* * *

Vauxhall, probably deliberately, was an impossible album to follow. But of course, Morrissey did. Retirement, even after such a public and professional self-suspension, was not an option, however attractive it might seem. However, even some of Morrissey's fans might have wished that these really had been his last words. By the time the cacophonous-portentous, and often almost unlistenable *Southpaw Grammar* — an album which begins with a one-and-a-half minute strings-backed drum roll — was released the following year, in 1995, Morrissey appeared to have lost both his ruffian and his *relative* peace of mind. And also his muse.

There is no mention of Jake on the sleeve, but one of the better tracks is an uptempo, hilarious, bitingly sarcastic song called 'Best Friend on the Payroll', about that point in a relationship when someone realises they've made a terrible mistake, not just about the other party, but also perhaps about the very nature of love (that it's not about you it's about *them*): '*More breakfast in bed, and I'll bring the paper in later/the best friend on the payroll/No, no, no, it's not going to work out*'. Morrissey is still not the marrying kind.

> *When were you in love for the last time?*
> It's quite recent, but it's not a very realistic story, rather a sort of dream. Someone concrete, real, but an impossible romance.
>
> LES INROCKUPTIBLES, 1995

This friendship, however short-lived it may have been, does appear to have achieved something which no one else and nothing else had ever done before — it changed him. Or at least, it broadened his hope-less horizons ever so slightly. It no longer appeared to be just outsiders, lost boys and rebels without a cause that captured Morrissey's imagina-tion. In *Southpaw* he allows himself to show open envy for the ease-in-the-world of ordinary, working class boys happy going nowhere (rather than mocking them as in *Viva Hate*). In the affectionate, endearingly daft, if monotonous 'Dagenham Dave' (also the title of a Stranglers track) Morrissey abandons his ambivalence, asks Sandie Shaw's roofer nephew out on a date, and declares himself a hopeless admirer of the apparent lack of self-consciousness of the 'ordinary boys'.

Dagenham Dave is a lad with his 'head in a blouse' and 'a mouthful of pie', everyone loves him 'and I see why'. Dagenham Dave is happy going nowhere, rattling around in his car: *'"I love Karen, I love Sharon" on the window screen/with never the need to fight or question a single thing'*.

> It's pure nostalgia, really, and there's very little truth in it. I'm well aware of that. I know that it's all pure fantasy really, and 50 per cent drivel. Everybody has their problems and there is no way of being that is abso-lutely free and fun loving and without horrific responsibilities. It just isn't true . . . I don't think I'm missing anything because I'm not a roofer from Ilford.
>
> THE OBSERVER, 1995

The fantasised bliss of normalcy — possibly of idiocy — is conveyed by the constant repetition of the name 'Dagenham Dave', which so irritated many reviewers and fans, for whom it meant nothing except perhaps a rather embarrassing, artless crush on the part of the per-former. But to Morrissey the words 'Dagenham Dave' are a magical mantra, literally music to his ears, conjuring up as those two avowedly ordinary words do, all the things that he still doesn't have and knows he'll never have: happiness, contentedness, peace of mind. And whose absence he feels even more after having experienced some kind of con-nection, however flawed and fleeting, with anOther. It may seem like a very small thing, but Morrissey's ability to 'come out' as an admirer of such 'normalcy', albeit of a highly retro and fetishised variety, was for him something of a breakthrough.

Happily though, he can't behold such contented, healthy mascu-line innocence, even to idolise it, without corrupting it a shade or two: apparently Dave *'would love to touch'* but the problem is *'he's afraid he might self-combust/I could say more, but you get the general idea'* — the last line, of course, also being Morrissey's comment on most of his back catalogue. (Deliberately contrasting with Dave's all-conquering likeability, the 'B'-side to the single release of this track is the sinister 'Nobody Loves Us', another paean to disgruntled outsiders... like Morrissey.)

Even the album title hints at 'self-combustion': 'Southpaw' is boxing slang for 'left-hander'. Hence 'Southpaw Grammar' could mean simply 'the school of hard knocks'. But 'left-hander' is also synonymous with deviance. 'Southpaw Grammar' is, in other words, also the syntax of deviance, rather like Morrissey's Palare.

As ever, though, Morrissey can't quite make up his mind. In 'Boy Racer' a driving, literally driven song (this singer has a thing about being 'driven' and taking the passenger seat: e.g. 'This Charming Man', 'You've Got Everything Now', 'There is a Light That Never Goes Out', 'Break Up the Family', 'Ammunition' — not to mention the fact that Jake was his driver...), Morrissey complains that the animal beauty and contentedness of such carefree creatures that speed through life without *'ever getting pulled over'* is really too much to bear. As in 'Dagenham Dave' the two words of the title are repeated over and over again, though this time in an increasingly frustrated, ultimately murderous fashion. The resentment is much more openly expressed here than in 'Dagenham Dave': *'He's just too good-natured and/he's got too much money and/he's got too many girlfriends'*. However, Morrissey doesn't rationalise his resentment. Instead he frankly states: *'I'm jealous, that's all . . .'* It's entirely understandable, really: *'standing at the urinal/he thinks he's got the whole world in his hands'*. Morrissey obviously agrees. When he promises, over and over again, 'we're gonna kill this pretty thing', it hardly seems so shocking. Even the use of the word 'thing' seems unremarkable — creatures such as these are not fully human or even 'animal' in the vegetarian scheme of things since *they don't suffer*. (*Southpaw* also contains the track 'The Teachers Are Afraid of the Pupils', an interesting reversal of the message of 'The Headmaster Ritual' from *Meat is Murder*, an acknowledgement of changing times and, perhaps, advancing years.)

157

* * *

By the time *Southpaw* was released in the mid-Nineties, three years after *Your Arsenal*, envy of the working class 'lad's' imagined lack of self-consciousness, his sexy physicality and ease-in-the-world, his unshakeable sense of who and what he is, and above all his authenticity, had become the dominant cultural trend in Britain.

The ruffian was no longer on the stair, but in the front room. Britain was entertaining Mr Sloane in all mediums: music, fashion, television and cinema. 'New Lad' as this tendency was dubbed, was ostensibly a reaction to the nappy-changing, sensitive 'New Man' of the Eighties and the emasculating effects of feminism. However, as its later uptake amongst women indicated ('new ladettes') it was as much a reaction to the inauthenticity and self-reflexiveness of modern life, where identity was increasingly uncertain and subject to massive change. Laddishness was in vogue and everyone had fallen for Dagenham Dave because, it seemed, 'lads' knew who they were, what they wanted and how to have a good time when more and more people were less and less certain of these things.

The bitter irony of the Nineties was that now that the working class had ceased to exist as a political force, as a class of itself and for itself, everyone was for it. Now that everyone aspired to be middle class home-owners, everyone wanted to be 'working class', or rather, wear working class-ness (no one wanted to be really working class — least of all the working class). Everyone wanted to like football, or at least be seen to be liking it. Everyone wanted to buy the football-terrace anthems of Oasis, the 'singing plumbers' (as they were dubbed by Brett Anderson) from Manchester, who cannily upped their cultural capital by pretending they were car thieves when teenagers. Everyone, not just posh Indie boy-band Parklife tourists Blur, wanted a 'sexy', downwardly mobile 'mocknee' accent. Everyone had an unhealthy fascination with 'low life' and gangsters and everyone, not just the rich art students of Pulp lyrics, wanted to sleep with common people. It even seemed as if everyone wanted a skinhead or suedehead haircut (especially if they worked in The City). And everyone, from Britpopsters to the Labour Party wrapped themselves in the Union Jack.

But no one wanted Morrissey. *Southpaw* (an admittedly 'difficult' album to the point of distraction) disappeared almost without a trace.

Ironically, many of the journalists spearheading this mainstream exploitation of rough English lads, writing excitedly in the new booming business of politically incorrect glossy men's magazines full of ads for men's vanity products, about English football hooligans, gangsters, boxers, bar-room brawls and 'yobbish' behaviour in general, were journalists from the very music paper that had lambasted Morrissey for his unhealthy and uncouth interest in 'scum' a few years earlier. (The first and most famous of these 'lad' titles was produced by the publisher of the *NME* , and was edited and staffed by *NME* journalists.

Morrissey's unhealthy personal obsessions turned out to have anticipated the 'hot' cultural trend of the Nineties — just as he had done in the early Eighties when, with his narcissistic naked male Smiths cover sleeves, feminist-inspired politics and sexually ambiguous lyrics, he anticipated, fathered even, the so-called New Man. Which is hardly surprising, since, contrary to the propaganda, New Lad was an organic development of New Man — both were, after all, marketing strategies, both were wannabe products of glossy mens' magazines (though New Lad turned out to be much more successful at selling men glossy, girly things), and both were forms of masculine aestheticism. Of which Morrissey was the supreme, dandyish connoisseur.

However, the ruffian's greatest and most thoughtful admirer could not be allowed to benefit from the ruffian's new-found fashionability. Partly because that's how commercial exploitation of art works, but mostly because Morrissey was the living, self-conscious, embarrassing proof of the connection and continuity between Eighties and Nineties masculinity — and the (homo)eroticism and aestheticism at its heart.

The literally hysterical disavowal and denigration of male-male erotics — at the same time as exploiting them to the elbow: e.g. the pretty-boys-together gangster films of Guy Ritchie — was an essential requirement of New Lad in its drive to reach a mass market. But this disavowal was symptomatic of an even guiltier secret which just the name 'Morrissey' threatened to blow the gaff on: the closeted, self-conscious and nerdy spectatorship of New Lad. In order for it to be saleable to millions it had to be advertised as something 'natural' and 'unaffected'; a cure for the symptoms rather than just more... symptoms. Worst of all, Morrissey wasn't terribly interested in the commodification of working classness for the middle classes to wear.

The very first track on *Southpaw*, 'Reader Meet Author', is a scathing attack on the middle class tourism of working class life, in which Morrissey declares: '*You don't know a thing about their lives/they live where you wouldn't dare to drive*'.

Morrissey gets straight to the heart of the strange, somewhat queer attraction, but also of the disingenuous appropriation of Otherness: '*You shake as you think of how they sleep/but you write as if you all lie side by side*'. Moz of course isn't blind to the irony of his own position as a sensitive mother's boy who hid in his room for most of his adolescence and then became a somewhat pampered pop star, exploring his idealisation of the boys who used to chase him down the street on his way back from the library (but then, he does appear to have occasionally actually lain side by side with one or two of them).

In live performances he has been known to amend the lines in 'Reader Meet Author' from: '*And if a fight broke out here tonight/You'd be the first away, because you're that type*', to '. . . *I'd be the first away because I'm that type*'. As if by way of explanatory equivocation, he has also changed a later line in the song from: '*Have you ever escaped from a shipwrecked life?*', to '*Have you ever escaped from a* Manchester *life?*'

> *Is 'low life' the right term for what you write about?*
> No, it's my life actually. It's not affected in the least. Working class culture isn't particularly going anywhere. On 'Reader Meet Author', I sing, 'The year 2000 won't change anyone here' and that's true. It won't change their lives. They won't be catapulted into space age culture and mobile fax machines. The poor remain poor. Someone has to work in Woolworth's. *And it could have been you.*
> No. I haven't got the legs.
>
> Q, 1995

For the final verdict however as to whether Morrissey is really a ruffian or just another 'tourist', perhaps we should look to a higher authority, a professional expert on such wayward boys, someone skilled in passing judgement on bad lads. Someone like Judge Weeks, a High Court Beak.

As Morrissey himself had predicted several times, his pop career did indeed bring the judiciary cracking down on his unruly head, but perhaps not in the precise manner he might have imagined. In 1996 he found himself in court with Johnny Marr contesting ex-Smiths drummer Mike Joyce's claim to 25 per cent of The Smiths' perform-ance royalties against the 10 per cent he and Rourke had been allo-cated by Morrissey and Marr, the founders, creative talent, and *de facto* administrators and managers of the band (working class lads together or no, Morrissey was certainly not going to pretend that everyone in The Smiths was equal).

In court Morrissey showed that, matured or not, when confronted with magisterial paternal — and class — authority, he still couldn't and wouldn't be a 'good son'. His rebellious streak shone through and he displayed, perhaps for the first time in his life, a lack of reverence for men who dress in wigs and stockings which the Court inevitably interpreted as insolence. Morrissey was used to being cross-examined by middle class men with degrees in pedantry, even if usually they were equipped with tape-recorders instead of legal briefs, so for him it was just more of the same. The difference was, however, that on this occa-sion there was no jury — or readership — to play to.

> QC: *Could I please finish my question?*
> It's much too time consuming.
> QC: *It's more time consuming if you don't allow me to finish the question.*
> I don't agree.
>
> MORRISSEY IN THE HIGH COURT BEING CROSS-EXAMINED
> BY JOYCE'S QC, 1996

Arguably, this Wildean loftiness was to cost him and Marr a cool one and a half million pounds, as Judge Weeks appeared to decide not so much for a polite Joyce (who was praised for his "straightforward and honest" testimony) as against the unbowed Morrissey. In a phrase which was immediately turned into crowing banner headlines by a deliriously grateful British press, which naturally saw this case as noth-ing less than a criminal trial with Morrissey's personality in the dock, the very grand Mr Weeks (so grand in fact that he reportedly had to have *Top of the Pops* explained to him) pronounced the evidence of this northern working class Anglo-Irish radical who bears more grudges than High Court judges as being 'devious, truculent and unreliable when his own interests were at stake'.

Of course, the first four words were the ones generally reported and were presented as a judgement on Morrissey's entire life.

It is open to debate what a High Court Judge, or for that matter any member of the legal profession, might mean by 'devious' and 'unreliable'. However, the use of the word 'truculent' is more telling. According to the *Concise Oxford English Dictionary*, 'truculent' means: 'fierce . . .; aggressive, savage; pugnacious'.

An' they catch 'im an' they say 'e's mental

* * *

So much for the verdict. Who actually, finally won this confrontation, this showdown between Morrissey and the English Legal Establishment is another matter however. Seven years and several appeals on, Morrissey was still defiant while Joyce was still waiting.

He may have to suffer and cry slightly longer.

I was working class and I was made to feel like a peasant.

ON JUDGE WEEKS, *THE IRISH TIMES*, 1999

take me back to dear old blighty

Only England could have produced him, and he always said that the country was going to the dogs. His principles were out of date, but there was a good deal to be said for his prejudices.

OSCAR WILDE

I don't really think black people and white people will ever really get on or like each other. I don't think they ever will. The French will never like the English. That tunnel will collapse.

MORRISSEY

11

If the past is another country, then Morrissey, for whom England is the past he never had, has always been a stranger in his own land, an exile in the present. Long before he moved to LA in the Nineties, Morrissey was propped up at the bar of the Olde English pub in Santa Monica, drunk on nostalgia for a Mother Country that never really accepted him, that he never really liked, and which probably never really existed.

Despite the fact that Morrissey has come to be seen as 'quintessentially English', his personal history runs counter to received 'Englishness': Anglo-Irish, working class, provincial, northern, *literate*. Even within the Northern, Irish-descendent working class sub-grouping of Englishness, his literacy marginalised him as a mummy's boy and a bookworm; philistinism and uncouthness is prized in England by all classes, North and South.

In retaliation, Morrissey broke off diplomatic relations with the actual existing England, blockading himself in his bedroom for most of his adolescence, starring in his own remake of *Passport to Pimlico*, holding a torch for a preposterously idealised and romanticised Albion. He watched, observed, noted, analysed and desired ravenously from afar, trying vainly to consume, to possess her through old films, books and records. England would be his; it would owe him a living.

In other words, Morrissey was a wannabe. Just like his literary role model, that other Anglo-Irish wannabe, Wilde, he was determined to become more English than the English — partly because he ached to belong, to be loved, to be accepted by England, to wrap himself up in her green hills and satanic mills, and partly because he ached to destroy her. As the lover-destroyer of nineteenth-century polite society put it himself: Each man kills the thing he loves, the brave man with a sword, the smart man with a pop single.

> I am only attracted to the things I can never become or get. My pop career would be finished if I found total harmony.
>
> Dagens Nyheter, 1997

Morrissey's relationship to Englishness is, next to his relationship to fame itself, perhaps the most contradictory of all his contradictory relationships. How can such a radical be such a patriot? How can such an anarchist be such a nationalist? How can someone who wanted to drop his trousers to the Queen, who went one step further than the Sex Pistols and named an album *The Queen is Dead*, who sang 'Margaret on the Guillotine' and openly regretted that the IRA bomb which exploded at the 1984 Tory Conference in Brighton failed to assassinate the British Prime Minister, be so fiercely loyal to the country of his birth which has tormented him so? How, in other words, can such a cynic be such an idealist?

* * *

> I could never live anywhere else — I absolutely adore England, I really do. Not many people see what I see — so many romantic elements of English life buried beneath the corrosion. I'm the only person I know who can take a day-trip to Carlisle and get emotional about what he sees.
>
> Melody Maker, 1987

Just as behind every cynic there is a disappointed idealist, the rebel, however much of a bastard, literal and metaphorical, he might be can't help but love his Mother Country. Which is why he finds it intolerable. The rebel patriot, like the ex-pat, is in love with an idea, which is always the most passionate, most dangerous, most *artistic* kind of love (D.H. Lawrence, another home-grown product of Mother love, also loved to loathe England). Splendidly complicating matters, the rebel is often adamantly attached to the very things which oppressed and suffocated him and which turned him into a dissident and sent him into internal exile: Manchester; flat, grey days; pitiless rain; numbing boredom; narrow minds; petty jealousies; warm beer; dole queues; every day like Sunday; class despair; pub fights. England was the Other for Morrissey, which he needed to tell him who he wasn't and thus who he wanted to be.

> I'm really chained to those iron bridges. I'm really chained to the pier. I'm persistently on some disused clearing in Wigan. I shall be buried there, I'm sure, and I shall be glad to go at that point.
>
> MORRISSEY, 1984

Morrissey's patriotism, like his attitude to life, was a form of sulking — but then, so was that of many other fellow islanders. After the realisation began to sink in, post-Suez, that the UK had lost both the Second World War and the Empire to the United States, Englishness had itself begun to deteriorate into a form of sulkiness, a kind of petulant pouting, exemplified by the endless, but sometimes rather diverting, industrial tantrums of the Sixties and Seventies. And, most famously, most gloriously, with punk, and its affected sneer to all things English which, like Johnny Rotten himself, was fiercely in love with England and her blowsy beer gardens, her litter-strewn car parks, her hopeless housing estates, her ridiculously cluttered and overbearing history, and probably, yes, her ugly, kitsch, ludicrous monarchy, even as it gobbed in her face.

With perfect, supernatural, timing, Morrissey arrived on the scene in the post-punk early Eighties with his own fully-formed, poetic, sulky, sullen, I-want-it-back-I-don't-want-it Englishness when British sovereignty was being surrendered to Europe, the British Establishment and Monarchy was on its last gouty legs, undermined by their own Tory Party (which was now treasonously in love with market forces), British society was beginning a process of crash, crass and compulsory Americanisation which seemed designed to produce a nation of crap Americans (by the next decade it had succeeded spectacularly), and 'Britishness' itself was beginning to unravel under devolutionary demands. (Significantly, presciently, Morrissey generally preferred to speak of 'Englishness' rather than 'Britishness').

Where do you go for your holidays?
I don't go on holiday. Not since they shut down Butlins at Bognor. No, I just hang around the East End in a long black cape.

Q, 1995

There was only one other figure in the Eighties whose relationship to Englishness was as complex, powerful and important as Morrissey's, and that was his hated Margaret Thatcher. Maggie was his dodgy doppelganger, sharing not only his fondness for hairspray and old-fashioned blouses with frilly collars, but his animus. She was an outsider and a wannabe. She was utterly self-possessed. She didn't suffer fools gladly. She was northern (from Grantham, the first truly Northern town as you motor up the A1). She spoke her mind in a profession where insincerity was the lingua franca. She was a Little Englander. She possessed a gender that was all her own. She was the product of an especially intense and never properly resolved family romance (Daddy's girl instead of Mummy's boy).

And she was lower middle class, which to the Tory Party in those days, before she refashioned it in her own petit bourgeois image, was literally as low as you could go. Maggie was in some senses the Northern Woman of Morrissey's dreams (and nightmares) — common, comic, glamorous, forceful, unstoppable, grotesque, driven and quite, quite mad. No wonder he was obsessed with her.

In fact, if the Iron Lady had embarked on a recording career instead of a political one, and somehow acquired the two attributes of the Northern Woman she lacked — a heart and a sense of humour — Morrissey might have written her fan mail instead of hate lyrics.

Like Morrissey, Maggie was a rebel-patriot with chips on both shoulders, whose resentment against the British-English Establishment was as strong, if not stronger than her love for England. Gleefully she set about destroying the institutions which made England... Britain. The BBC, the universities, the corporate state, the Monarchy were all put to the torch of the marketplace, though some of these edifices turned out to be slow-burning and were not entirely consumed until long after her departure from the political scene. She was Janus-faced, idolising the past in the shape of the Nineteenth Century rather than Morrissey's Sixties, which she despised, seeing it, quite rightly, as the decade which cut England off from *her own* past, but she changed this island more than Cromwell (his Revolution, unlike hers, failed to endure).

Posing as Britannia wearing Boadicea's face-paint, she oversaw Britain's last Imperial adventure, the Falklands War ('the wishes of the islanders must be paramount'), and loudly broadcast her steely Europhobia, while quietly taking Britain further into Europe, pushing Scotland into the arms of the secessionists and opening her legs to America, her real love. She may have destroyed the British working class, but she also ultimately destroyed the British institution which was their historic enemy and which had brought her fame and success and which she had taken to the absolute limits of its endurance – the Tory Party.

> I don't like anything new – I'm really not modern to any degree at all. Take houses – I like old, dark properties, Victorian or Georgian preferably, with very old furniture. I can't stand maisonettes. It's really nothing to do with coming from the north – southerners always regard having lived in the north as a strange medical phenomenon or the reason for having an unusual diet or peculiar haircut.
>
> MELODY MAKER, 1987

Likewise, Morrissey also effectively destroyed or exhausted the British institution which had brought him fame and success and which he had taken to its absolute limit – pop music. He was also a Janus-faced figure in the world of pop in the Eighties, countenancing both an exaggerated respect for British pop and the final destruction of it (as well as a secret Yankophilia). After Morrissey there could be no more pop stars, which was actually how he wanted it. Like the Iron Lady, he was an impossible act to follow. And also like her, the much-reverenced bygone era was merely a plinth on which to mount his statue, where it would cast a long shadow over the future. His oft-repeated predictions about the imminent demise of pop music were accurate enough, but were also plain wish-fulfilment, born out of an intensely ambivalent, nay *apocalyptic*, love for pop. Like him, it was too good for the world.

> Popular music is slowly being laid to rest in every conceivable way . . . the ashes are already about us if we could but notice them.
>
> THE SOUTH BANK SHOW, 1986

Morrissey was the ultimate, preposterous incarnation of English pop. He was the moaning Messiah that it had prophesied for so long. Fathered by the unholy spirit of English pop culture, his was a virgin birth, and this was born testament by his life: pop music took the place of human contact. He was both the final evolution of English pop and the fatal mutation spelling its doom; its apotheosis and its nemesis, its final justification and its final solution.

Not only was there no competition, there could be no descendants. His unrivalled knowledge of the pop canon, his unequalled imagination of what it might mean to be a pop star, his loopy ambition to turn pop into great art, and his total, single-minded, *desperate* investment in pursuing these things, could only exhaust the form forever. Moreover, Morrissey's mastery of English and Englishness was so self-conscious, so ironic, so intense, so devout, so creepy and finally so played out that English pop and even Englishness itself could never hope to recover from it. The unnatural, analysing, stripping heat of Morrissey's love of Englishness, the knowingly iconic Smiths sleeves, the arch lyrical references, the longing nostalgia, the pronounced eccentricity, the humdrum towns, the frustration, the fucking iron bridges ended up separating Englishness itself from anything solid, anything lived – anything corrupting – turning it into a free-floating signifier.

When The Smiths expired in 1987 following guitarist and collaborator Johnny Marr's exit from the group, Morrissey may well have risen again on the third day (at Wolverhampton) and pursued a successful solo career, but it's now possible to see that English pop remained in the tomb, hopelessly extinct, wrapped in back-issues of the NME. A large rock blocked the entrance, rolled there by Morrissey himself.

✳ ✳ ✳

The so-called 'Britpop' phenomenon of the Nineties which so excited some newspapers and a couple of hairdressers for a while, may have had one or two interesting moments, but it certainly did not represent a resurrection of English pop, merely a galvanic motion induced by the application of large amounts of lucre (and cocaine). Britpop was little more than a commercial footnote to The Smiths, a belated and massively overhyped attempt by the record industry to cash in on the legacy of the original 'Indie' four-boys-and-guitars band whose commercial potential was never fully realised in their lifetime. It may be difficult for a generation raised on a diet of media hype to comprehend, but The Smiths, the band who are now almost universally hailed as the greatest group of that decade, *were never played on daytime radio*. Their record company, because it really was Indie, spent less on publicity than most Britpop publicists (the real stars of the show) spent on cocaine. As a consequence, with the exception of 'Sheila Take a Bow' which scraped in by the skin of its buck teeth in 1987 at the height of the group's 'popularity', their singles always stalled before reaching the Top Ten (and often didn't even make it into the Top Twenty — in fact the highest chart position of any Smiths single was the re-release of 'This Charming Man' in 1992, five years after the group's demise it reached the giddy heights of number eight, which was an improvement at least on its original, criminal, high water mark in 1984 of number twenty-five). They certainly never made it into the popular press, except to be denounced; while the 'serious' nationals merely ignored them. And, to cap it all, they *refused to make pop promos*.

By today's slaggy standards then, they were a bunch of complete losers.

Yet they had a large, fanatical following, across all classes, the like of which will never be seen again and are now hailed as that decade's greatest band and in fact the most influential band ever. The media-PR-recordbiz-fashion conglomerate known as Britpop, by contrast, had all of these things handed to it on a BPI monogrammed velvet cushion with a complimentary line of charlie. While it may have been more 'popular' — 'Indie' after all now meant 'mainstream' — Britpop failed to inspire even a single Kleenex worth of the devotion and passion The Smiths did when they were hidden under a (Gary) bushel. Under the arc lamps they kissed, and although they ended up with sore lips, it just wasn't like the old days any more.

Throughout the Nineties, the blood pressure of English pop, measured in overall record sales, especially of singles, continued to plummet. The Britpop bands themselves seemed strangely deathly, much more slavishly, icily retro than The Smiths — who were denounced at the time for their nostalgia — had ever been. Blur were The Kinks for students and confused teenage girls from Epsom who mistook Damon Albarn for someone sexy. Suede, who arguably began it all, and did to be sure show some early promise, were fronted by a man who seemed to think he was Ziggy Stardust exhumed from his shallow grave in the dressing room of the Hammersmith Odeon (and reanimated with countless *NME* front-pages). Oasis, by far the most successful Britpop outfit and in fact its standard-bearers, were a Beatles tribute band for New Lads and New Labour MPs, who by only their third album *Be Here Now* managed the extraordinary and admittedly rather impressive achievement of becoming their own tribute band.

These working class Manchester boys with Irish antecedents were seen as The Smiths minus the troublesome, effeminate, evil genius — which is to say, Marr without Morrissey (a point of view supported by the doggerel lyrics of Oasis songs). And indeed, Marr, the scally Beatles fan fond of partying, might perhaps have possibly trodden the same football-crowd-pleasing path if he hadn't had the Sandie Shaw-worshipping, Oscar Wilde-quoting, abstemious introvert from Stretford to nag and pervert him in a more difficult direction. Legend has it that Oasis's songwriter and guitarist Noel Gallagher decided to become a pop artist after seeing Johnny Marr perform with The Smiths on *Top of the Pops*. (Typically, Blur's Damon Albarn decided to form a band after watching Morrissey on the *South Bank Show*.) Marr himself bestowed his avuncular blessing on Oasis, and became very friendly with the Gallaghers; it was even rumoured that he loaned Noel the sacred guitar with which he had recorded *The Queen is Dead*. It was promptly, so the story goes, smashed onstage.

> If I were knocked down tomorrow by a passing train, I would be considered the most important artist ever in the history of English pop music, which today I am not considered to be. That's just a rough guess.
>
> Musician, 1991

In a sense, the whole point of Britpop was to airbrush Morrissey out of the picture. Morrissey had to become an 'unperson' so that the Nineties and its centrally-planned and co-ordinated pop economy could happen. (Which, of course, was exactly what occurred after the Madstock gig in Finsbury Park in 1992, the year before Britpop took off.)

> If there's one thing I've grown to NOT expect it's good reviews. The ONLY thing from me that the British press will review positively is my death.
>
> ROLLING STONE, 1999

With the possible and very brief exceptions of fabulously skinny northerner Jarvis Cocker, who threw it all away with that embarrassing tantrum in front of Michael Jackson at The Brits (Jackson was being very annoying, but did the world really deserve to see Jarvis' bottom? Besides, doesn't turning up at such a record industry pig-trough event somewhat compromise your self-righteousness?) and Taff band Manic Street Preachers' even skinnier Richey Manic — who sensibly disappeared before the Manics became famous, fat and fatuous (*This is My Truth, Tell Me Yours*).

Britpop failed to produce a single star worthy of the name.

> Stand me next to Primal Scream and I'll eat the lot of them alive — and I know you worship the very hair that they stand on — but next to someone like that there is no competition. Intellectually there is no competition at all in pop music any longer! Everybody is so boring! Relentlessly boring! Even those who are considered not to be, bore me stiff. And I can forgive people of anything except dullness.
>
> Q, 1994

But then, it wasn't meant to. Pop stars in the Nineties had devolved into mere celebrities, nothing but painted wooden horses for the media merry-go-round; Noel Gallagher's then wife sensibly formalised this arrangement by hiring out her celeb friends for openings and launch parties. The Gallagher brothers themselves, though undoubtedly talented, behaved like lottery winners with guitars, white trash with stacks of cash who spent it recklessly on the front pages of the tabloids. To be sure, the monotonous monobrows represented a kind of working-class revenge, but mostly in the form of drunken looting and snorting amongst the ruins of English pop.

The bragging materialistic self-importance of all this was somewhat punctured, however, by the fact that by the late Nineties, the Spice Girls, the manufactured 'girl power' band whose professed inspiration was Margaret Thatcher, and who seemed to be a feisty, bollocked version of the eunuch boy band Take That (who in turn seemed to be modelled on The Village People), outsold the main boy bands Oasis, Blur and Suede put together. Teen girls, not teen boys and thirty-something New Lads, were the industry's paymistresses. Geri Halliwell sweating bovinely in a stretchy Union Jack dress – the pop version of those tourist shops on London's Oxford Street full of Union Jack mugs and Houses of Parliament ash-trays – was the real face of English pop in the Nineties.

> How come, regardless of what happens, I'm 'alternative'? And when alternative starts happening I'm still 'alternative'?
>
> ONSTAGE, BOSTON, 2000

What was to turn out to be the official wake for English pop was kindly laid on by Oasis fan and ropy Margaret Thatcher impersonator Anthony Blair, the New Labour leader elected by a chart-busting landslide in May 1997, ending nearly twenty years of unbroken Tory rule (though many would later dispute that Tory rule had actually ended). Having decided to 'rebrand' Britain as 'Cool Britannia', 'Tone', enjoying pop star levels of approval, invited the usual suspects of Britpop round to Number 10 for a drink and some mutual publicity. After all, since everyone else was gnawing at the corpse of pop, why shouldn't politics? So the new executives of the English political establishment and English pop finally met in a morbid celebrity embrace for the cameras, and it was much more difficult to tell them apart than it should have been.

It was left to Elton John, that old Seventies pop rocker turned panto dame, to sing the music at the actual funeral of pop later that year in Westminster Abbey, in the form of the best-selling single-to-end-all-singles, the Diana dirge 'England's Rose'. To the hundreds of thousands lining the streets of London on a warm September day, and the hundreds of millions watching live around the world on what was effectively the last ever *Top of The Pops*, Diana was the nearest thing to an English pop star in the Nineties. Which was of course the greatest indictment of that decade.

Morrissey was probably thousands of miles away in Los Angeles (or perhaps hiding at his Mum's in Cheshire). Nonetheless his scornful, spiteful laughter still echoed through Westminster Abbey that day, unnoticed by the assembled feudal dignitaries and their heirs and successors the celebs, but mightily frightening the pigeons nesting in the gargoyles and Dame Elton's wig.

* * *

Britpop would have been forgiven everything if it hadn't failed in the only thing that would have justified it and which it was trumpeted as having already achieved — halting the advance of 'dance music', or even just treading on its toes a little. In fact, since the late Eighties, dance and its attendant drug culture had continued its speedy assimilation of England's youth without pausing to check its pupils in the gents' mirror. The programmed bass lines and drum sequences laid down a murderous barrage not only on pop music, but on Englishness itself. After all, Englishness relied on repression — class repression, sexual repression, emotional repression, any bloody repression you can mention. Repression made the English all that they were and, even more importantly, all that they could not be (and was the most 'naturally' English aspect of Morrissey's character). Dance music, however, pushed the ear of English youth up against a ten-foot speaker, told them to 'loosen up', to 'groove with the beat', to have a 'good time', to lose themselves in sensuality — or in the words of a Nineties TV ad for a Swedish designer furniture store: to 'stop being so *English*'.

> To me Acid House was never about music but a doorway for the drug culture . . . people realised that they could take enormous amounts of drugs. Which the English never used to. And suddenly, on one or another, it was part of everybody's lives. It was, if you ask me, the only thing Acid House achieved. The music was rubbish, just as the people who made it.
>
> THE HUMAN DAFFODIL, 1998

174

Of course, dance music couldn't achieve this historic victory over the English all by itself; chemical warfare had to be deployed. To loosen their dependency on the magnificently ersatz drug of pop music, the English had to be persuaded to take drearily real drugs. English youth would be weaned off beer, pub fights, sharp dressing and pop singles and on to designer drugs, chill-out room neck massages and baggy clothes. Ecstasy — even the word was fiendishly un-English: (until c.1989 its use was only permitted by football commentators describing England winning the World Cup five nil on the Queen's birthday) — was secretly added to lager supplies by fifth columnists parachuted in from Ibiza. Ecstasy was nothing less than a nerve agent that destroyed the English sensibility. Unlike the love affair with aggro-inducing amphetamines in the mod Sixties and punk Seventies, this was really poisonous stuff that made your teeth fall out. By loosening inhibitions, releasing endorphins, provoking a sense of well-being and warmth towards others, and by giving straight white boys the notion that they actually had a sense of rhythm, it promised to destroy English culture and its edge forever.

> England may be a very small country. But why is it so important for pop musicians all over the world to be famous in England of all countries? Why? I tell you why, because the English have always been born with a sense for good taste. And in this particular case, we've had a lot to offer. Probably more than anyone else.
>
> BLITZ, 1992

'E' was ingested religiously by millions of young people every weekend. It broke down class barriers, racial barriers, gender barriers, taste barriers. English lads and lasses were turned into vacant, sunny-natured Californians: ' 'avin' a good night, mate?' became the Anglo version of 'Have a nice day'. Billions of conversations full of embarrassing, redundant intimacy were conducted with complete strangers, some of them foreign. Most horrifying of all, Ecstasy made the English finally feel worthy of love, at least for a night or two or three (if you had some really good shit). In an England of all-weekend raves, every day was no longer like Sunday. Even Sunday wasn't Sunday any more, it was just the second half of Saturday. And there were no more stifled Friday nights.

I know people for whom drugs make them very happy. And I personally know of many relationships that are built simply upon Ecstasy. On the surface it may seem like a good thing but one day it may all wear off. And physically, a lot of people will be in terrible, terrible trouble. The way I see it is people just breaking out and saying, 'No more depression, no more repression. I'm not going to stay on the dole queue. I'm going to go out and dance and meet people.

THE FACE, 1990

It was no coincidence that the invasion of England by dance music and its massive uptake by her youth began in Morrissey's gloomy home town, The Rainy City. Funnily enough, most Mancunians were not cut out for a life of maudlin introspection amidst the mossy post-industrial landscape and redundant wreckage of a once proud working class culture. Given the choice, they would opt for partying or Ibiza every time. Even Morrissey, for all his protestations of eternal fidelity to those iron bridges, chose escape: he left the North, travelled South and knew he could never go back home again. Everyone wants to leave home, especially those who protest they never will. And drugs are the cheapest and perhaps the safest way to leave home.

The career of New Order, possibly Manchester's *second* most influential band, and one that also promised faithfully never to leave its home town (living in Manchester, like Englishness during the Blitz, is or was a form of 'don't worry we're all in this together'), symbolises just how much Manchester has to answer for. They began as the gloomiest and most – gloriously – pretentious of gloomy pretentious Manc bands, called, perversely enough, Joy Division (actually this was a double perversity as the name was originally assigned to those forced to work as prostitutes in concentration camps). After their angst-ridden lead singer proved his sincerity/took it all too seriously and hanged himself in 1980, they understandably changed their name and direction, began getting more interested in electronic music and hanging around in gay discos necking Ecstasy.

The New Order that bassist/songwriter Peter Hook and his initially charmingly, mumblingly reluctant and uncertain new lead singer Bernard Sumner would usher in was to turn out to be rather more interested in levity (though, thankfully, it would never quite manage to completely lose its mournful, almost tragic quality: Sumner's

176

vocals still sound like a lonely boy crying next door with his window open). Hence the transitional 1983 mega-hit 'Blue Monday' — a dance record whose greatness, like New Order's, owes as much to the way it is fighting against its inner disco-dolliness as to its innovative bass line. However, throughout the Eighties this resistance was to decline, as the Dionysian gained over the Apollonian (i.e. they appealed less and less to the head and more and more to the 'handbag'), finally producing the MDMA-soaked end of the Eighties 'Ibiza' album *Technique* and the literally crowd-pleasing 'World in Motion' 1990 World Cup England team anthem — originally called 'E Is For England'. (Admittedly, even their 'Ibiza' record, bless 'em, never really got away from that happy-sad-drunk-on-a-wet-Tuesday-afternoon-in-Whalley-range feeling).

It was highly symbolic both in terms of the Manchester scene and the English pop scheme of things that after leaving The Smiths in 1987, reportedly after a long bout of depression, Marr joined up with New Order's Sumner to form the dancey-prancey-portentous Electronic; Morrissey was infamous for his implacable opposition to electronic music and dance. Their first collaboration was with the Pet Shop Boys' Nil Talent who predictably, triumphantly seized the opportunity of this association with Marr to realise the ambition with which he had started his pop career: penning the limp lyrics for the debut single 'Getting Away With It', he regaled the world with his bad Morrissey drag — 'It was me doing Morrissey' he has since confessed eagerly, if somewhat self-deludingly to anyone who would listen.

However, pop's flirtation with dance, which, granted, had a certain charm (though perhaps the best thing about it was that you couldn't really dance to it) didn't so much provoke a re-invigoration of English pop as a merciless, final gang-bang of it. A whirlwind of hard drugs and a stampede of unadulterated dance was to effectively undo New Order, and also their legendary label, Tony Wilson's Factory Records, the batty Svengali force behind much of Manchester's phenomenonally creative pop scene since the Seventies. Fittingly, it was the famous Manchester dance club the Hacienda, central to disseminating the new dance culture and its drugs, built and run by Factory with New Order profits, that proved, like the Happy Mondays (New Order's label-mates and anti-thesis) a swaying Frankenstein monster of Dionysian chaos

— the 'big wheel generator', where boys didn't get so much stabbed as peppered with semi-automatic fire — which eventually consumed the Apollonian, Factory records and with it much of Manchester's pop scene, as well as most of New Order's earnings. (It's difficult though not to admire the enthusiasm and consistency with which Mr Wilson fed, trained and encouraged his own baggy gravediggers.) New Order were then forced into the terrible, unimaginable humiliation of breaking their promise and leaving Manchester and moving to despised London, and, worse, signing to a label called... *London Records*.

Little wonder then that by the early Nineties, Manchester's youth had lost themselves in bass-heavy gay disco rhythms from Detroit — another decaying post-industrial northern town — and were taking masses of mind-altering drugs (instead of merely listening to music made by people on drugs, the more usual British division of musical labour). The rave scene ruled and djs, the spawn of Jimmy Saville but with less style sense, were the new pop stars. Once again Manchester and the north proved itself the heart of the nation's youth — as pretty soon the whole country began really, like, feeling the music inside them. And forgetting they were ever, y'know, English. Man.

> *What do you think of the Criminal Justice Bill? Do you think people in leggings have a right to live wherever they choose?*
> I don't think people in leggings have a right to live. I don't think people should hold raves because I don't like rave music. I suggested the Criminal Justice Bill, so I'm glad that it's been taken up.
>
> Q, 1995

Admittedly, E culture was as much a curative as a calamity. The drugs that dance prescribed and the incessant fidgety movement, sweatiness and garrulousness it provoked represented a therapy for English melancholia — a jubilant, warm dampness in place of a unhappy, cold, drizzly one; a sense of belonging and contact instead of awkward isolation. After all, Ecstasy had originally been developed to treat depression. *E is for England*. But as is often the case with life-long and congenital illnesses, if you remove all the symptoms, how much of the patient is left?

All the same, Morrissey understood that like the pop music they were replacing, dissolving, drugs could be a route out of suffocation. In the 1989 ballad single 'Interesting Drug' (the 'B' Side featuring a track called 'Such a Little Thing Makes A Big Difference'), he calls for some plain speaking amidst the moral panic that was endemic at the time: '*interesting drug/the one that you took/TELL THE TRUTH – IT REALLY HELPED YOU.*'

Unlike almost any of the other pop songs about drugs that emerged in the late Eighties/early-Nineties, it doesn't beat around the bush, and actually uses the word 'drug', instead of resorting to sniggering nudge-nudge wink-wink 'Ebeneezer Goode' (sub-Palare) type references. Moreover it puts the use of drugs into a political, class context of late Eighties post-boom-heading-for-bust Thatcherism: '*there are some bad people on the rise*' who are '*saving their own skins by/ruining people's lives...*'. And in a reference to Government 'job creation' programmes which echoes what is possibly his most well-known lyric ('*I was looking for a job and then I found a job/And heaven knows I'm miserable now*') he sings of kids being '*On a government scheme designed to kill your dreams*' before asking '*look around...can you blame us? CAN you blame us?*' The backing for 'Interesting Drug', provided by Kirsty McColl, has an angelic-sounding 'Village of The Damned' childishness to it familiar from 'Panic' (the video is set in a school and writing on blackboard spells out '*there are some bad people on the rise*' as 'there are some bad people on the *right*').

Morrissey doesn't appear to have a moral problem with drugs themselves, they make perfect sense to him, it's their disastrous effect on English culture he cannot abide. Attached as he is to the very things which oppressed him and made him what he was and what he wasn't, and forced him to invest so much in pop music, a substitute for drugs, sex, love, life which at its best far surpassed what it stood in for, he couldn't help but lament their dissolution. The drugs were fine, but by removing the very critical faculties which imprisoned the English within their own self-consciousness they made for banal music – which was, as we know, a hanging offence in Morrissey's book.

> England is not England in any real sense of the word, it has been internationalised and that's screechingly evident wherever you look around the country. The English people are not strong enough to defend their sense of history. Patriotism doesn't really matter anymore. So I think England has died.
>
> SPIN, 1991

Morrissey's dogged defence of English self-consciousness can take some oddly provocative forms, however. *Viva Hate*'s 'Bengali in Platforms' (1988), complete with an arrangement by Stephen Street which sounds as if it includes a sitar, could possibly be interpreted as mocking immigrant attempts to *assimilate*: '*he only wants to embrace your culture/and be your friend forever/...Bengali.../Oh shelve your Western plans/and understand/that life is hard enough when you belong here*'. It hardly needs pointing out that Morrissey, the unrivalled pop sovereign of England and Englishness is himself a product of immigration and assimilation.

'Bengali in Platforms' is a rather more ambiguous song than 'The National Front Disco', though, oddly, is generally not cited so often by the Morrissey-is-an-evil-racist-don't-play-his-records-or-you'll-burst-into-flames brigade. From a certain perspective the song seems to question the Bengali's right to be 'here' at all. From another, it is merely a mischievous examination of alienation. However, unless you really *want* to believe that Morrissey is actually advocating the forcible repatriation of Bengalis in platforms, the most likely, most obvious interpretation, the one that is carried by the wistful tone of the music, is that Morrissey, the self-confessed grotesque, the homeless Anglo-Irish bedroom hermit who prizes his Englishness but also claims he doesn't belong anywhere, who is both a triumph of assimilation and also a tragic failure, is unable to resist poking heavy-hearted fun at someone else's social/cultural/sartorial displacement and their uncertain attempts to fit in.

When you realise that the song is, like Morrissey's disastrous childhood, and his fragmented head, clearly set in the context of the Seventies (platform shoes were a staple of glam rock) then it becomes even more apparent that he is singing, once again, more about his own awkward subjectivity than about anything else. The ambiguity of the song is at 'worst' a symptom of Morrissey's artistic self-indulgence, or at 'best' another example of his reckless refusal to write about a subject in the officially approved fashion.

There are many people who are so obsessed with racism that one can't mention the word Bengali; it instantly becomes a racist song, even if you're saying, Bengali, marry me. But I still can't see any silent racism there.

180

Not even with the line, 'Life is hard enough when you belong here'?
Well, it is, isn't it?
True, but that implies that Bengalis don't belong here, which isn't a very global view of the world.
In a sense it's true. And I think that's almost true for anybody. If you went to Yugoslavia tomorrow, you'd probably feel that you didn't belong there.

SOUNDS, 1988

It was rap which provoked the most bitter assault from Morrissey, going much further than any of his denunciations of dance. Perhaps this was because for him rap represented an acceleration of the Americanisation of England, by far the most powerful foe of Englishness. And perhaps this was also because rap unlike dance music, appears to use words seriously. After all, like Morrissey, it uses rather a lot of them; likewise it also refuses moon-in-June sentimentality, and demands that you listen to them, in this instance by actually refusing to sing them.

The increasing popularity of rap in the early Nineties in the UK, and its attendant culture of 'rap-ismo' could be interpreted – by an old-fashioned pop star – as an assault of the lyrical heritage of English pop (replacing it with a regime that had no use for Morrissey). There was also the disastrous aesthetic impact of rap which has to be taken into account. By the early Nineties, every white male in Britain under twenty-five was required by a local authority bye-laws to wear basketball shoes and a baseball cap the wrong way round, and constantly talk about 'bitches' 'hos' and 'motherfuckas', especially if they attended public school. (If Britpop can be credited with anything at all, it did at least succeed in making baseball caps unfashionable – though apparently no one thought to mention this to William Hague, the balding 'young' leader of the Conservative Party in the late Nineties.)

Perhaps jealousy also played a part – after all Morrissey's highly successful, acclaimed lyrical fascination with hoods and hard men was being replaced and supplanted by a music form which presented itself as actually being made by hoods and hard men. The propaganda of rap held that there was no need for the artist middle-man any more. Rap was coming direct from 'da streets' (in the case of much of punk, which made the same claim, and certainly of Morrissey, it was more a case of coming from a box bedroom overlooking da streets).

> Rap is the degree zero of music. I know that what I'm saying sounds really corny, but I'm struck by the fact that it's enough for a rap group to break itself laboriously on a song with the thinnest of melodies to make people call it a work of genius and hail the song to the pantheon of classics. I know as well that the same speech has been held about punk. Except that punk didn't last. It had the virtue to bring us The Ramones and, above all, to revitalise rock and shake the system. On the contrary, rap never fails to repeat itself. It must be assumed that its only use is to sort out the swingers from the fuddy-duddies. Blokes who suffer while listening to rap just because they're scared to death not to be hip – I see some everyday! Sorry, but I'd rather be corny.
>
> ROCK SOUNDS, 1993

Morrissey's criticism of rap music is nothing if not forthright. It may be a tad over-stated, it may be a little out-of-touch, but it is not entirely groundless. More to the point, almost no one else (white) dared say it. Inevitably, Morrissey's honest critique of rap was used as more kindling by those that wanted to burn him at the stake: rap was 'black culture' therefore white Morrissey was being racist in daring to criticise it. Of course, this argument is itself segregationist racism of the most patronising kind.

Early rap in the form of groups like Public Enemy and NWA was vital, creative, revolutionary even — artistically and politically. But rap quickly institutionalised itself, going through the rebellious motions, assembling the stale iconography of outsiderdom and, with 'gangsta rap', finally becoming a form of 'carni' bling-bling bragging showbiz. Even though it managed to produce the occasional dead (black) body, rap had largely become a smoothly-oiled mechanism for making record companies very rich and conservative white suburban boys who wanted to piss off their Mid-West/Home Counties mom very happy.

Perhaps this is why at the end of the Nineties hip hop finally produced a white rapper from Detroit called Marshal Mathers, aka Eminem, aka Slim Shady whose songs and ranting interviews and in fact whole mothafucking point, or so he would have you believe, was all about pissing off his mom and revenging his allegedly 'fucked up' childhood. With Dr. Dre (formerly of NWA) standing behind him, gifted hands on the mixing deck, Em's neurotic, twisted, and highly sexually confused investment in words, delivered over a fat, funky very non-neurotic bass line, seemed to have produced a new music form, a genuinely pop hip hop.

The troubled-troubling smash-hit single 'Stan' from *The Marshall Mathers LP* (2001) told a tragic, twisted and hilarious Gothic love story about a male fan who becomes obsessed with him and ends up killing himself and his pregnant girlfriend in a fit of pique, driving off a bridge, because Slim didn't write back. His young male and (mostly) female fans cut and died their hair like his bleached blond crop, becoming queer-looking clones of this bastard star, disowned at an early age by his father, who reconstructed and then reproduced himself through the perverted alchemy of pop/hip hop. Controversy followed him everywhere and he was denounced (by Lynn Cheney, the Gay and Lesbian Alliance Against Defamation, the National Organisation of Women, and his mother) for his violent and hate-filled lyrics. Not surprisingly, comparisons with Morrissey began to be made.

However, aside from the observation that Morrissey's lyrical chainsaw was rather sharper and funnier, and that he wouldn't be seen dead in dungarees, the crucial difference was that the British music press did not campaign to silence this 'alarming' man Slim Shady.

Eminem is the new Morrissey. Discuss.
Pigfarmer's Weekly is the new *City Life*. Discuss.

CITY LIFE, 2003

On the contrary, American-born big mouth Slim Shady was awarded gongs by the *NME* and accorded the honour of being defended by British broadsheet journalists (anxious to show how hip hop happening they were), as 'great artist', 'humorist', 'genius lyricist', 'free speecher' and 'truth-teller' who was anatomising the way things are rather than they should be — despite the fact that he sang gleefully and unambiguously about beating and murdering women (including his own wife) and the joys of raping lesbians and stabbing gays in the head, and was even arrested for threatening someone with a gun and pistol-whipping them (smartly, blacks were not targetted by Em, who was not exactly an 'equal-opps' misanthrope).

By contrast, when home-grown big mouth Morrissey had been accused of the 'r' word after being found in possession of a Union Jack and some vaguely ambiguous lyrics there was no general stampede to his defence.

I didn't invent the Union Jack, you do realise that don't you? I didn't knock it up on a spinning wheel in the front room. I can't account for people's reactions. Some people adore it; others are embarrassed by it. I don't get it. I don't understand the Fascist implications of it. I think it happened because it was time to get old Mozzer. Nothing more sophisticated that that.

Q, 1995

Despite being an artist of much greater achievement and nuance — or perhaps, because of this — Morrissey the Mancunian misanthrope was not afforded a smidgen of the creative freedom later awarded the Michigan maniac who, it was to turn out, after countless actressy acceptance speeches at record industry awards ceremonies and some dubious duets with Dame Elton, was anyway rather less interested in artistic integrity and truth-telling than suckcess).

✳ ✳ ✳

If you were forced to leave England at the point of a gun, where would you go?
Jersey, Guernsey, anywhere with a decent postal service.
Not Los Angeles?
No. I need grit and struggle and Los Angeles is terribly nice but people once they get there cease to be real. Constant and repetitive fulfilment is not good for the human spirit. We all need rain and good old depression. Life can't be all beer and skittles.

Q, 1995

During the early Nineties Morrissey himself had begun looking to Los Angeles, if not for the language he used then certainly for his audience, record sales and record label. As his popularity began to plummet in the UK, as he denounced the Americanisation of Britain most loudly, his popularity in the US reached unheard of proportions, selling out the Hollywood Bowl in just ten minutes, and the Los Angeles Forum in fourteen. In the States he was hailed as a living sign and invited on prime time TV chat shows; in England he was branded at best irrelevant and a clapped out embarrassment.

As the Nineties progressed, his stock in the US continued to wax as much as it waned in the UK. Inevitably, he found himself spending more and more time in the US, especially in LA. In 1996 he bought a house in Hollywood designed by Clark Gable for Carole Lombard, with cult actor Johnny Depp for a neighbour. Morrissey; the arch patriot, found himself in the very situation he would have lambasted ten years previously: an English pop star 'selling out' to America, betraying his roots... and perhaps – most unforgiveable of all – finding some kind of approximation of contentment.

> Initially I had a naïve view of America. I hated the fact that it seemed to have so much while I had nothing. I feel differently now. Guess why?
>
> THE BIG ISSUE, 1997

But of course it wasn't a betrayal, or, at least, it was no more of a betrayal of England than his whole pop career had been. The anti-Americanism of his past, like his anti-Southernism before he left Manchester for London, was the simultaneous product of envy and a refusal to admit his aspirations even to himself. In an important, if off-beat sense Morrissey was always American – and not just because he was a James Dean devotee. His ambition was much too big to be contained within The Old Country with its petty resentments, class envy and twitching net curtains, (even if he himself was responsible for much of the twitching). He was always heading for that West Coast penal colony for uppity working class English types.

Above all, Morrissey's *loneliness* is quintessentially American: all Americans are strangers in their own land. The Native Americans were wiped out or forced on to unfamiliar reservations not just to steal their land, but to make them as rootless as the white man – to make them 'American'. The 'United States' is a big, draughty, empty place without enough history or public houses and fish and chip shops to go round, and so Americans wrap themselves in the flag, hug the Cross, huddle on the sports field, or religiously attend the movies. From time to time they even invade foreign countries hoping to make friends with the newly conquered/liberated peoples. Most famously, they invented

185

popular culture and consumerism to keep them company and have very generously exported this form of canned loneliness around the world.

For his part, Lancashire's patron Saint of solitude, perhaps the strangest but also perhaps the aptest product of pop culture, its ultimate victim and ultimate master, probably admires American affability, friendliness, *neediness* as much as he finds it ludicrous and frightening. Besides, he often performs Englishness just as self-consciously, just as desperately — and endearingly — as Americans perform American-ness (though since England is on the verge of extinction while America engulfs the globe in its smotheringly friendly bear-hug his performance is perhaps somewhat more arch).

> Everything that happens in America is constantly reported on the English news while in America, England is never referred to and British politics are completely meaningless. I mean the country could completely explode and disappear into outer space and America would not mention that on the daily news.
>
> ALTERNATIVE PRESS, 1993

Morrissey's Englishness was virtual — an idealised Englishness that could actually be much better sustained in the US, away from the increasingly compromised contemporary reality; in a Californian town where 'England' only existed as an underused set on the backlot of Universal Studios. With the perversity that he is famous for, by settling in 'Loose Angela' as much as anyone can settle in such an insubstantial place, Morrissey was being true to his vision of Englishness, which increasingly had even less to do with the actual existing England than it ever did.

> Please don't imagine I came to Los Angeles to surf or work out. I know it's happening here somewhere but I could never do any of that.
>
> WORD, 2003

Morrissey in LA is a joke, of course, but a predictable one, not just because LA is the natural home of narcissistic, dysfunctional, agoraphobic types with great profiles everywhere, but because in a globalised postmodern world where, so it seems, all meanings become 'free-floating', all meanings and those interested in producing them gravitate to the city of signs. Arguably, Morrissey himself, through the success of his art, finally separated England from Englishness forever, watched it drift across the Atlantic like an untethered fairground balloon caught in a prevailing wind, and then upped and followed it.

Besides, America offered this Anglo asylum-seeker uncritical, all-embracing, all-conquering love. And to someone from England's resentful shores, America in love is an awe-inspiring, intoxicating, life-transforming revelation; one far more potent and therapeutic than even Ecstasy.

Everyone leaves home in the end, especially those who say they never will.

> I'd like all the vilification to end now and just the love to come through and feel, for 24 hours a day, unbridled support from all quarters.
>
> Q, 1994

Of course, Morrissey's pessimism, misanthropy and 'miserabilism' are technically capital offences in the US, but he is from the Old World, which everyone knows is a terrible cross to bear and so allowances are made on compassionate grounds. By the same token, if America was in love with the future and Morrissey was in love with the past, then that was OK, since the past that Morrissey was in love with was an English one and Americans all consider the Old Country washed up anyway.

> Everybody is beautiful all the time and that heat, every single day ... I understand that some people find it unbearable. It really is the Mamas And The Papas all the time. It really is.
>
> POP, 1998

To young, perhaps slightly unpopular Americans, Morrissey represents not so much 'Englishness' (which, quite rightly, most know little about) as a country, or world in his own right — Morrisseyworld is a place where they can wander through his vast back-catalogue, lose themselves in his mysterious references, ride his ready wit, tour his Gothic neuroses and childhood hang-ups. With his impressive oeuvre, now spanning over two decades, Morrissey has created an unrivalled richness, depth and, yes, peculiar kind of love from his own imagination. Morrisseyworld is a place to meet other outsiders, a community of loners and losers; alienation and shyness is nice, but it's better to have someone to share it with. Hence Manchester's prodigal son has spawned myriad fanzines in the US and a host of web sites where lonely young people typing in their bedrooms can connect with other lonely young people typing in their bedrooms and talk about the lonely records they like to listen to... alone.

> I like the light. It's astonishing to wake up in the morning and see that light and say, yes, you can do things today. That really doesn't happen in Manchester.
>
> THE BIG ISSUE, 1999

To a certain American audience, Morrissey is familiar but exotic, American but un-American, alternative but timeless. He is the pop cultural soul in a world made soulless by pop culture; a distinctively Catholic voice in a distinctly Protestant country. A man who lives between borders, an insider-outsider. Which, along with his refusal of rap music, his tendency to wear his heart on his sleeve, his fascination with, exploration of – and penetration of – machismo, his dramatic defiance, and of course his highly cultivated sideburns, is probably a factor in his famous appeal to many young Mexican-Americans – effectively California's hidden, and 'homeless' working class. Or perhaps it is merely down to Mexican-American evident good taste.

Oddly, the people sweating, without health insurance, frequently for less than the minimum wage to sustain California's luxurious lifestyle (including of course the one that Morrissey enjoys), maintain those immaculately clean homes, those neatly tended gardens, those shiny cars, those sparkling swimming pools, that staggering abundance of food and eateries, tend towards a doomed and romantic view of the world, one at odds with that of cosseted, entitled 'realistic' mainstream prosaic middle-class Californians for whom these things appear almost by magic, or entitlement: *It's seems when you're rich and white you'll be alright* ('Mexico').

> I spend hours just driving around the small rundown Mexican areas of Los Angeles – that is, the areas where the small, rundown Mexicans live. And have become quite fascinated by that. And so, yes, you could say I've come from Salford to Lincoln Heights. It's a short walk, really, and there are very familiar types in each place.
>
> THE TIMES MAGAZINE, 1999

188

Morrisseyworld is also a place where malcontented, adolescent Americans of all descriptions can go and drop out, going against the jock-prom-queen-college-fund values of the suburbs and the piped, choreographed snarly 'rebellion' of MTV. Morrissey is after all, much cheaper than Paris, and slightly less hassle than a High School massacre. On the American scene, Moz remains a resolutely almost-mainstream cult performer, triangulated somewhere between Kurt Cobain, Lou Reed and Benny Hill.

* * *

Then again, maybe this is patronising Old World horseshit. Maybe American fans, like Morrissey fans anywhere else in the world, simply recognise him as an authentic individualist — and in a country ostensibly built on individualism but frequently more slavishly conformist than Switzerland, this means a lot. In particular, this is seen in the fatal integrity which shines through his work and his career choices like a beacon (luring the innocent on to the rocks). His refusal to compromise, to chase the money, to give the audience what they want, to listen to the record company men with their focus group findings who tell him how much there is to be made if he cashes in his chips and goes chasing the Serious Moonlight, is an especially extraordinary thing to achieve in a land — a world — where the customer is always right, the artist is always wrong and money does all the talking.

> I've lived for the best part of the last two years in Los Angeles, where I remain, and which I even quite like. All the awful clichés about Los Angeles are, of course, true. But I feel less affected by them than most, because I happen to think that ALL PEOPLE EVERYWHERE are mad.
>
> ROLLING STONE, 1999

With the exception perhaps of Oscar Wilde and that other failed Morrissey prototype, Quentin Crisp, who were at least fortunate not to have to deal with record companies, most other English pop stars who have found success in the US have promptly lost themselves. Since the Beatles, the 'British invasion' of America has been a constant motif of British pop music, if not the whole point of it. Making America notice us, or at least hear their daughters screaming at us, seems the greatest form of success we can conceive of. After all, 'success' is an American idea and hence it isn't quite the genuine article until it is something that Americans recognise too.

But we're terribly conflicted. We condemn our bands for 'selling out' to America, but ridicule them for not selling in America. We in England like to imagine that we can reverse the result of the War of Independence with a fancy hairstyle and a few catchy tunes, that we can stake our claim in the American sun without having to sacrifice our charming English pallor or penniless integrity, only to rudely discover that America always, always wins. It is too big, too coarse, and the climate altogether too intemperate for the overdressed-underdressed urban dandies, professional eccentrics and out-and-out psychotics who periodically launch themselves from these shores in an attempt to stamp their image on the place.

It's also far too grown up. The naïve cult British artist says coquettishly to the almighty dollar 'Let's Dance', but the American record company just bends them over their three album deal, reams them out and pins their broken hymen to the Washington Monument. Like Antaeus, the undefeated wrestler of Greek myth, or for that matter David Jones, the kabuki mime artist from Bromley, English pop stars find their power ebbing away when their feet are no longer touching their Mother soil.

Does this include Morrissey, the most 'English' of English pop stars? Probably. Possibly. After all, since he moved there in 1996 he has not exactly been what you would call *prolific*. But not inevitably. Whilst LA may represent the nearest thing to retirement for Morrissey, and possibly a kind of mummification (it is after all, Hollywood, that crumbling, crypt-like part of LA guarded by the ghosts of Bette Davies and Marilyn Monroe that he has immured himself in), he may yet turn out to be the most durable Limey pop star in the New World precisely because he has always been homesick, he's always been an Englishman abroad. Like an Anglo Count Dracula, he carries his Mother Country around with him, the soil in the bottom of his coffin is his books, records, films — and his own back-catalogue.

It's very important that you heat the pot before you put the water in — if you use a pot, I know most people just throw a teabag into a cup. But in England of course, you have to make a pot of tea. And you have to heat the pot first with hot water, and then put the teabags in. I can't believe I'm saying this. And then put the hot water in and then just throw it all over yourself. Rush to outpatients and write a really good song.

EXPLAINING TO AMERICANS HOW TO MAKE TEA, K-ROQ, 1997

✳ ✳ ✳

And then, just when you had got used to, resigned to, relaxed to the notion of Morrissey buried in LA. Forever. He turns up with a flourish of his cape in... Whitby. Well, the Royal Albert Hall to be more exact.

The year 2002, the same year in which he was acknowledged as 'most influential artist ever' by a recanting *NME*, saw a triumphant, albeit brief return to the UK for The Prince of Gloominess to play two sell-out nights at the Royal Albert cake tin. On-stage Morrissey, looking leaner than he has done for years, performing songs mostly from his early solo period and also some new material, including the exquisite 'The First of the Gang To Die' ('*he stole all hearts away*') and the celeb-bashing 'The World is Full of Crashing Bores' ('*so scared to show intelligence/it might smear their lovely career*'), was devastating, his voice, stronger and more seductive than ever, easily overcoming the prim resistance of the Victorian building's notorious acoustics, not to mention its sense of morality, filling the packed, odd-shaped building with his strange, odd-shaped music hall love.

He began by setting about the audience with an enervatingly boisterous, shockingly youthful, note-perfect performance of the Smiths song 'I Want the One I Can't Have', the song that is literally the song of his life, but that night, the last night of the Poms, it seemed addressed to the whole of England.

England responded by shouting out she was his for the taking. For the first time since the early Nineties Morrissey was greeted with adulatory notices in the press; even the auld tabloid enemy *The Sun* sniffed which way the wind was blowing and saw fit to rave about his show and assure us that 'Morrissey is on his way back'.

Rehabilitation was definitely underway for one of England's most famous exiles. After all the years of vilification the prophet without portfolio was finally being honoured in his own land.

Why?

Perhaps because the Nineties were finally over. Perhaps because Britpop and in fact English pop music itself was dead and buried, just as Morrissey had predicted, supplanted by TV talent contests, tacky show-biz values and makeover programmes. Perhaps because no one could be bothered to pretend to believe he was Manchester's answer to Adolf Eichmann any more, or could even remember the reasons they had in the first place. Perhaps because it was some time since he'd released an album and reminded them of how difficult and contrary to fashion his work can be. And perhaps because it was hoped that Morrissey, now forty three, had lost most of his teeth and could be indulged as the Grand Old Gummy Man of Pop (if so, they were in for a sharp surprise).

Or maybe, just maybe it was because everyone had forgotten what a true star as opposed to a celebrity looked like and what they were capable of until Morrissey showed up again with a quip and a flash of his disdainful talent.

And perhaps it was also because the media, and the world in general, now had within its upper echelons quite a few ageing Smiths and Morrissey fans: Beautiful Bastards grown older but not necessarily up — just hideously compromised. Probably these clever swine were engaging (rather like this author) in a little personal thirty-something nostalgia for a poorer, less sophisticated time when they were just better more likeable people, dreaming big dreams and planning big plans, before the big ship sailed on the alley-alley-o. A time when they still had tremendous, tremulous, foolish faith in the power of pop music and words and their lying promises. A time when that charming-alarming man, the unchallenged and wicked master of both, accosted them and stole all their hearts away in a swooning, crooning manner that no other performer or for that matter any 'real' 'live' person whatever that may be, ever came close to matching.

You see, of all the disappointments the pop Cassandra sat and prophesied about, none proved truer than his claim that there would be no one like him again. Ever.

Does it scare you that you still inspire such devotion in people?
No, but it might scare them.

CITY LIFE, 2003

By the following year Morrissey began to be sighted more frequently in the UK, particularly in second hand cardigan shops near his mother's home in Cheshire. Unusually, he granted interviews to magazines other than his 'arch' favourite, the homeless weekly *The Big Issue*, threatening to become, well, almost *ubiquitous*. He also popped up in Manchester's *City Life*, who had just voted him 'Manchester's Greatest Ever Frontman', beating Liam Gallagher, Ian Curtis, Shaun Ryder, Ian Brown, Richard Ashcroft, Mark E Smith and the blessed Tim Burgess — and promised to play in Manchester soon, ending the (real or imagined) feud with his hometown which had lasted over a decade: the last time he played Manchester was in 1992.

How does it feel to be voted Manchester's greatest ever frontman?
I'm absolutely exhausted from sending all those votes.

CITY LIFE, 2003

He was even seen on the box in his first major UK TV appearance since 1987: an hour-long Channel Four documentary about him made over the previous year was aired in May to a frisson of media excitement. Most of the talking was done by various famous fans, including JK Rowling, Bono, Kathy Burke, Noel Gallagher and Alan Bennett, expressing their admiration for this prickly star; Morrissey for his part gave very little away and pulled off the remarkable feat of appearing a reluctant guest on his own doc. Perhaps the most significant moment was when he was filmed outside his eccentric Hollywood home that looks like a gingerbread windmill, squinting against the Southern Californian sunshine and promising us that he hadn't 'adapted' to Los Angeles.

In the same week, after six long years without a record contract, it was announced that he had signed to a British record company Sanctuary Music Group, home to Black Sabbath, the Libertines and the Strokes and also, following a takeover in the early Nineties The Smiths' old record label Rough Trade. Morrissey threatened to begin work immediately on a new album reportedly called *Irish Blood English Heart*, the title of one of the new songs he performed at the Royal Albert Hall the previous year; a song which bragged, all-too credibly, '*There is no one on this earth I'm afraid of...*', and went on to look forward to a time when to be English '*is to be standing by the flag, not feeling shameful/racist or racial*'.

Morrissey, it seemed, really had come home.

Why did it take so long to re-sign? You can't have been short of offers...
I honestly didn't have any decent offers. For example, three major US labels said 'We want you, but we don't want your band,' so I turned them down. Another label said, 'We want to sign you, but we'd first like you to make an album with the musicians from Radiohead,' and another label said, 'We'll sign you if you agree to make an album with Tracey Thorn'. Absolutely bewildering. People don't know what I've been through.

CITY LIFE, 2003

In a classic, deeply Morrisseyan twist (of the stilleto), it emerged that he had so impressed Sanctuary's Chief Executive with his connoisseurship of their Trojan catalogue that he had readily agreed to his request to resurrect for his use the old 'Attack' label, which in the Seventies brought the world the Pioneers, Gregory Isaacs and the Upsetters, giving Morrissey the licence to its back catalogue and the power to sign any new talent that caught his eye.

In other words, that alarming man who had once famously outraged the *NME* by daring to criticise music that happened to be black in origin, who was nearly destroyed by his criminal refusal to feel ashamed of Englishness, and who would not save his skin by genuflecting to political correctness and talk loudly about the black music he did happen to like (and which, of course, was the favourite music of real skinheads, as opposed to Nazis with no hair), was a decade later back in town, back in business and in charge of a reggae label called 'Attack'. Irony is probably the only sensual pleasure which rude boy Morrissey enjoys more than pouring scorn.

If all identity is based to some extent on contradiction, Morrissey's is all contradiction.

I once said, "Reggae is vile", did I? Well, several tongue-in-cheek things were said in those days, which, when placed in cold print, lost their humorous quality. 'Swan Lake', by the Cats, along with 'Double Barrel' and 'Young, Gifted and Black', were staple teenage necessities to me.
Anyway, annoying the *NME* always has value.

EXPLAINING THE INCLUSION OF A SKA TRACK ON HIS COMPILATION
ALBUM UNDER THE INFLUENCE, WORD, 2003

fame, fame, fatal fame

I have often wished I had time to cultivate modesty . . . But I am too busy thinking about myself.

DAME EDITH SITWELL

Sisyphus, proletarian of the gods, powerless and rebellious, knows the whole extent of his wretched condition, it is what he thinks of during his wretched descent. The lucidity that was to constitute his torture at the same time crowns his victory. There is no fate that cannot be surmounted by scorn.

ALBERT CAMUS

If George Michael had to live my life for five minutes, he'd strangle himself with the nearest piece of cord.

MORRISSEY

12

Everyone knows that Morrissey is mad.

It's an official fact of which every household is informed by a Government leaflet pushed through their letter boxes every year, usually around Whitsuntide.

The stories proving his madness are legion: the cancelled concerts; the cancelled tours; the refusal to be interviewed; the refusal, when he actually agrees to be interviewed, to be nice to interviewers; the imperiousness; the spontaneous disappearances; the unanswered telephone; the unanswered telegrams; the unanswered doorbell; the summary excommunications (sometimes by postcard; legend has it that one hapless former confidante, after some perceived betrayal, received three postcards through his letter box, one after the other, with a single word allocated to each: 'LOSE', 'MY', 'NUMBER'); the ditched record companies; the sacked managers; the refusal to get married in *Hello!* magazine. Above all, the refusal to be a proper pop star and do all those proper pop star things that pop stars are supposed to do, that anyone in their right mind would be happy to do, and which are in fact the only reason that most people become pop stars in the first place.

A churlish refusal, in other words, to suck Satan's cock.

196

Morrissey's 'madness' is actually a passionate, not to say rabidly jealous self-possessiveness rare enough in ordinary punters, but almost unknown in the tarty world of pop. Morrissey's 'looniness' is an extreme form of self-preservation, self-regard and self-love which compels him to say the one thing people don't want to ever hear from a pop star: 'No'.

Over and over again.

No to the loss of himself. No to the ravenous, slavering demands of everyone who wants a piece of him: fans, the music industry, associates, biographers, even and especially friends. Albert Camus once asked, 'What is a rebel?' and came up with the answer: 'A man who says "no"'. Obviously he meant to say: 'Morrissey.'

The resentment felt by Joe Public at his refusal to paint a vulgar picture is understandable. After all, they're used to the idea that a pop star belongs to them, that he or she is their creature, entirely and always available for their pleasure and, most particularly, their displeasure. It's not a groundless expectation. Most people who become famous do so by inviting the public to buy shares in them. They float themselves on the stock exchange of public opinion, surrendering their destiny and personality to interested parties and spending the rest of their pop careers trying to manage, play off and reconcile the various interest groups that own them. Morrissey, on the other hand, a self-capitalised and very private company, will not let his fame and his success be about anything other than *him*. He wants recognition, he wants adoration, but not at the cost of his self-love. Morrissey's madness is really just a simple form of meanness: he refuses to pay anyone else a dividend in his own fame, a percentage of his own personality.

So he rejects the deal that almost every other star strikes with the world — a world which says, We will make you a legend across the globe, a giant among men, an Immortal of the early evening news and a regular on The National Lottery, on one tiny, teensy-weensy condition: That it is not actually you whom we make famous. Yes, we will put your name in lights, but it will not be your name any more. Your face will rotate round the clock on MTV, but it will not be your face. You may cash the lottery-sized cheques we send you, but it is not really your money. You will sing to millions, but you will not sing your life. You will be loved, but not for who you are, rather for who we decide the audience wants you to be. And in the meantime, don't you EVER unplug your telephone again or leave town without checking with us first, OK?

> *Which words or phrases do you most overuse?*
> 'No I won't', 'Why should I?', 'What's the point?' and 'I'd like to termi-nate our agreement'.
>
> K<small>ILL</small> U<small>NCLE</small> T<small>OUR</small> B<small>OOK</small>, 1991

To describe this deal as Faustian is to do a disservice to Dr Faustus's business sense. In his deal with Old Nick he at least gained a lifetime of doing exactly what he pleased before the Sulphurous One came for him. Most pop stars happily sign away not just their immortal souls (which, frankly, no one is terribly interested in), but their mortal lives as well. They live in a gilded cage paraded around town by their record and film company who hand out tridents to the public with which to prod the star for their amusement. Why do celebs agree? Why do they sign such a patently bad deal with their own blood? Because their ambition is just so desperately mundane. Most pop stars are, by definition, second-handers. They don't want the world, just acceptance. They don't want to be great, just popular. They don't want to be feared, just rich. They don't want to destroy, just to belong. They sign away their lives because they want the sweet, fluffy, sticky celeb trappings of fame, not its bitter, lonely essence. And the essence of real fame is . . . revenge. While the essence of revenge is . . . Morrissey.

> *Do you regard success as a form of revenge?*
> Oh absolutely and entirely a form of revenge, yes I do.
> *And is it sweet?*
> Remarkably sweet. I like the taste, yes. More, please!
> *But revenge for what?*
> Well, for everything, on everybody... So now I can just sit back every night – when *Minder* is finished – and just chuckle, deafeningly.
>
> T<small>HE</small> H<small>IT</small>, O<small>CTOBER</small> 5, 1985

Just what does a strong-willed but oversensitive boy sitting out his adolescence in his bedroom do after he has memorised *The Picture of Dorian Gray* and masturbated three times that afternoon already? Why, he plans his *vengeance*! Every day he rehearses his boundless vindictiveness against a world that tramples him underfoot with its indifference.

Over time his anger cools, but it solidifies it into something tangible, something familiar, something that he could love as the most valuable and virtuous part of himself. Hence, his hunger for fame was not for a cure for his misanthropy, a walking into the light and the laughter, as it so often is – or is hoped to be – with lesser talents, but a bubble for it that would sustain and channel his enmity beyond his excruciatingly disappointing adolescence. Fame was the route by which Morrissey could leave his foetid bedroom but continue to breathe the same air, a way of entering the world without ever having to change, without having to compromise, without having to relinquish his familiar passions. Without ever having to grow up: *I'd like to drop my trousers to the world . . .*

How do you want to be remembered?
As Manchester's answer to the H-bomb.

KILL UNCLE TOURBOOK, 1991

Inevitably, this victory over the world was a pyrrhic one. It meant that some things would never change. In a sense, he never *did* leave his bedroom. In the Eighties the success of The Smiths allowed him to leave Manchester for the arms of national fame – which inevitably meant London. But by the Nineties he found that London had become Manchester (and so he left Britain for the arms of America). Moz was still the strange boy on his own whom everyone round these parts laughed at; the 'nutter', the 'basket case'. His bedroom may have been more spacious, better decorated and now came with room service, and he may have had rather more pen pals, but he was still living in a mental bedsit. As in those grey, resentful Manchester days, people suspected that this secluded, introverted creature thought himself that most unforgivable of things – particularly in a star – 'special'. And they were right.

> I'm not a phone person. I can't quite get used to the telephone.
> *Why? Lack of intimacy?*
> Lack of interest. There's usually a person on the other end.
>
> MODERN ROCK LIVE, 1997

This isn't to say that Morrissey wasn't sorely tempted by the promise of global fame. The desire for recognition and acceptance always sits alongside the desire for retribution and destruction (though it is always a mistake to see the former as merely being masked by the latter, as in: Oh, he's a nice person really — he's just a bit bitter, that's all). In the days of The Smiths he frequently boasted about their/his world-wide ambitions, and songs such as 'Frankly Mr Shankly' and 'You Just Haven't Earned it Yet Baby' appeared to pour scorn on the 'righteous' and 'holy' scruples, or simple incompetence, of those such as his hippy Rough Trade boss Geoff Travis, who he deemed to be standing between him and the vast unlimited fame he felt should be his by rights.

> I'm ready to be accepted by everybody. I want to be heard and I want to be seen by as many people as possible.
>
> MELODY MAKER, 1983

But his own actions spoke differently, betraying an unconscious refusal to grant the necessary concessions, to make the necessary dilutions of himself to achieve the level of fame he craved. Morrissey's ambition was bigger than that of the rest of The Smiths put together, but he was the one persuading them, often against their better judgement, to renounce Satan and all his works and live on a diet of fame gruel and celeb abstinence. He wanted The Smiths to be as big and as modest as the Beatles but with the (early) cred of the Rolling Stones — the Beatles, in other words, without Brian Epstein. Later, it became clear that he wanted to be Elvis without Colonel Tom Parker. Of course, this was just more evidence of his 'madness'. Without Colonel Parker, Elvis was just a hillbilly truck driver no one had ever heard of. Everyone knows — even Jesus H Christ, who would have been just another bastard carpenter who thought he could walk on water without his go-getting Jewish manager St Paul — that what is Caesar's must be rendered up to Caesar, because Caesar is the master of this world and all who would succeed in it. But no one had told Morrissey.

> Sometimes I do have a great physical need to be reasonably blunt, which most people find quite taxing. That's the side of me which is unmarketable, totally unpromotable . . . But the songs, and the album title, and the sleeve, and whatever else you might wish to investigate, are simply . . . me.
>
> MUSICIAN, 1991

So, with the brief and reportedly reluctant exception of the venerable Joe Moss who managed The Smiths on an ad hoc basis until the first album, he refused to deal with managers. He signed to an Independent record label without the resources to market his records. He wouldn't make pop promos (which meant, amongst other things, that they didn't get played on MTV, and so big, sleepy America didn't wake up to The Smiths until they were The Stiffs). And he cancelled major international tours, literally at the airport gate. Given that Morrissey's fear of flying seems metaphorical as well as literal, Marr's departure from The Smiths at the very moment that they were threatening to go global makes one wonder whether he jumped, or was unconsciously, half-intentionally, pushed, however bereft Morrissey was at the break. (Self-sabotage is a proud Mancunian habit: e.g. Oasis' antics in the US and Ian Curtis, the lead singer of Joy Division, who hanged himself on the eve of his first American tour.)

> Can you imagine anything so boring as world domination. I mean, what would you do in your spare time?
>
> Q, 1995

The bizarre story of 'Hand in Glove' illustrates Morrissey's total disrespect for the way of the world, the workings of the pop business in particular, and his refusal to give the public what they think they want instead of what he knows they need. When it was originally released in 1983 'Hand in Glove' disappeared almost without trace, barely charting at position 124. Morrissey, however, was not satisfied with this unambiguous public verdict on his debut and instead of drawing a veil over his stillborn firstborn, began an unprecedented campaign of browbeating. He proceeded to bang on and on and on about the song in every interview, insisted it appear on *The Smiths*, *Hatful of Hollow* and the US compilation *Louder Than Bombs* — even including the taunting lines 'Hand in glove . . ./the sun shines out of our behinds' at the end of *The Smiths* track 'Pretty Girls Make Graves'. He finally beat the British public into abject submission and made it a Top Ten hit after he persuaded Sandie Shaw to cover it in 1984 (only a year after the original).

> *What brings you here today?*
> The 138 to Streatham Hill.
>
> TO AN MTV REPORTER AFTER HIS ACCEPTANCE OF AN
> IVOR NOVELLO LIFETIME ACHIEVEMENT AWARD, 1998

In his solo career Morrissey may have relented and given Caesar/ the record industry some burnt offerings of pop promos, but only because now, with most of his audience in the United States, he would simply fade away without them (mind you, MTV exhibit an extreme aversion to actually showing them). However, this appears to have been his only concession. Far from becoming more pragmatic, more pliable with age, this stubbornly, devoutly self-obsessed character shows no signs of relinquishing his 'control freakery'.

> As soon as people get to work with a group they have the impression they have full powers. Guided by money and covetousness they start doing anything. It's one of my biggest regrets in life: I've never found any person clever enough to represent me. This person doesn't exist.
>
> LES INROCKUPTIBLES, 1995

By dint of a sustained and superhuman effort of skill and cunning Morrissey managed throughout the Nineties to snatch defeat from the jaws of victory and prevent his career going supernova in the US, somehow keeping it forever bubbling under, just short of major, fully-fledged, all-formats, all-media, general-release, vulgar fame. (By 1998 he had managed to bring about a state of affairs where he was such a 'special' pop star that he was actually without a record deal of any kind, and was to remain that way into the early Noughties.)

> I know I'm making your stomach churn as I say those words, but I do feel like a one-off. You can hate the sight of me, or you can cherish every word

I've uttered. But I do feel reasonably unique, I do. It's a terrible, terrible curse. I wish I could just blend in.

MUSICIAN, 1991

Despite his tendency to blame record companies/the press/the Marylebone Cricket Club for these things and the fact that he stubbornly remains 'merely' the most famous cult performer in the world, one that everyone has heard of even if most don't actually own any of his records, he knows he has no one to thank but himself. His solo career has turned out to be a perfect rendition of that truth. His solitary image on the album covers, his lonely mono-moniker (without even a first name to keep it company), hovering above like a halo, like a crown of thorns, like a bloody albatross. The way, post Marr, his voice occasionally seems to be trying to impose a melody where there isn't one by sheer willpower. And above all, his strangely moving stage performance, where he seems a thousand miles away from his band, from his 'profession', and in fact from any kind of human society at all — except the adoration of his fans — is a distillation of the essential drama of Morrissey's life: one man and his 'madness' against the world.

> *What does it feel like to see your proliferated image about, on hoardings, in magazines, to hear your voice on the radio?*
> It's very odd. I was in a shop once, buying scented candles, and on the radio came Steve Wright with a collage of Smiths songs, and I got a distinct chill, almost as if the hand of Death was tapping me on the shoulder, saying 'put yer candles down, it's time to go!'
>
> MELODY MAKER, 1988

Whatever it might do for your mental health, not to mention your bank balance and marriage prospects, this is a great strategy for holding on to one's artistic edge. Nosing into middle age, surrounded by the evidence of his past successes and acclaim, and of course the continuing love from his fans, Morrissey is still a voice sobbing in the wilderness, still complaining bitterly of the things he complained about to himself as a child: that he is unloved, underrated, overlooked, neglected. His love, in other words, is still as sharp as a needle in our eye.

> Dirk Bogarde sent me a card the other day, and I almost cried with joy when it arrived. I thought, Put it this way, Mozzer, you have a card from

203

> Dirk Bogarde here [and he slapped the settee]. You have Alan Bennett
> sitting in your kitchen having tea. You have David Bowie having sung one
> of your songs quite beautifully. What else are you looking for? What right
> do I have to be sour-faced and complaining, queuing up at Waitrose in
> Holloway being annoyed because somebody in front of me has got a leg of
> lamb? What more could there be?
>
> SELECT, 1994

Anyone needing to be convinced that he has held on to his edge
— and exclusion — with white knuckles needs only to listen to his eve-
of-middle-age 1997 album (his eleventh) which was not called *Help Me
Put My Kids Through College* but *Maladjusted*. Although much of the
music ranks several celestial circles beneath the sustained brilliance
of *Vauxhall & I* or *Your Arsenal* and was not received well by the critics
or fans, it has moments, such as the shudderingly powerful 'Trouble
Loves Me', which more than equal anything from his back catalogue
and which have a directness and unaffected, uncloying poignancy and
pathos which, say, Radiohead or their many (very) well-brought-up
imitators, such as Coldplay, will never achieve, no matter how much
angst they sprinkle on their Coco Pops of a morning. Moreover as a
document of an artist's wilful failure to 'settle down' *Maladjusted* is
incontrovertibly, startlingly genuine.

Remaining true to the thirteen year-old promise of 'Suffer Little
Children' to make society pay for causing such suffering (by paradoxically, if perhaps inevitably, reversing its subjectivity) is a track
called 'Ambitious Outsiders', a mournful string arrangement with
threatening kettle drum accompaniment over which Morrissey croaks
eerily, poking fun at the imagined security of domestic bliss, apparently speaking on behalf of faceless, threatening figures committed to
spoiling other people's happiness: '*top of the list/ is your smiling kids* . . .
DON'T UNDERESTIMATE US'.

While this may be the universal ransom note of all pop music at
its best, this really isn't the sort of thing a wealthy, famous, globally
acclaimed thirty-eight-year-old should be singing. It's an irresponsible
statement of a continuing artistic identification with those on the
fringes who avenge themselves on society; a statement which performers half his age and with rather more piercings wouldn't dare make.

204

Nevertheless, pop's most unapologetic and most pernicious Pied Piper is perfectly well aware that he's also his own worst enemy, especially when he's blaming someone else. The piano-led 'Trouble Loves Me', reminiscent of 'I Know it's Over' from *The Queen is Dead*, builds and falls like the self-intoxicating moods of, well... a manic-depressive — a heart-rending mixture of confession and accusation. Musically it's the tortured anthem that Queen were forever trying to write, but just didn't have the neuroses. With a hymn-like piano-chord intro (Morrissey is our Ancient and Modern), he croons in at the high end of his range in a voice on the verge of cracking: '*Trouble loves me/trouble needs me*', asserting these are two things '*more than you do/or would attempt to.*'

Quavering and wobbling in that characteristically engaging-annoying way, he 'attempts' the high note of 'attempt to', confiding the drama and pathos of his scorn. And indeed, the more he considers his condition, the more he reflects on his treatment, the more agitated he becomes and the worse he makes things for himself: '*Just when it seems like/everything's evened out/and the balance/seems serene . . .*' — the accompaniment escalates from warm piano to searing electric guitar as he begins flagellating himself with gusto decrying his foolish 'ready-wit' and deluded desires that keep him 'running 'round'... '*on the flesh rampage — at your age!*'

As he implies, his famous ready-wit is both function and cause of his disenchantment. He won't allow himself the peace he says he craves, even after all these years. He's still chasing his demons, stopping to catch his breath, and then turning around and inviting them to chase him again. He is discontented, malcontented with everyone and everything, most especially himself and his achievements: '*Show me a barrel/and watch me scrape it*'. He wants not to want. Almost.

Contrary as ever, in the very next line he's proudly resigned to his condition, his art and its consequences: '*Faced with the music/as always I'll face it*', a line whose very sub-Morrisseyean weakness is powerfully evocative of his despair. Often, Morrissey's songs seem to take the form of an imagined conversation with an imagined lover (which is literally true in a sense: he's addressing his fans almost as much as he's talking to himself). 'Trouble Loves Me' is a classic example of this. The opening lines suggest that the lament is directed to, in typically accu-satory, ironic fashion, an 'ex' (certainly 'Trouble' could be the name of any or all of the ruffians he admires). By the end of this turbulent song, fraught with emotional drama, defiance and weary resignation, he finally confesses that at midnight *'I can't get you out of my head/a disenchanted taste/still running 'round'.*

The frustration and anger in the dark, midnight thoughts still run-ning 'round his head is emphasised by the unusual, almost clumsy length of the line: 'I-can't-get-you-out-of-my-head', which Morrissey shakes out with musically balled fists. It is a syllable longer than the next longest line which occurs in the earlier, more tranquil part of the song: 'and the balance seems serene'; a caressing, sibilant phrase which the longer line with the shorter, harder words have deprived him of.

But is it Morrissey himself or his 'ex' that he can't get out of his head, and who leaves him with a disenchanted taste? Is it an unhappy experience of love, or is it the uneasy residue of his life which leaves him sleepless and anxious at nights? As ever, and as in most people's experience, it isn't clear. The lines *'go to Soho, oh/go to waste in/the wrong arms'* could be a dismissive rebuke delivered to a former, un-faithful, perhaps male lover (Soho is famous today as the gay district of London, but also as a 'party' district, especially for media types; though in Morrissey's much-loved Fifties and Sixties it was the centre of bohemia and criminality).

Or it could merely be Morrissey offering himself some more sarcas-tic advice: that it is better to acquiesce, to be the person society wants him to be, to embrace the predictable and the inauthentic. Settling for the attainable — which is to say, what you don't want — and going to waste in the wrong arms, is at least a safe option and certainly less trouble than pursuing the unattainable. At your age.

Whatever his enemies might attack him for, whatever the crimes they might accuse him of, Morrissey always beats them to the punch. No one is harder on him than himself; no one would want to be Morrissey.

There's nothing difficult about going to a psychoanalyst. Especially not for me, who is by nature rather keen on confession. I've given a great number of interviews in my life, which has probably constituted an excellent warm up . . . I'll certainly need centuries to settle everything.

LES INROCKUPTIBLES, 1995

The title track, 'Maladjusted', is perhaps the most powerful and mordant statement of Morrissey's awareness of his position in the world — and the seriousness of his condition. It opens with some distorted feedback followed by a sample from the classic stiff-upper-lip British war movie *Cockleshell Heroes* (1955), an account of ten Royal Marines' heroic if slightly silly attempt to take on the might of the Nazi Navy in canoes (almost all were killed). Before the mission the lads get into a punch-up with a pub full of sailors. Black and blue and back in the barracks but in high spirits, Anthony Newley, grown up from his Artful Dodger role and playing a cheeky-chappie bootneck from the ranks, announces mock-formally, '*On this glorious h'occasion of the splendid defeat*' — which can only be Morrissey's own wry appraisal of his own career and life (*Maladjusted* was released in the year following his drubbing by Mike Joyce and m'learned friends in High Court.)

Sounding like a voice from beyond the grave and before the womb, Morrissey moans, '*I wanna start from before the beginning*' (a twisted echo perhaps of 'Do-Re-Me' from *The Sound of Music*, which opens: '*Let's start at the very beginning/a very fine place to start*'). Morrissey is almost speaking the lyrics over doom-laden drums and guitars; it seems as if he's making a statement to the police, or his Maker. Then, suddenly changing his mind, he grabs his car keys and trilby and takes us on a night out where we loot some wine, avoid some 'Stevenage overspill' (Stevenage is a deathly dull dormitory town half an hour north of London, as well as a pun on his disowned 'dull' first name) and, as usual, toss a half-brick at normality — '*jeer the lights in the windows of all safe and stable homes*' — without bothering to hide our resentment: '*but wondering then, well what/could peace of mind be like?*'

The lights of the Fulham Road (a lively, well-to-do part of London, full of bars, restaurants and animal life) '*stretch and invite into the night*' but somehow their promise is not delivered, at least not to us: '*Oh Christ, another stifled/Friday night*'. Life fails us again and instead we end up back where we started, with Morrissey complaining and boasting of his masochistic relationship with the machinery of fame and the pimping record industry (and the lawyers that infest it): '*with a soul full of loathing/for stinging bureaucracy/making it anything/other than easy/for working girls like me*'.

But his loathing isn't all outer-directed. Self-loathing, after all, is always the 'B'-side to self-loving: '*I flop on your bed/with a head full of dread/for all I've ever said*'. Then comes the discordant central refrain: '*maladjusted, maladjusted/never to be trusted*'.

It's an astonishingly brave, not to mention despondent, confession for an artist of Morrissey's stature to be making; the idea that he might entertain such profound doubts about the merit of his work, that he might even have taken that remark of the Lily Law Lord to heart, when his genius is founded precisely on his singularity, his wilfulness, his arrogance, his self-conceits, his scorn, is perturbing. Then you re-member that, of course, without the self-doubt, without the merciless, neurotic questioning of everything, the disrespect for all assumptions, even about his own achievements, there could be no genius. Self-in-dulgence might not be altogether uncommon in Morrissey's life, but self-deceit, a necessity for most people in order to survive life, is to him a luxury he rarely affords himself.

This, after all, is the terrible personal cost of Morrissey's greatness — but it is a price, you sense, that Morrissey, for all his brilliant whinge-ing, is ultimately willing to pay. 'Maladjusted' ends with an ethereal repeated falsetto, '*There's nothing wrong with you, oh*', ironically recalling the echoing, falsetto line '*I need advice, I need advice*' at the end of *The Smiths*' 'You've Got Everything Now'. Though here, thirteen years on, the irony works in the opposite direction — actually, he really does need advice (not that he's going to take it, mind).

Yes, the refrain '*There's nothing wrong with you*' could be interpreted as yet another rebuff to his critics, the press, the courts, the music business, the family — all the institutions which have effectively sec-tioned him and packed him off to the funny farm — but it is just as likely that Morrissey is actually mocking those around him, including himself, who like to tell him that it's not him that's a wrong 'un but the world.

Taking the self-analysis and humility of 'Maladjusted' one stage further is 'Ammunition', a bizarre splutter-inducing track which, by

Morrissey's standards, is almost Buddhist: he claims that he '*doesn't need more ammunition*' or to '*dwell on the things I'm missing*' and that instead he's pleased '*with the things I've found*'.

For a moment it seems as if poor old Mozzer has finally accepted that bitterness doesn't become someone of his years and jaw line, that he ought to try on a more dignified sensibility. That he ought to become a distinguished old man of pop, resting on his comfy and extensive laurels, take up painting and perhaps launch an Internet service provider. Gratifyingly, 'Ammunition', which otherwise would seem to mark the end of Morrissey's serious musical career, is violently contradicted by the splenetically and unremittingly hateful (not to mention tuneless) 'Sorrow Will Come To You in the End', a song whose concept of bad karma is just a little bit too pro-active (perhaps for this reason it was dropped from the UK release of the album). Addressed to '*Lawyer . . . liar!*' it advises him not to close his eyes because '*a man who slits throats/has time on his hands/and I'm gonna get you*'.

> *Hey! Um, yeah, Morrissey, your new song 'Ammunition' you talk . . . you say that you have not place or time in your life for revenge. I was wondering is that true, and did something happen that triggered that?*
>
> It's not true, I'm afraid. It's not true. It's a nice idea, but not true. I've got lots of space for revenge and, uh, long may it live.
>
> MODERN ROCK LIVE RADIO PHONE-IN (USA), 1997

It is left to the mellifluous (if perhaps somewhat pale descendant of 'Everyday Is Like Sunday') 'Alma Matters', to explain what really keeps him going. He admits the choices he's made '*may seem strange to you/ but who asked you anyway?*' And then asserts, in the words of that wilful 1960s Northern girl Jo, the pop star manqué, that have brought him to this pretty pass, '*it's my life to wreck my own way*', adding, punningly, '*You see to someone somewhere/Alma matters*'.

'Alma' is probably a reference to Alma Cogan, the 'girl with a giggle in her voice' who was the Fifties prototype of the Sixties girl singers Morrissey still worships, and who died in 1966, underrated and largely forgotten. But the word has many resonances. 'Alma' was also the name of Mike Baldwin's wife in *Coronation Street* in the 1980s-90s. Baldwin was the show's live-in 'love-rat', while Alma was a classic example of the tough-but-vulnerable Northern Woman suffering valiantly the slings and arrows of outrageous fortune especially in matters of the heart, whom Morrissey still identifies with and, in fact, as the pun on 'alma mater' (old school or college) implies, this autodidact early school-leaver was tutored in during his Manchester childhood. In a further Morrisseyan twist, 'alma mater' is also the name given to a university or college song. The line *'it's my life/to wreck my own way'* is from his favourite hymn-sheet, Shelagh Delaney's *A Taste of Honey*, which is Morrissey's college song.

Just as his connection with such misfit, touchingly freakish, gender ambiguous characters sustained him when he was young, the connection his fans have with him today when he is not so young but not very much older either, sustains *them* in their misfit, freakish confused years, however long they might last. *To someone, somewhere . . .* And the knowledge of that sustains him now. Quite possibly, it maintains him in his perpetual adolescent agony.

It is this peculiar, decidedly unhealthy relationship with his fans that explains the oddly intense nature of Morrissey's cult fame, which more than makes up for in devotion what it lacks in numbers. The unique and unrivalled fervour with which his fans love him is a function of their certainty that their relationship is something special, that it isn't like any other love, that this one is different because it's just *us*. They know that their love affair with him is as pure and unadulterated and as direct as it gets in pop music. There is no percentage proof higher, no stronger distillation available, even under the pop music counter for ready money, than the Morrissey brand. They know that he has always been true to them, in his own strange, sick way. *Because he's remained true to himself.* The very thing that has cost him his happiness — his bitter integrity, his scorn — is the thing they love him for.

> *Do you receive a lot of fan mail?*
> Yes, a great lot. Mostly complaints, actually . . . It's often parents of fans who write and ask me to stop existing. Someone wrote that she couldn't manage to walk past her daughter's room, because she constantly played records by a man having his legs sawn off.
>
> BLITZ, 1992

Through his work he gives them the only love he knows — himself. Never what he thinks they might like to hear (although his music is full of jokes at his expense shared with his audience e.g. the end of 'Disappointed': *'This is the last song I will ever sing* [audience cheers] */No: I've changed my mind again* [audience boos]' — and perhaps the whole of *Kill Uncle*). It is all, apart from the occasional half-decent tune, that most Morrissey fans want. Even the cancelled concerts that some point to as evidence of a fickle or callous attitude towards his fans, are, in a sense, merely part of the package, a reminder that Morrissey is not and never has been an *entertainer*; that in the end, although he may depend on his relationship with his fans rather more than most performers (partly because it stands in for real flesh and blood ones), and take strength from the knowledge that his love is arming them in their own struggle with the world (or withdrawal from it), it's definitely, decidedly about him and not about them.

> *What is the source of this extraordinary love your fans display?*
> Trust. I think admiring me, shall we say, is quite a task. Because if you say you like Morrissey then you have to explain why.
>
> DETAILS, 1992

When the fans rush the stage, flattening hefty security guards, and succeed in wrapping themselves around the indulgent singer, head on his shoulder or pressed against his neck, or somewhere in his bosom, beaming preposterously rapturously, like an adopted child reunited with their (un)natural mother, they're proving their love, forgiveness and acceptance of him and all his glorious shortcomings in an outpouring of demonstrative affection which no other contemporary performer comes close to provoking.

They are also, of course, also hugging themselves, trying to claim his wilful loneliness and the tremendous, foolish strength it betokens as their own — without, hopefully, actually having to suffer the full consequences of it in their own lives. They are consoling themselves with the entirely fanciful notion that the world can reward integrity, when as they know very well, no matter how much they try to change the fact of it with their adoration of him, Morrissey is the exception which proves the rule of mediocrity. The Way of the World is the Way of the World for a very good reason. Only a blessed man, a man of saintly and perhaps slightly unhinged virtue can resist it. Such a man is admirable, but definitely not enviable.

> I think that there is a great sense that I have been always overlooked. I think that the audience is perfectly aware of this and they feel that I have been enormously short-changed . . . By the entire music industry and all of their relatives! I've been dumped into the 'out' tray.
>
> *SPIN*, 1992

Truth is, Morrissey is far too preoccupied with posterity to achieve full-blooded, real, here-and-now *News of the World* fame. The hereafter is what he has his eyes on. It is fatal fame he really wants; every song must be sung as if it were his last.

Hence the obsession with suicide — death as a performance that the suicide hopes will be extensively reviewed. After all, taking one's own life can, like fame, also be a form of revenge. The wrists slashed, the neck snapped, the brains spattered, are symbolically someone else's ('*now* they'll be sorry . . .'). The suicide's body is a metaphor; the most violent and powerful of all. Perhaps because, unlike most metaphors, it can only be used once. In the self-mutilating self-perpetuating words of Richey Manic, it's '4 REAL'.

So how much revenge is there to be had in a famous suicide! The famous suicide is an artist-zealot who dies in the service of an idea, which is the sign of true dedication and fanaticism. Jesus Christ was, of course, the most famous artist-zealot. His death, an elaborate form of suicide, was literally the linchpin of his fame, turning him into an idea — transcendence — as well as a timeless logo (one which a famous vamp[iress] named after his mother would find, a couple of thousand years later, rather kinky). Even ordinary, common-or-garden suicide can be a stab at immortality, or at least notoriety. Not so much the ultimate victory over Death as the ultimate revenge on... Life. (The Universal Church of course decreed that Christians who were unable to persuade someone else to martyr them and who decided instead to cut out the middle man and organise their own martyrdom, were guilty of an irredeemable sin, otherwise known as cheating, and would be buried in unconsecrated graves.)

I look upon suicide as this incredibly brave thing, having maximum control over one's body, yet ludicrously suicide has been looked upon as some severe disorder of somebody who doesn't know what she or he's doing. I always saw it as the height of self-awareness and control over one's destiny . . . The desire to live for as long as possible is really quite cowardly. I find these issues quite easy to confront in the comfort of one's living room, but perhaps in a high speed jet I'd rather talk about something else.

SQUARE PEG, 1984

Suicide, in other words, is the most spectacular form of sulking, but also perhaps the ultimate form of self-possession, a refusal to become what the world wants you to become: pragmatic, reasonable, sensible, corrupt, older. St Augustine saw it as nothing less than a defiance of God; perhaps not just because it was the 'easy' way out of this veil of tears but also because, in the right hands, it could be a blasphemous attempt at godhead. Rock and roll recognises this very well and has always been an extremely 'morbid' art form (though not quite as morbid as Christianity), preoccupied with the idea of an authentic life, which of course means a life that can't be lived: 'Death is the only thing left to respect,' as Jimmy Dean, that strange boy who crucified himself on the steering wheel of his Porsche and will now never grow old, put it.

Even when the death of an idol is not officially suicide, we like to imagine that it amounted to as much — Marc Bolan's crash, Janis Joplin's/Jimi Hendrix's/Johnny Thunders' overdose, James Dean's smash, Buddy Holly's disappearance, Elvis's heart attack. Of course, it was a 'terrible tragedy' on the one hand. But, on the other... well, they were *asking for it*, weren't they? We like to conceive of them, if not actually, literally taking their own lives, then at least loitering with intent in the Garden of Gethsemane. Kurt Cobain's shotgun fellatio in 1994 was not, in rock and roll terms, a 'mad' or 'sad' act, but a perfectly logical development, a sign of his dedication to his art. Suicide was, as it was for Ian Curtis before him, his greatest hit.

What did you think of Kurt Cobain's suicide?
I respect his decision.

MORRISSEY

Some thought Morrissey might be miffed that Cobain had beaten him to it. After all, the theme of suicide, premature death and being remembered is a constant in his work, and had been long before Kurt's brand of grungy sulking arrived on the scene. In fact, the suicide note as a musical form is Morrissey's speciality, e.g.: 'Shakespeare's Sister' (*And the rocks below say:/"Throw your white body down!"*); 'There is a Light That Never Goes Out' (*'and if a double-decker bus/crashes into us/to die by your side/such a heavenly way to die'*); 'Well I Wonder' (*'Gasping – dying – but somehow still alive/this is the final stand of all I am/Please keep me in mind'*); 'Death at One's Elbow' (*'Don't come to the house tonight . . ./because you'll slip on the/trail of my bespattered remains'*); 'Asleep' (*'Don't try to wake me in the morning, for I will be gone'*); 'I Know It's Over' (*'Oh Mother, I can feel the soil falling over my head'*). To name just a few.

And, of course, the suicide note to end all suicide notes, the spectacularly, *heroically* passive aggressive 'Speedway' from *Vauxhall & I* (*'you won't rest/until the hearse that becomes me/finally takes me/oh you've done it now'*) a song so blasphemous in its disdain, so astounding in its self-pity, so moving in its self-dramatisation that it seems, like the Galilean Fisher of Men, to offer the ultimate 'yes' to the world that is in fact the ultimate 'no', one so perfectly beautiful that it almost renders suicide unnecessary, or at most a bureaucratic formality hardly worth bothering with. Morrissey enacts his own death every time he performs it, usually as a last number, in a single spotlight surrounded by darkness, nimbly stepping out of the circle light as the final trap-door drum beat falls, the spot extinguishes, and gliding away quickly into the backstage gloom.

Of course, this means that unlike most suicides, Morrissey can read the notices the next day.

Arguably, if childishly, the only authentic and genuinely free response to being given a life you didn't ask for, the only way to own it, is to give it up — which is perhaps why we talk about 'taking one's own life' (in both hands).

But Morrissey, as his fans know very well, is not very likely to take this option — it isn't nearly as dramatic a gesture as continuing to live, in spite of everything and, most importantly, everybody. To live on... *in spite*. As he sings in 'He Cried' on *Maladjusted*: *'he was stoned to death but he's still living'*.

214

For all the dark hints of Dean-inspired auto-thanasia in his work, Morrissey is not likely to exercise his final artistic option and bring down the curtain at the moment of his choosing by veering cliffwards or into the path of an oncoming double-decker bus. Partly this is because he doesn't need to. He has achieved in life the transcendence that other performers have only achieved in death (or real, clinical, certifiable madness). This is the twisted miracle of Morrissey's life that his fans, his congregation of Beautiful Bastards, bears witness to. Morrissey is the only 'saint' to be canonised before his death, and the only one to intercede on behalf of his supplicants not from heaven but from his bedroom.

As 'Speedway' chucklingly implies beneath its morbid but undeniably witty death-wish, the old moaner is not likely to be found swinging by his neck from his antique Victorian chandelier. The cord that binds him to this world, keeping him dangling here, choking and gasping, but somehow still alive, is not simply his defiance, or even his sense of drama, but more importantly his very twisted sense of humour. Staying alive and staying Morrissey is just too big a joke to play on the world to pass up.

> Do you find that there are certain subject matters where you might belittle it by putting it in a three-minute lyric?
> No.
>
> GREATER LONDON RADIO, 1999

Humour, albeit of the funereal-black variety, permeates almost all of Morrissey's work, making him easily the funniest and most self-mocking lyricist around. Yet Morrissey's black crêped comic talent is resolutely overlooked by all his detractors, who, inevitably accuse him of being humourless. Perhaps this is partly because his humour is quintessentially Northern, both in its darkness and its self-deprecation: 'as the flames rose to her Roman nose and her hearing aid started to melt'. Perhaps also because there is something to his gallows humour which is frighteningly Other and yet familiar at the same time; as old as the hills yet original; impossibly wicked but also somehow too good for this world.

But mostly it's because, for such people, recognising or even acknowledging Morrissey's sense of humour would compromise the useful defence mechanism they have that Morrissey is mad and/or sad in some simple, hygienic, fashion that doesn't implicate *them*. It would no longer simply be Morrissey's problem. After all, to laugh at Morrissey's jokes is to let him inside your head, something which, understandably, terrifies most normal people.

> I have always had to laugh at myself. If I hadn't found my social position when I was a teenager so amusing, I would have strangled myself.
>
> *BLITZ*, 1988

Nonetheless it is precisely Morrissey's 'darkness' that is so liberating. Just as a joke makes us laugh because it, shakingly, releases an idea or feeling we hadn't dared or thought to express ourselves, Morrissey's 'miserable' songs have saved many fans from suicide – when someone on this 'unhappy planet' has gone to the trouble of expressing your own dark thoughts so charmingly and so wittily, and in a fashion that makes it clear he's lived with them for a thousand years before you were born, it would be the height of bad manners to leave it prematurely. And anyway, Morrissey has blocked all the exits with his own talent, he's met us at the cemetery gates on a dreaded sunny day with some muscle in the form of Mr Wilde at his side: he's felt it, thought it, looked at it, sung it, quipped it, and laughed his head off at it infinitely better – and much more exquisitely – than you or I could ever manage. So why the hell should we even *bother*? We'd only make a bloody mess of it.

Another reason why Morrissey isn't about to make a quick getaway, is the small question of where he would actually *go*. A question addressed in the teasing, ticklish but 'tragic' final track on *Maladjusted*, 'Satan Rejected My Soul'. A breezily bleak parting shot, 'Satan' suggests that Morrissey was so desperate to find some kind of peace, some kind of home, that he tried to cut a deal with Old Nick, but found himself rejected even there: '*he knows/my kind/he won't be dragged down/ he's seen my face around.*'

It's a joke of course, but one that relies upon us knowing that Morrissey's entire career, avowedly depraved as it is, has been a struggle to renounce Satan's works in the form of the Way of the World – or corruption. He is much too originally wicked for old Beelzebub, and his soul much too heavy for hell, or, for that matter, for the balance of a Manichean universe. Morrissey is forever trapped somewhere between heaven and hell, life and art, good and evil, lying in his bed thinking about life, thinking about death, and neither one particularly appealing to him. Even purgatory would be a relief; like Gatwick Airport, there may be a long wait, the food may be execrable and the décor distasteful, but at least the lost souls there, unlike Morrissey, know they're eventually going *somewhere*, they're just not sure whether they'll have a sea-view or not.

> Artists are not really people are they? Not really. Because eventually you end up having had a lifestyle or an experience which most other people have never had. Because before you had the fame or success you were working towards it. And your mind was very locked into that. And then when it happens to you, it takes you further away from the human race. But it is a great journey.
>
> MELODY MAKER, 1997

Understandably, Morrissey, the poor dear, becomes desperate and begs, '*so take it please/it's free*' — even when actually trying to make a deal with the Devil, Morrissey can't bring himself to put a price on his immemorial soul. He goes on, trying to reassure Satan, '*you'll never see/all the fun in life it's cost me*'.

Wicked and vain as Morrissey might be in his heart and in his art, his lived life has been anything but sinful or venal, if it has been anything at all. Morally speaking, he is The Picture of Dorian Gray in reverse: all the sin and corruption and genius has gone into his ravishing art, which walks the world while he remains locked up hanging in his attic. Hence Lucifer won't be persuaded, not even by Morrissey's seductive, depraved cooing '*oo-ooh, oo-ooh*' noises over the last few bars of the song. Contrary to the time-worn phrase, you can't go to hell in your own way, and Morrissey can't even give his soul away. He's stuck with it, poor lad.

And so are we.

Morrissey may not be happy in his own special purgatory, but at least it is unquestionably his own. This is the real Faustian pact that the boy from the mean Stretford streets who refused to forgive or forget the trick that life, love and lust played on him has made, not with

217

the Devil or with a record company or even with his hairdresser but with himself.

His art, and what passes for his life, bears testament to his greatest virtue and his greatest vice: He would always rather be unique than happy.

But then, isn't that the nature of True Love? The kind of love that pop music is always whispering in our ear about if we would only hear it, encouraging us to feel so singular in our sadness, so achingly good about feeling bad — to hug ourselves and never ever let go?

The kind of love that isn't like any other love, the kind that if you go about it the right-wrong way, shines out of your behind.

I've always been true to you in my own sick way I'll always stay true to you.

index

SAF and Firefly Books

Order Online

For the latest on SAF and Firefly titles, or to order books online, check the SAF website. You can also browse the full range of rock, pop, jazz and experimental music books we have available, as well as keeping up with our latest releases. There are also:

Special pre-publication offers
Signed copies
Monthly offers
Book reviews and extracts
Competitions

You can also contact us via email, and request a catalogue.

info@safpublishing.com

www.safpublishing.com

Recent titles:
Morrissey, Devo, Mountain, Alex Harvey, The Pretty Things, Cabaret Voltaire, Coil-Current 93-Nurse With Wound.

Forthcoming titles:
U2 Encyclopedia (updated), Thin Lizzy, Shirley Collins, Genesis, Gentle Giant, Nirvana recording sessions,

Backlist titles:
From Frank Zappa to Alice Cooper, From Captain Beefheart to Prince, From Robert Wyatt to The Residents, From Kraftwerk to the Ramones,
And many, many more.....

saf publishing

saf publishing

www.safpublishing.com